AN AEROPLANE, A G A I N?

AN AEROPLANE, A G A I N?

ISRAEL OSITA EJIOGU

AuthorHouse™ UK
1663 Liberty Drive
Bloomington, IN 47403 USA
www.authorhouse.co.uk
Phone: 0800.197.4150

Published by AuthorHouse 02/12/2015

ISBN: 978-1-5049-3763-4 (sc)
ISBN: 978-1-5049-3764-1 (e)

Print information available on the last page.

This book is printed on acid-free paper.

Chapter One

That night, she had a dream and in the dream she saw her husband. The dream was rather brief but appeared very real. When she woke up, she was no longer sure whether her husband was alive or truly dead. All she needed was to feel him beside heself to confirm that he was really there beside her. She pondered a while trying to recollect her encounter with him a short while ago, her eyes still closed, her mind, racing fast. But the more she tried to recollect it all, the more confused she became. Her confusion increased when she became no longer sure of where she was. And in the prevailing confusion, she opened her eyes and glanced around but could not actually determine where she was at that time. She began to ponder again this time trying to recollect exactly where she was. Still confused, she rubbed her left hand against her eyes and thereafter opened her eyes wider and glanced round the little bedroom for the same purpose. Unfortunately, she still could not get a positive result. It was very dark all over the room. She hissed. Moments later however, she instinctively, realized that she was in bed in her bedroom. This precipitated a dual feeling in her. First, she felt relieved at realizing where she was. As a result of this, she heaved a sigh of relief. But this made her unhappy also. She had encountered Tasie else where other than in the house for all she could remember. This therefore gave her another concern. "Can this be a mere dream?" she mumbled, feeling disappointed. Suddenly an impulse flashed through her mind. "Could he have gone outside?" she mused. She began to strain her ears so she could hear any noise outside that could turn out to be him. There was no sound, it was rather still everywhere. She hissed again, feeling more depressed. At that moment, her son Osita turned in sleep in his own bed. Violet became quiet. She did not want to wake him. However a few minutes later, he slept off. When she felt that the boy had slept off, she turned her small body this way and that way, and as if this had injected some energy in her, she lazily rose up and sat down on the bed. Suddenly she felt a movement on her cheek and using her left hand, she traced the movement. That turned out to be sweat. She mopped the sweat with the back of her hand, hissing as she did. Frustrated, she lowered her body and went back to sleep. The obvious had dawned on her. Her husband and the father of her children was not really the person she saw. "So that was a mere dream", she bemoaned, hissing. And as if in a trance, her memory began to unfold the unfortunate events. It began to torture her, reminding her of the incident about four years ago. It was as if it were taking place right away. She and Osita were cracking palm kernel together, that fateful Tuesday afternoon, when suddenly, a knock came on the door; "Kwai kwai kwai, kwai kwai kwai," sounded the knock on the door. And quickly following the sound of the knock, was another sound, but one of a familiar female voice. "Please where are the people who live in this house?" the voice had called out, and the caller had at the same time tried to peep into the house through the only door that served as the outlet to the house. And to be able to see through, the caller partially folded and held the faded curtains at the door in her right hand. Although the voice sounded familiar, Violet had demanded who the caller was. "Who is calling please? We are right at the back of the house, do come right in there," she had called back."Oh it's you, my husband's wife, Agbonma," she greeted as the woman emerged. "How are your children?" She added. As she spoke, she slanted a glance at her visitor, while her hands remained busy, cracking palm kernels. "We're doing well," Agbonma replied, her face full of smiles. "And how are your own children?" she inquired in return, while her hands equally busied, trying to hold her almost loosed wrapper back in place. And after further pleasantries, she unfolded the purpose of her visit. "My husband's wife," Agbonma had begun, "please release my son, Osita to come and help me lay my articles of trade on my head, for I am billed for the market now," adding "each day that he helps me carry my wares, I make a tremendous sale in the market. That is the reason why I have come to ask him to also help me now". "Everyone in this village seems to share this same opinion that Osita wears good furtune on his forehead", Violet remarked, grinning, and quickly added, "God will keep me alive to see what this lad grows up to become" "He certainly does not only wear good fortune on his face, he equally wears God's favor," Agbonma said matter of factly, as she turned her back to leave, adding "I see in him an Iroko tree in the making." "Amen, my sister. We, I mean the child and I, do completely accept that prophetic assertion by you." Violet enthused but quickly added, just before Agbonma finally turned her back to leave, "the lad will be with you in a moment's time."

However, no sooner had Agbonma left, than two young men, each wearing faded jean trousers as if in uniforms, knocked on Violet's door. "Come right at the back of the house," Violet called, raising her head to see who it is this time around. Violet was later to find out that one of the two young men turned out to be her husband's younger brother, Ezekwem. Ezekwem came in with a distant relative of the Tasie's. "Oh it's you, my husband's brother, you are very welcomed," Violet greeted, momentarily suspending what she was doing. This she did as a sign of respect for her brother inlaw. "Please do sit down," she added, pointing at a wooden bench near Osita. "Thank you very much my wife," Ezekwem replied, adjusting the bench for the sitting comfort of both himself and his companion. When Ezekwem and his companion accepted to sit down, Violet knew that she had to completely stop work, at least, for as long as they stayed. It would amount to gross disregard to her guests if she continued with her work while they were in her house. It would not matter whether they were staying long or not. Tradition demands that she suspends what ever she had at hand. That is not all. She had to give her total attention to them. That way, she would know their purpose of coming. Failure to do so, she would have portrayed herself in the light of a poorly brought up woman. This was unthinkable to her. She therefore brought her own sit close to them.

Ezekwem was the first person to speak in this gathering. "I can see my son, Osita and yourself here, where are the others.?" he enquired, caressing Osita's head with his right hand. But as if he was not expecting any response from

Violet, he went on. "I hope that they are equally doing very well." As he spoke, Violet noticed that Ezekwem tried as much as possible to avoid her own eyes. This made her feel somewhat uncomfortable, but she swept the matter under the carpet. "We are all fine," she answered back, but kept stealing glances at her guests even as a sense of premonition began to build up in her mind. "What shall I offer you?" she asked, after a brief period of silence. As she pronounced the last word, she rose on her feet and made to enter the only bedroom there was in the house for some kolanuts. She was, however, asked to leave out kolanuts by her brother-in-law. "No, my wife, there is no need for kolanuts," Ezekwem had said, gesticulating with a wave of the hand. That was when Violet began to suspect that all was not really well after all, but could not make out what the matter was all about.

Ezekwem would not turn down any offer made to him by his relatives. He would rather accept everything with thanks. It does not matter whether such offers appear in form of food. It does not matter, either, whether they appear in form of presentations that are as little as alligator pepper. What ever was presented to him, as long as it is edible, he was sure to receive with smile. It is based on this premise that Adanna, one of his elder sisters, nick named him, 'Ori wom wom', 'he who eats every thing, and at any time'. That was long before Adanna got married. However, the name had persisted till today even though no one dares mention it to his hearing.

And so Violet was taken aback when Ezekwem turned down her offer of colanuts. At first she thought he must be sick. But by merely looking at him, she discarded the idea that ill health must be behind it. "Some thing very serious must be in the offing," she mused. "I hope it's all well?" she found her voice almost immediately and inquired, fixing a steady glance at Ezekwem. Ezekwem tried to open his mouth and speak, but could not. He felt a lump in his throat. This did not allow him to speak. Trying hard to swallow the lump therefore, he merely succeeded in nodding his head.

Although the men had agreed to, and had tried as much as possible to put on a front that all were well, something in Ezekwem had caused him to falter. In addition to avoiding Violet's eyes, his voice took a progressive down ward disposition that was not akin to him. The Ezekwem's voice that was familiar to Violet was a typically masculine voice, deep and hoarse. In contrast to that, however, the voice that was speaking now, sounded confused or out right jittery. This was apart from the incoherence that dotted the voice's speech. All these had summed up to confirm Violet's fears. As a result, she inadvertently rose on her feet, unsure of the reason, though. Unwittingly too, she dragged herself into the bedroom. But realizing that she had no tangible reason to leave her guests on their own, she returned to the place where they were and took back her seat. In the prevailing circumstances, she was no longer sure whether her exit from that place was responsible to the uneasy calm that ensued or Ezekwem's demeanour. However, in spite of herself, she decided within herslef that whatever be the cause of the uneasy calm, must be broken. That was when she summoned courage and spoke as she had never spoken before. "Are you sure that all is well, my husband? If there is any problem anywhere, please tell your wife, and stop tormenting me with this silence," she heard her own voice demand. "It is all well," Ezekwem answered again, but almost inaudibly. But quickly added, "I brought this to you, I mean you and the kids". And having said that, he produced a special kind of soap and some other body care products. He moved closer to Violet with the cosmetics in hand. And feigning a smile that turned awkward, handed the materials over to Violet. She hesitated before accepting the gifts. With the gifts in her hands, she stood there as if transfixed to the ground. But as if she had later consulted with herself, she opened her mouth and hurled at the young men, a series of questions. "Thank you my husband's brothers," she had began, "but can I know what purpose these gifts are for? Are you not really trying to conceal something from me? How can I really accept this gift when you are treating me with secrecy?" And as if the walls of his resistance had collapsed, Ezekwem still standing on his feet, facing Violet, let the cat loose.

"My companion's name is Ebuzo," he said, pointing at Ebuzo. "He is the grandson of Okoroigbo. While Okoroigbo, himself, is a brother to my mother's elder brother."

But without waiting for Ezekwem to go on, Violet turned to Ebuzo and formally greeted him. "Welcome, my husband," she said and genuflected. She did not like Ezekwem's preambles, though. All that she needed to hear was the real purpose for this visit. It was not that Ezekwem never visited in the past. He did. But she had never felt the way she is feeling now, at any of Ezekwem's visits in the past. And on the other hand, Ezekwem had not behaved the way he is behaving today in any of his visits in the past. "So why all these odd feelings?" she mused, but finding her voice, she spoke out. "I do not know the reason why you are introducing this man to me. I wish….." She was in turn, cut short by Ezekwem. "I was not trying to introduce anybody to you. I was rather trying to deliver a message to you," he tried to correct.

Chapter Two

"Ebuzo was invited a few days ago, to a hospital at Oguta. The purpose was to meet with one Mazi Ojo Ole," Ezekwem had said, but had paused awhile. This was to see how Violet would react. And when he thought that she was stable, he went on. "Ebuzor and Ojo were servants together to a particular man at Ishiokpo." He however, could not continue with his story, as a drama had ensued, and had cut him short. Apparently, Violet had become apprehensive at hearing the word ' hospital'. It had jolted her to the marrow. And as she stood there, listening to Ezekwem, she felt her heart beat very hard against her rib. This made her feel as if she were collapsing. She had therefore tried to steady herself with the mud that made the walls of her husband's hut. But when she felt that Ezekwem's story was getting too long and her legs had begun to cave in under her slim body weight, she lowered her body and sat down on the bare ground, crying as she tried to do so. "'O-s-i-t-a-ee, O-s-i-t-a-ee," she began to lament, "your father has killed me. My God has killed me."

In this part of the world, it is believed that if one's guardian spirit or 'Chi' does not let any harm reach him, no 'external' force can harm the one. That was the reason why

Violet had accused her 'Chi' for 'killing' her. Furthermore, it is believed that it is not only when life has been completely squeezed out of a person, that the one can be considered killed. Rather, there is a magnitude of harm that befalls a man, or a woman, as the case may be, that is considered as being tantamount to killing the one. That was the reason why Violet lamented her own death rather than the supposed death of her husband.

"Shut up your mouth, woman, what information can you claim to have heard so far, that is responsible to making you cry now?" Ezekwem retorted, fixing a hard look at Violet, his face deeply furrowed, while Ebuzo looked on, his mouth wide open. A few minutes later, other close relatives who heard Violet lamenting, began to gather at the scene. As the men folk tried to pacify Violet, they exchanged glances among themselves, even as the women folk tried to hold her in their hands, in a bid to steady as well as comfort her. Some of the women were also carefully watching her waist. This was to checkmate her wrapper from loosing off her waist. With their eyes, those who were uninformed about the accident asked if Tasie were already dead. And with their eyes too, Ezekwem and his companion, assured them that he was still alive.

Violet was later to understand that Ezekwem's informant, Ojo, was himself a younger brother to one of the victims of the accident that involved her husband. "A road accident?" She lamented, crying pathetically, thrusting both hands to the heavenly. "'Chim,' you have killed me indeed," she lamented on, as tears flowed down her cheeks uncontrolled, but found their way to the ground.

After pacifying Violet, Ezekwem began his story afresh. But not to Violet alone, this time around. Ojo was to link Ebuzo with Violet's husband, Tasie, at the hospital for onward message to Violet. But Ojo and Tasie were not familiar with each other. For that reason, Ebuzo, who was familiar to Ojo was to serve as a bridge linking Tasie's family with Ojo.

When Ebuzo got to the hospital, he met the gateman who promptly arranged for a meeting with another man who was to lead him to Tasie. Fortunately, the man turned out to be another distant relative of the Tasies. "Oh it's you my brother, Ojo," Ebuzo greeted, as soon as they were brought together. "My mission has been simplified by the fact that you are the one to bring me to my brother, Tasie," he had added, reaching out for a hand shake with him. He was however taken aback when Ojo did not return his greetings with enough warmth. He rather offered him a casual hand shake, muttering something that was not very clear to him. This had precipitated a sense of fear in Ebuzo's mind. He took a second look at Ojo. That did not satisfy him and so he reached out his hand and took Ojo's own hand in his own. "How is he doing now?" he heard his own voice ask, his eyes boring on Ojo's own. And as if he wanted to confirm his fears, Ojo gave out a sign with his right hand, motioning him to come along with him. He had taken him straight to one of the casualty wards for men. Mesmerised, Ebuzo stood by the bed on which the wounded Tasie lay, heavily bandadged at the head. It was as if he had seen a ghost. He stood still as if transformed to the ground. Initially, he could not utter a word. But as if he had been prompted by an unseen force, he suddenly recollected himself and exhaled deeply, hissed, and began to shake his head in anguish, gnashing his teeth as if he would find solace in that. Ojo on the other hand, stood beside Ebuzo and stared at Tasie as if seeing him for the first time. And as the two men stood there shaking their respective heads as if in an arrangement, an uneasy calm enveloped the entire ward.

However, the meeting between Tasie and his kits and kin, came to a close when the doctor on call demanded that the meeting should end. "Please do not expose him to further talks. He has spoken at length, let him get some rest now," he said, as he turned his back to leave. "Thank you very much Sir, for the time allowed us," the two men said almost in unison as they equally turned and lazily moved out behind the doctor. This was however, after bidding farewell to Tasie.

When Ebuzo finally got home, he made straight to Ezekwem's house and narrated the story to him, but admitted that he could not grasp the full details of the story. "It is something that demands the attention of more than one person," he said matter- of- factly.

Early the next day, Ezekwem was accompanied to the hospital by Ojo. And although they arrived later in the morning, they were given the details of the accident much later in the day.

The Pepsi Cola van en route to Umuahia from Oguta had somersaulted at the dangerous Njaba Bridge, due to failure of the brakes. The vehicle was carrying some goods as well as some personnels of the company. There had been many casualties. Some people died at the spot. Others sustained severe injuries and Tasie was among the latter.

"God, this is terrible," Ezekwem had cried, letting out a few drops of tears down his cheek. And at the sight of tears on Ezekwem's cheeks, Ojo tactically led him out of the ward, his right hand wound around Ezekwem's shoulders. "Remember that you are the one to console your brother's wife and children. You are expected therefore, to exhibit the real man in you," he admonished him. And at the time they dragged themselves back to the ward, it was a somewhat stable Ezekwem that met his elder brother. Later that same day, Tasie gave some money to Ezekwem. This was meant to buy soap and other body care, which were to be delivered to his wife, Violet. The message was an assurance to her that her husband was alive, while the gift was to serve as the evidence. "This is a token from me and to you as evidence that I am still alive," the message had borne.

However, typical of every woman, Violet had become hysterical, and had cried herself hoars. Hours later, the extended family clan had gathered to commiserate with her. And after the initial shock, the men folk appointed a team of delegates who were to leave the next day with Ezekwem to bring a wider picture of the incident. "Please be thorough," the men had been charged. The delegates really did a good job. There is a saying in the land that "'ezuoka aha eri udele, atotuo ngiga', meaning that 'when the titans and great minds converge, they brainstorm on important issues."

So when the delegates came home with the information that the doctor who was a white man had told them that the war made drugs and other medical facilities inaccessible to the hospital, and that the extent of wound sustained by Tasie, coupled with the spot concerned, all together posed a great threat to his life, the 'Umunna' sat together again and subsequently brought him to a nearby hospital in Owerri.

Unfortunately, it was not long after, that the beloved Tasie, left for the world beyond. Thus Violet became a young widow, a widow with six children.

Chapter Three

"My husband's brother," said Violet, Osita's mother, "what on earth shall we do? His teachers seem to have taken it upon themselves to put pressure on me. It is as if there is an agreement that is binding to all of them. I mean his teachers, to try and convince me on the same issue. Maybe, they think that I need to be convinced about it. Last Eke market day," she tried to recount, "A man came here. He introduced himself as Mr. Nduka, a teacher in his school. There was no man in the house that evening. And I had only come home from the farm. And so I did not bring him into the house. I rather came out and met him at the threshold of the door," she said, pointing at the spot near the door leading into the small parlour.

As she spoke, she tried to force herself to smile. It was as if she was troubled inwardly but did not want to betray her real emotional feelings. And so, the smile she put on was neither broad nor natural. It was somewhat awkward. But she spoke on nonetheless.

"Initially" she continued, "her hands clasped in front of her, her left palm on top of her right palm, both hands trying to demonstrate how taken aback she was at seeing the man, a total stranger, knocking at her door at that time of the evening, her eyes fixed at Michael." I thought he was going to ask which one of the houses was yours or Nnadi's own or any of the men's own.

"Wait a minute," Michael said suddenly, gesturing at Violet, thereby interrupting the gist. "Ebere, Ebere," he called, looking towards the back of the house. There was no answer. "Ebere, Ebere," he called again, his voice rising, his attention focused towards the same direction. "Where has this boy gone to? he querried, still focusing towards the back of the house. He was about calling again when Ebere's voice came on air. "Oh o- o- o-," he answered, a frown on his face. "I wonder why papa would not allow someone a moment's rest in this house," he grumbled, adding, "he would always have one errand or another to send one to." "Please bring us two benches from the kitchen," Michael said, gesticulating with his hand as soon as Ebere appeared. Having said this, he turned back and faced Violet. "Please go on, woman," he said as soon as Ebere had left, his ears rapped up in an apparent keen interest. "As I was saying," Violet began again, repeating what she just said "I initially thought that he was having problem trying to locate the house of any of the men's folk in this compound including your own. I was surprised when he rather said he had come to see me".

No sooner had Violet made the last statement than Ebere returned, carrying two benches in his hands. Michael promptly took one of the benches. "Give that one to Ostia's mother," he said, lowering his thick set body on one he had taken from Ebere.

"Me? I thought in my heart, but tried to conceal my fears," Violet said, lowering her onto the bench. "I hope it is alright?" I inquired. "Yes it is for good", the man promptly said, fixing a glance at me.

"I hope you are Ostia Tasie's mother?" he asked, his gaze still fixed at me. "Yes," I stuttered as my heart promptly skipped a beat. But the man quickly came to my rescue as if he realized that I had been somewhat disturbed in the heart. He went straight to the object of his visit. "That boy is a very bright star, though one in the making," he had said and quickly added, "please do give him a broad enough opportunity to acquire western education, even if it entails selling all the landed properties that you have. If you do, you will be fostering a great star," he had said and paused, still staring at me, as if waiting to hear from me. Unfortunately, I could not say a word. I opened my mouth to speak, but the words, the rights words, eluded my mouth. And as if he understood how worried I had become, he turned his back and left. I stood there as if transfixed to the ground. Frankly speaking, 'Nnam ochie', as I tell you this story, I cannot recollect when or how the man left this compound. Rather than open my mouth and speak, I allowed my brain to take me along memory lane. I remembered, an encounter of this sort. That one was however, between a fellow woman and myself.

It was on the last Eke market day. One of the teachers, who introduced herself as Mrs. Echeanyanwu accosted me on my way to the farm and stopped me. It was this same matter that she brought up. "Please mama Osita" the woman had said to me, "do something about that boy. Let him be given all the education that he can get in this life."

And as she spoke, she laid a great deal of emphasis on the word 'all' as if education were free.

Matter - of -fact, my husband's brother, that did not go down well with me. She did not sound like one who had a feminine blood in her system. She rather sounded like one who was trying to teach someone else her responsibility. At least that is how her sermon sounded to me and I hate the idea of someone else trying to tell me what my responsibilities are. After all you and I know that it is my uttermost desire to offer to these children the opportunity to get to the highest educational level that they could attain. You men have a way of believing that women hate themselves. It is actually not true. But some of us women do not know how not to talk to another person or in the public, she stressed, her forehead slightly contorted. As she made her last statement, Violet felt that she had betrayed her fellow women. That was not what she came to talk over with her husband's elder brother. She promptly changed the picture. She tried to reproduce a finer image of the women folk. That woman's sermon to me made a whole lot of sense, now I know it. What she said made a whole lot of sense, just like most women make sense in their talk. I was the one who was wrong. I probably was in bad frame of mind when she and I met. You know some of these problems like the issue of Osita's education can weigh even the strongest of all men down. How much more a woman, I mean a widow like me. As she made the last statement, Violet lowered her face, shaking it as she did, her eyes suddenly turned red, her nostrils stuffy with mucus.

"Well, my wife, I have heard your story. I feel a great pain in my heart each time this matter is brought up," Michael began, shaking his own head as well, his face also lowered to the ground, his heart aching while he tried to muster enough strength to stop the hot tears that were also brewing up in his eyes. He did not want Violet to notice the tears that had almost coalesced in his own eyes. It would amount to sheer cowardice to shed tears in front of a woman. So he vehemently withstood the tears as well as the urge to weep. "This is not the first encounter that I have had with the men who teach my son Osita in the school," he stressed on, his deep masculine voice cracking as the weight of emotion took its toll on him. As he spoke, he paused at intervals. This was to allow Violet absorb his speech step by step. That man who came to you, I mean Mr. Nduka, has met with me on several occasions with this same matter. It may be that he thinks that I do not take what he said seriously. That could be the reason why he had decided to come to you on the matter. It might further interest you to hear that many of his teachers in addition to this Mr. Nduka had taken turns to come and meet with me over the issue. He was the first man to approach me on the issue, though. The first day that he came here for that same mission coincided with the day that my first son came back from the township. The man was offered a fresh and sweet palm wine as kola on arrival by my son. Soon after that visit he came again. I think I made the same mistake that you made. I thought that it was because of the palm wine that was offered to him the first day he came that induced him to come again. 'Why don't people mind their own business,' I had thought. But when he came again and again without any body offering him any kola, I began to think otherwise about him. I discovered that he had my son's interest in mind. Now as if that is not enough, his colleagues, both males and females have toed the same part. That is to show that they have seen something in this boy."

This last statement was followed by a pause. The two in-laws sat opposite each other, each bearing his head on his hand as if in agreement. And as if so agreed too each also got enveloped in thoughts.

After what seemed like ages, Violet found her voice and spoke "'Nnam Ochie' My husband's brother, what shall we do, then?"

This queston precipitated another period of silence that was so thick that it seemed as if it could be felt with the hand. Moments later, Michael heaved a sigh. It was not clear, however whether that was a sigh of relief or otherwise. He opened his mouth to talk but soon closed it, again. No word came out. He lowered his face again, but raised it up after a few moments, anguish clearly written on his face. He heaved another sigh, hissed and shook his head. It was as if somebody that is very important was lost in the family.

However, after what seemed like another age, Michael finally found his voice. It was as if he had been infused with strength from an unseen being. "Woman, I mean, my wife, please go in and have some rest. Our elders have a saying that 'Inspite of how challenging a situation proves, it is not actually insurmountable." As he said this, he rose from the bench, went into his room, and threw himself on the hard bed, his face focused on the ceiling, his eyes open, but seeing nothing.

Chapter Four

Osita's father had died a few years earlier. He died at the middle of the war, a few months after his forty-second birthday. No one was expecting his death even in the next four decades. No. No one, not even himself.

When he was alive, there was something he incessantly told his children. And he said it as candidly as he envisaged it. It was as if he thought that by saying it out daily, that vision would come into manifestation. He said. "Look, I passed through hell, in my growing up years." And as he spoke, he glanced at his six children, one after another. As if he was not satisfied with that, he lowered the stake. He used a simpler expression. This was to ensure that, everyone understood him very well. "I, I passed through the thick and the thin", he would say, shaking his head, as he spoke. "How do you mean, Papa?" Osita once asked him, his face raised up to face his father's own. "I suffered in the hands of poverty," he tried to explain, hissing and shaking his head at the same time. After a pause, he went on. "But as God grants me long life, none of my children would suffer in this life." He said this, matter-of-factly. Did he have it as he planned?

Unfortunately, as a result of his death, his widow, Violet, Osita's mother, had been compelled to do certain odd jobs which she could not have done were her husband alive. These she did in order to make ends meet.

One morning, little Osita was cracking the shell of oil palm seeds, along with his mother as they were wont to do. Intermittently, his mother brought up a song, and Osita joined in the singing. And bathing in the euphoria of the music, they achieved the rounding off of what they termed the first phase of the job, without feeling the strain or stress that is associated with the job.

"Mama," Osita, suddenly called with a chuckle, "I'm faster than you in this phase." Violet smiled back at him, and momentarily suspended the work she was doing. "Have you forgotten that Agbonma called me and I went to see her, though briefly, or was it not at the course of this phase?" she replied, her face still full of smiles. "Oh yes, Mama, I remember" Osita admitted, nodding his head even as he smiled back at his mother. "However, my son," Violet began again, her eyes fondly focused on her son while she momentarily suspended work the second time, the same day. "You are truly fast. You seem to learn quickly, even in school. That reminds me," she recounted, this time, resuming her work. "Your teacher came here, yesterday." "My teacher?" Osita asked, looking surprised. But as if he was not expecting any reply to his first question, he came up with another one. "Do you know my teacher?" he asked again, still surprised. "She was the one who told me that she is your teacher," Violet explained, grinning. "Please, mama, I can't wait to hear what she came to do," Osita grinned, tilting his sitting position in order to enable him sit face to face with his mother. "My son, go ahead and crack the kernel," she replied, her face suddenly turned solemn.

“Those teachers of yours,” she went on, “I hope they won’t kill me one of these days. What else did you think she came to do?” she asked, a frown now on her face. “Perhaps they do not understand what it means to be a widow. A widow who does not have a helper of any sort”.

She began to recount Mrs Echeanyanwu’s recent visit to her house. As she tried to do so, hot tears began to gather in her eyes. Moments later, she began to mope her eyes and nostrils which had become damp with tears, using one end of the worn out wrapper which she was wearing. Osita’s blood ran cold when he noticed this. He could no longer continue with his questions. As it were, he intuitively suppressed the curiousity that surged in him. And in the minutes that followed, the atmosphere around became moody as if in sympathy with the feelings of this young woman and her son. This was followed by an uneasy period of silence that seemed so thick that it could be felt with the hand. This was one mood in which Osita hated to see his mother to appear.

That was however not the first that she had appeared so moody. Osita had tried as much as possible to get used to it, but had unfortunately failed to scale through. The mood on the other hand seemed to stubbornly continue to raise its ugly head every now and then. Now that the ugly situation was up again, both mother and child had continued with their work in silence as if in agreement. However, when he felt that his mother was not coming forth with his last question, and the brief period of silence had begun to seem like ages to him, Osita could not help but had broken the silence by bringing up the issue again. “Mama,” he had called, but had hesitated almost immediately. He could not form the right words to use, and so had stopped short.

Violet heard her name. She raised her head up, and looked enquiringly at the boy. But when Osita would not utter a word, she felt that he was getting emotional and thought it right to break the silence. "You called me, Osita," she said, fixing a glance at him and momentarily suspended her work. Osita now considered this as a clear opportunity to go on with his questions. "Did she come because of my schooling?" He asked, his voice low, his head somewhat lowered too, and his eyes hooded. "You are still asking questions. I have told you that she introduced herself as Mrs. Echeanyanwu, and said that she had come to repeat her plea that I should send you to a secondary school by the time you finished your primary school next year," Violet tried to narrate, unwittingly letting out a few drops of tears which found their way to the ground.

Osita and his mother thus chatted while cracking and separating the palm kernel seeds from the shells. They did so every day, between the morning hours and the afternoon, when the sun shine was still mild. And at the end of every week of eight days which coincides with 'Nwafor' or 'Afor Obodoma' market day, whatever quantity of the palm kernel seed they collected, she would sell in the market. This was their means of livelihood.

Chapter Five

Nwafor market is located near their home. On each market day, Violet would leave very early in the morning for the sale of the palm kernels which they had processed. She would buy all the food stuffs which the kernel sale could afford. While buying the food stuffs, she would also buy more uncracked palm kernel to compliment whatever quantity that was remaining at home. But if she came home and realized that there were some items she forgot to buy, she would not mind going back to the market to buy the items, since the market was only a stone throw from their house.

While his mother was away in the market, Osita would remain in the house. His heart would be saturated with prayers that God might grant his mother a good sale so that she might in turn buy enough food stuffs for their use before the next market day. He usually takes up this prayer passionately. The reason is that the amount of money realized from the sale of the product was directly proportional to the magnitude of food stuffs she was able to buy. Those days when God seemed to have granted his prayers, his mother added a little luxury to her purchases.

The luxury was usually in form of fish, especially smoked ones. Aside from those exceptional weeks, soup which was usually prepared on market days, were without fish, only crayfish, enough vegetables and other condiments, when available, were used.

On one occasion, Osita's mother had forgotten something in the market, and had asked someone else who was coming back from the market to ask him to bring the thing to her in the market, while she waited at a designated place, usually at the stall of one of their numerous relatives.

Initially, Osita, while he moved along the roads in the market, would expect to see those who took it upon themselves to shout 'woooooohh', once they got to the market square. He was however disappointed when all he could see were people busy negotiating either the sale or purchase of an article of trade, but the sound was not stopping, nonetheless. This had continued to pose a puzzle to Osita's young mind. One day, he had summoned courage and asked his mother about the issue. "Mama," he had begun, "do you partake in the sounds that I hear in the market?" "Which one?" asked his mother, looking confused. "Aren't you hearing the heavy noise that I hear emanating from the market? It seems some people are shouting 'wooooh' at the market square," he added. The amused young woman had right away explained out the puzzle to him. "There is no shouting in the market," she began, "it is just that there are very many people in the market," adding, "What you hear is the collective sound of the voices of these people as they talk randomly. That is actually what constitutes the sound you hear," she tried to explain thoroughly, and at the same time reached out for a palm kernel seed which she picked up and threw into her mouth.

"How was the sale?" Osita asked, trying to change the subject matter. And having observed what little quantity of food items which his mother was able to buy in the market, he digressed a little and commented on that without waiting for the answer to his first question. "Mama," he had called, fixing a glance at his mother.

"You didn't buy enough garri?" "Yes my son," Osita's mother began, frowning as she spoke."The sale was poor today. I had gone round the market hoping that somebody may pay even a little more than what others had offered, but that was not to be," she said, hissing. Osita knew what that entailed. In moments like this when his mother buys a little quantity of garri, he was not to worry. He had gotten used to such predicaments. What they did was sure, though unpalatable. They would eat garri and soup on some occasions, but at other times, they cooked a large quantity of soup. This would serve as food, as both mother and son would pick a spoon each, and helped themselves to the delicacy. After eating, each felt satisfied momentarily, only to feel otherwise after urinating twice.

Chapter Six

The next day after each Afor-Obodoma market day, mother and son resumed their business of palm kernel cracking. They did not have to waste any day. If they did, that would tell on the quantity of seeds they would produce for the week. To enhance their speed, mother and child adopted a competitive stance. An equal quantity of the uncracked kernel was deposited in front of each of them. Water or any other item they might need was provided enough, too. This is to ensure that none was disadvantaged against the other. They were to start simultaneously. By the time both of them rounded off the small hip in front each of them, they counted the end of the first phase. Sometimes, the young Osita rounded off his own a little earlier than his mother, but on many occasions however, the mother toppled the son. Music, they say, is the spice of life. And so, soft songs were raised up, one after another, in the course of the work. "'Odighi onye yiri ya..., odighi onye yiri ya...' There is none to compare with him...," they sang. Another song that piqued Osita's mind each time it was raised was rather, a long one, but one that encouraged unity of purpose. At least that was according to his own youthful mind's understanding. The song tries to remind humanity of the fact that all peoples, irrespective of tribe, colour or race, descended from one creator and so should view one another as belonging to the same nationality. It says, "One body, one body, one GOD, one GOD, one nation, one nation, oh praise His name." The purpose of the singing was to add speed to their work. But in addition to adding to the speed, the singing also impacted on the work by reducing the monotony of the work. To cite an instance, any day that Osita's mother experienced melancholy, the singing did not go far as she would not join in any of the many songs that Osita would raise. She would rather sing her own type. "Dear ...dear...dear" she would burst out "'asi na onwu n'eri ego,.. onwu o n'eri ego, ayi ga-atu ego nye onwu......'" This was one of the songs which she sang in painful mourn for her late husband, Tasie. On such days, the work went on rather less swiftly before boredom sets in. "Mama," Osita would complain, a frown on his face. "Why do you like this song? I have told you that I do not like this song and I do not want to learn it either." If his mother however, continued in this state of mind, it would not be long before one of them, usually Osita, starts yawning. The end point here is obvious, a reduction in their gross production.

Although Violet had tried to suppress the grief in her heart, many times however, she lost a little of the battle due to human weakness. Ordinarily, she had resolved to minimize the rise of any situation that caused grief to Osita. If it were possible, she would live her remaining life with her family facing only the future, while forgetting the past. But life could be cruel when it wants to be. Otherwise why would she almost always keep her son, her dear son busy cracking palm kernels while his mates were out there playing and enjoying their cradle. Sometimes she would console herself alongside her son, that she was doing what she had to do, in order to make of him, a well behaved boy. Oftentimes, she reasoned that she was trying to shape him into a prospective and responsible husband and father, just like his father, when he was alive. "But is that totally right?" her mind would nag."Did they not say that all works and no play on the other hand, was not the best for a growing child?" she heard herself mumble. Each time this thought sweeps through her mind, she would lose control of her emotions. At such times, it would not be difficult for young Osita to ask, "mama, are you crying again? Tell me, mama, are you crying again? I have told you to forget the past and let us face the future." But in the course of trying to cheer his mother up, Osita's own eyes ended up getting wet with tears, too. And at the sight of the tears, Violet quickly mopped her own eyes up and began to cheer her son up. "Men are not supposed to cry or shed tears like women, especially in the presence of women, unless of course you want me to consider you as a woman or a child," she would say to him, her eyes slanted at him. This was to let him not see the tears in her own eyes.

Truly life could be very unfair, she mused, resolving for the umpteenth time that she would really try and forget the past this time around and face the future. But can she really afford to do that? Or forget the hardship which she had been plunged into? Was it not on account of the demise of her young and caring husband that she had become poor? Fortunately for her, it was nearing evening time, so she prepared whatever she could lay her hands on as supper, for the family and went straight to bed.

Chapter Seven

A thought passed through his mind. He suddenly became sober. The thought later developed into a puzzle. And in a short while, it began to unfold a series of pictures in his mind. And so as if in a daze, he lazily dropped the pencil he was holding in his right hand on the small table that he was using, where the book he was reading lay. He had borrowed the book from Udo. That was not the first time he had done that. Osita had been in the habit of borrowing books from his cousins who were privileged to attend school during the war. They called the school session 'win the war school'. His favourite book was the English Reader, Book one. He read the book in anticipation to the day he would be admitted into school like his cousins. His love for books had earned him the nick name 'Bukuru'. One of his many friends, Donald, had given him that nickname. Although he did not know the real meaning of the name, he had postulated that it meant either 'the critical thinker' or 'avid reader' or both. This was owing to the circumstances that precipitated the name. For instance, each time that he answered a question correctly, which answer, Donald considered, difficult, he was sure to hail him and call him by that name. Another time that Donald used that name on him was when he thought that Osita had been reading for quite a long time.

Each time he read the book or any other story book, his interest in such books seemed to soar to the high heavens. They had a way of arousing in him, the longing for the day when he would be able to write his own story book. “If I write my own book” he mused, “I hope that the publishers of the book would agree to write my name as the author on the cover of the book, instead of their own name.” As he thought of this, he glanced back at the name written on the front cover, as well as the picture of the person on the back cover of the book in his hand. He viewed them with admiration. He wondered if the name that was written on the book cover and qualified by the word ‘by’, stood for the writer of the book or its publishers. “Whichever is the case in this one, I will try and persuade them to write my own name not theirs on my book,” he mumbled, and tried to resume reading. But he could not read any further. As he sat down on his bed, his face raised up, his eyes focused ahead, but seeing nothing, he could not help, but allowed the thought to invade his mind a second time, hauling a series of questions at his young mind.

“Why on earth did father give that whole kolanut to me as if I were an adult or was he so drunk that he forgot my age?” he mused, leaning back. And as if a new question would give answer to the first ones, his mind came up with more questions. “Was there any underlying meaning to that demonstration? Why did he not give the kolanut to my elder brothers since they were both older than me?” he sighed, his pencil now held up close to his mouth.

He was still pondering over this when he suddenly heard a voice. It was his mother's voice. "If you are no longer reading, son, please put that lantern off and save my kerosene, did you hear that?" the voice said emphatically, thereby breaking the flow of his thought "No mama, I'm still reading," he answered quickly and lowered his face towards the book on the table. "Don't waste my kerosene unnecessarily please. Do put off the light as soon as you are through with reading," his mother grunted. "Alright mama," he replied, trying to concentrate back on the book, "I will soon put the lantern off."

Soon after, Osita adjusted his sitting position and read a few more lines. But soon too, he gradually began to loss concentration again, although he was unaware of the fact. Soon, his mind began to stroll back to the same issue. As the picture began to unfold itself, Osita began to feel a chill down his spine. Suddenly he felt his head swell ten times over its normal size. Soon too, goose pimples sprang up all over his body. Although it had been in the past, he still felt as if it were taking place now. He had heard Gold shout on top of her voice that eventful afternoon, every fear in the world manifesting itself in her voice, "'Agwo-oo, agwo-oo, agwo-oo, agwo-oo'. Here is a snake, here is a snake," she had cried several times. And as she cried, she held up both hands on her head, her eyes fixed on the snake, her right leg raised slightly up, making it rest on her toes rather than on her foot.

At the first sound of the cry, he had felt his heart suddenly jump into his heart. And quickly he had turned his face towards the sound of the cry. He was shocked to the marrow when he saw the long green snake, lazily moving up the few cement steps that lead into the outer door to their house.

As he saw the snake move on the steps, he felt his heart jump into his mouth and began to beat hard against his chest, his mouth wide open, eyes broadened as if they would bulge out, his hands also held up on top of his head as if he tried to emulate Gold. He quickly remembered that his father was sleeping right inside that room. This made him feel like flying into the house even before the snake entered so that he could protect the sleeping man. Fear and anguish increasingly filled his heart and all the hairs in his body cropped up. He inadvertently but urgently joined Gold and began to shout on top of his own voice. "'Agwo-oo, agwo-oo, agwo-oo'", he heard his own voice ring, overlapping Gold's own voice. And as if the snake heard its name, it suddenly turned right and began to move faster, trying to maneuver its way into safety. Luckily, that was not to be. In a twinkle of an eye, a handful of men and women attracted by the cry had gathered and gone into a calculated effort to kill it, yelling at one another as they tried to do so. "Hit it at the head, hit it at the head. No, not there. Mind your leg."

As the snake made its desperate move to get into safety, about three or four long sticks held by different, but able bodied and brave men, began to land on its smooth body while a larger number of people stood around advising who hits the snake and at what spot to do that. Unfortunately, some of the aims made at the snake missed their targets. However, it was finally killed when a hard stroke made by Uchenna landed on its head. It tried to curl itself. But as if that was not suiting it, it began to hit its long frame here and there on the ground. More strokes landed on its body, nonetheless. Soon its body went limb.

"It is dead," about three or more voices announced happily. "We will roast it and eat up the flesh," one of the men announced grinning. "Yes we will roast it," said another man, but quickly added, "we shall however not eat it without first cooking it, as well." "Who said that we shall not cook it before eating?" the first man snapped, his face slightly furrowed. "I thought that you suggested that we eat it up after merely roasting it," answered the second one. "Both of you talk as if you do not know that one could roast it up very well and eat without cooking it," a third voice chided, shifting his gaze from one of the men to the other.

"Have you chopped off its head?" he added in form of a question, whereas he was actually trying to make a jest of the other men. As he spoke, he reached out his hand and dragged the dead snake towards himself, using the long stick in his hand. "That is very true. Get a matchet and chop off its head, while I open up the ground where it would be buried." "Cut it from this point," the first man opined, pointing at a part of the dead snake's body close to its head. And effortlessly, the third man chopped off the snake's head using a long and sharp matchet. He however ignored that other man's opinion of the part where it would be chopped off, and cut it from another point. Blood gushed out at both the neck and head ends.

Osita was still seized with fear. He did not want to go closer even though he would have wanted to go and see his father in the room. The men who killed the snake were still chatting over the snake when Tasie, Osita's father suddenly appeared at the door, obviously oblivious of what had happened. "What is going on here?" he asked, shifting glances first at Osita, and then at the young men, one after another, as if trying to count them. And for an answer, they began to exchange glances as if that was what he said to do. There was no vocal answer. In place of an answer, the young men glanced back at him almost simultaneously as if in agreement. And in what seemed like an act of being amazed, they exchanged glances among themselves repeatedly, a mock smile on the faces of some of them. He moved closer and leaned against one of the door posts, and watched the men more closely. That was when he noticed the dead snake. "My God!" he exclaimed, shuddered and drew back a bit, his eyes propping out, his mouth wide open. Moments later, however, he returned to the door, his eyes shifting from the dead snake to the men and back at the snake. "Please what is going on here?" he asked once again this time, his eyes fixed on Osita, his hands spread enquiringly in front, his mouth wide open.

Osita had seen his father emerge at the door from the distance where he stood. As soon as he saw him, he moved quickly towards him but stopped momentarily at the step. That was because his father stood at the entrance to the room, thereby blocking his way into the room. Another reason was that his father was his concern. Having set his eyes on him, he momentarily felt relieved.

And at this point his father began to repeat his question on what had actually taken place. He was taken aback when he heard his father ask the question. He wondered why he did not hear the whole noise that was generated at the instance of the snake. "Did he not really hear the noise, or was he putting on a front as the adult that he is? If he did not really hear the noise, was there any significant reason for that? Or was it just coincidental. If anything was responsible for his not hearing the noise, what was it? Could it have to do with the snake?" All these questions and more flashed through his mind but he pushed them to the back of his mind.

"Please take the dead snake away from here," Tasie pleaded to the young men after hearing what had taken place. As he spoke, he shook his head repeatedly, a frown on his face, his forehead, somewhat furrowed. "I think I need some quietness and rest …," he added, concluding it with "thank you very much for all that you have done. If not for you, who knows what mission the snake was billed to carry out."

Father and son sat on the bed in silence after the men had dispersed. It was as if a moment of silence was being observed by both of them. However, a few minutes later, the father broke the silence. "Take this kolanut" he said offering a big kolanut to Osita, who was sitting by his right. "If I go to bed tonight but fail to wake up tomorrow morning, this kolanut shall serve as a symbol to you that your father gave his love out to you before he eventually died," he added, looking Osita straight in his eyeball, his own eyes looking emotional.

Osita had himself, become emotional too. Although he did not understand what it all meant, he had hitherto felt a sense of forboding sweep through his mind. He had heard of harbingers and things like that. "Now was the presence of the snake a harbinger of evil? Did his father think in that line?"

In that split second, another thought flashed through his mind. And an incident that took place a few years before flooded his memory. It was as if it took place only yesterday. He could see it all with his mind's eyes as if it were reoccurring at this time.

He remembered how his father would come back home after the close of work each day, eat his food and take a brief rest on the bed. Soon after the rest, he would take him out, lift him up and land him on his shoulders. So would he carry him on his shoulders. His two legs would hang low, around his father's neck and rest down on his chest. Then his father would reach his hands up and get hold of his own hands. His father's right hand would hold his own right hand and his father's left hand, equally held his own left hand. Carrying him on his shoulders in this manner, his father would begin to stroll around the neighbourhood, singing one song after another. "Osita the great… the Duke of chamber… ability, ability…." There was this other song that he also usually sang. This song always piqued Osita's interest. "I am a blessed man… Jesus makes me a blessed man… so I am a blessed man." As he sang these songs, his father's face beamed with smile. There was one other song that his father took delight in singing, too. That one seemed to last longer than others. It seemed to him that his father loved that song more than the others. Each time the song was on his lips, his strides changed. He would take his strides as if he was holding a match past. He would move his left leg first, and then his right leg. Each stride however, was wider spaced out than his normal strides. "The church is marching on, the church is marching on, the gates of hell shall not prevail, the church is marching on." As his father sang and demonstrated to this song with march-like strides, he swung Osita's own hands in the air with his own hands. This had a way of evoking laughter in Osita. He would laugh and laugh and laugh.

Athough these songs appealed to Osita's young mind richly, he did not actually get the clear meaning of their wordings. And so, he did not really understand what the songs were all about. For instance, when his father sang 'Osita, the Duke of chamber', this would sound to Osita's ears as, 'Osita, the Book of Chamber'. In spite of this, however, he tried to memorize some of them. He tried to sing some of them even at his father's absence. At times, he succeeded in getting the songs right. "You like that one?" his father asked him. "Yes," he happily admitted, his face beaming with smile. "Can you sing it alone?" his father asked, trying to look up and take a glance at Osita's face. "Yes, I can sing it" he replied, trying hard to sound convincing. "Now go on and sing it on your own," his father joked.

Thus he and his father would go on and have a good time. And as if to seal the good time up, his father would buy him a can of canned beef, or a bottle of fruit juice or a can of margarine and bread. It gradually became a daily exercise which Osita had habitually looked forward to, as the days rolled by. But now that his father was no more alive all these and many more had been all over. As this thought flashed through his mind, he felt some hot tears coalesce in his eyes.

Chapter Eight

Tasie's house or ancestral home as afore said, is only about a few kilometers away from the urban township of Owerri along Okigwe Road. From the time of our great grandfathers, the name Obodoma had evoked respect from the villages that were afar off, as well as those that were in close neighbourhood of this great and famous village. There is a saying that the average man from Obodoma was exceptionally industrious and patriotic. He is in fact so patriotic that people from other villages in the neighbourhood envied as well as tried to copy their method of doing things.

Nduhu is one of the villages in close neighbourhood to Obodoma. It shares a common boundary with the later. History has it that girls born into that clan or other nearby villages envy those that are married into Obodoma clan.

In the days preceding the war, it was a well known culture, that any Obodoman, as was the pet name for an indigene of Obodoma, who discovered a gold mine, came home and took some members of the youth and made them equally rich. That was how this urban village made her wave in the time of their fathers. This patriotic nature of the people spurred their fathers into giving the community, the pet name 'OBODO LONDON'.

Indigenes of Obodoma were a people who loved and helped one another too. To cite an instance, Madu, a prosperous textile merchant once came home for no other reason than to pick promising young boys who would serve in his numerous shops spread at various locations in the city."Udo, your son Ikechukwu, strikes me as a brilliant boy. If you give your consent I'd like to take him along while going back to my station, next week. I already have two other boys who are ready to go back with me," he had said to Okoroafor, one of his cousins who lived in the village. "God bless you my own brother. That's why I always ask our fathers to go on and bless you, because I know that when it is well with you, you'll remember your brothers here at home."

Thus, Madu, a textile merchant, resident in Lagos had picked promising young boys and equally made them, textile merchants. Such men as Madu are rewarded by Obodoma clan by giving them traditional titles. Today Madu is 'Ochiri Ozuo 1' or mentor of the youth. Unfortunately, by the third quarter of that year Obodoma began to receive her sons from various parts of the country. Every family got the number of people living in the house increased many times over its normal size. That was the reason why, before his death, Osita's father, Tasie, had revealed to his dear wife, his plan to expand the house they were occupying at that moment. Tasie and his brothers, had each, built a little house when they were younger and fewer in number. Relatively, the houses each had now been made to accommodate a number that is tumultuous to it. Violet and her six children now had to squeeze themselves in a room, both day and night. The same predicament was true with almost all the families in the whole village of Obodoma.

"Shift your legs, Ngozi, you're pressing me against the wall" Jane grumbled, frowning. "No Jane, it's Chika's fault." Ngozi replied, also frowning. "No, it's Chika's fault not mine," Jane protested. "It's Kelechi's fault. She would not keep her legs straight. Papa please tell Kelechi to adjust a little so we can have a breathing space." This way, the Ota family of eight, squeezed themselves on a mat, at bed times.

Toilet facilities became over used. It became a common sight to see defeacates at both sides of the village road. The flies in turn, spread an epidemic of cholera, and this also in turn, claimed many lives.

"S…s…e, see," Kwazema stammered, trying to alert Chibuzor of a sample of defeacate that was close to his left foot. But before the stammerer could say it out, Chibuzor had stepped upon the dirty thing. "Y…yo…you…have already stepped on it," he said, grimacing. This had so annoyed Chibuzor that he felt like striking Kwazema with a blow, but had restrained himself.

Furthermore, food shortage hit the village like a plague. The little available food meant for a few village dwellers, now had to carter for both the original dwellers, and returnees. To cite an instance, Afam and his family and perhaps all the villagers ate anything that came their way including unripe fruits. "This is a sweet paw-paw" Afam said, his mouth full with a lump of paw-paw "My own is not that sweet," Akudo grimaced, "It's even bitter." "Did you expect that it would be as sweet as the ripened one?" Her mother querried, "just go ahead and eat the thing so that you may have something deposited into your stomach," was her advice to the little girl.

The common sights of ripened mangoes, oranges and the likes, hanging on their mother trees completely vanished. Consequent upon these, the prices of food stuff escalated. And finally, this in turn raised the rate of theft. Prior to this time, Obodoma was calm and law abiding. It was devoid of most of the social vices that are rampant in many communities. Sadly speaking, this was no longer the case. Everything had changed for the worse owing to the war. Following this development, occasioned by hunger, a day hardly passed bye without Dick, Tom or Harry having to search for either one of his chicken, his goat or any other domestic animal. As a matter of fact, occassionally, reports of houses having been broken into were heard. At times the culprits were apprehended red-handed, while at other times, it was either that they escaped, having succeeded in breaking into and stealing from a house, or that their plans were foiled midway. Incidentally, one Afor-Obodoma market day, a distress cry and shout was raised in the market. Eye brows were raised and close follow-up was made. "Hollam, hollam." This was followed by another distress call, "'Obodoma, hei, gbaa nu oso, gba nu oso', my people of Obodoma, please hurry up here." And in a twinkle of an eye, a crowd had gathered. A woman had spread her wares by the side of one of the roads in the market square. Some other women had gathered to price the articles of trade. The seller who gave her name as Ojiugo suddenly lost her purse to a thief. Luckily, before the thief had gone far with the purse, somebody had bought some item, and in a bid to give the customer her balance, she discovered that her purse was missing. That was when she raised alarm. And one of the women, sitting opposite her, said she saw the woman pick the purse, but had thought it was her bona fide purse. When the lady thief was interrogated, she gave her name as Nnenna but denied stealing. "Steal? God forbid" she snapped. "In our lineage," she said, "the instinct or the drive to steal does not exist. "But Nnenna, you're accused of taking something that doesn't belong to you. What d'you term the act?" the market master querried, fixing a gaze at her. "This is Aka-ego," Nnenna replied casually, looking the other way. What she practiced according to her was mere 'Aka ego' literally meaning 'hand of cash'. This had erupted an air of laughter among all that thronged around her. "Yes," a voice tried to jest from the crowd, "'aka ego' indeed." The crowd was thrown into more laughter. Another occasion of theft that is worth mentioning here was a pathetic one.

There was an 'industrious' man in the village. His name was Oduruko. He was considered well to do because of the way his wife and children dressed and looked like, the hard times notwithstanding. While other people in the village looked hungry and emaciated, his family looked otherwise. One early morning, a large crowd was dragging someone along the road. The pace was however, sluggish. They hardly moved consistently, forward. There were times when they turned towards the left. There were also times when they turned in the opposite direction. This depended on the direction to which the wounded thief turned. "What is going on there?" a bicycle repairer asked, pointing towards the scene. "A thief, they caught a thief, and are dragging him to his home so that his people would see his severely wounded body," a little boy coming from the opposite direction tried to explain. "He had received a wound in his head that was bleeding badly and blood was gushing into his mouth," continued the boy. "'Ele Amadioha?' where is 'Amadioha' began the thief. And as he spoke, blood entered his mouth and he tried to spit it out.

"Amadioha told me that no man borne of a woman could harm me. Now, I realize how much I was deceived." People who knew the family told the story of how the man's wife would always nag at her husband. She would complain bitterly on how she lacked dresses and good shoes. At a point the man could no longer contain the pressure. He had therefore taken to home breaking. 'Every day' they say, 'is for the thief, but one day is for the owner of the house.' And so this man had gone to 'procure' wares as usual for the family, especially the nagging wife.

Nevertheless, Violet kept on working hard to sustain her family. She did that with the help of her children, especially Osita. Nothing could make her misbehave herself, no, not even the war could do that. "God forbid it," she had mumbled at the time the news of Oduruko's theft and death had reached her ears. "If people like Oduruko could turn to thieves on account of hunger," she had continued, "then the world must be at the threshold of collapsing," she had concluded, shaking her head. She was in the kitchen when the news filtered into her ears. Enyidiya and Agbonma had been chatting. Some of the things they said got into her ears. She was not really interested in what they were saying, though. She was however shocked when she heard Enyidiya say to Agbonma, "have you heard the latest news in the air?" "What is the news all about?" Agbonma asked. "They said that Oduruko died this morning," she heard Enyidiya say. At this point, Violet suspended what she was doing. She was fanning the fire at the centre of the tripod iron stand that served her as stove for cooking. The fire had gradually been reducing in intensity. Violet noticed this and picked the local fan made of raffia to revive it. It would go up appropriately, but would go down shortly afterwards. She bent down, checked the firewood and fanned again. The same result had taken place. "What is the matter with you?" she said and tried to wipe the mucus that had collected in her nostrils with her hands, and tried to clean her hands with the worn out wrapper that she was wearing. It was as if the fire could hear her voice. She had done that severally with the same result precipitating. She therefore rose up, took more firewood and added up into the fire. This induced more smoke. Her eyes began to release more tears. She mopped her eyes with her wrapper. When the smoke could not give way, she began to make use of the fan once again. The fan produced sound as the air generated by it met head on with the fire wave.

That was when Enyidiya spoke to Agbonma about the death of Oduruko. Violet could not hear clearly if she continued fanning the fire. She therefore suspended that in spite of the smoke that was all around her. "They said that he went thieving last night but was caught red-handed," Enyidiya said, and quickly added. "They severely wounded him on the head and right hand with a matchet, before bringing him home to his people." "My God!" Agbonma exclaimed, grimacing and at the same time throwing out spittle from her mouth. "S…, so…," she stuttered but was almost immediately cut short by Enyidiya. "So he bled profusely and died later this morning." "What about his wife and children?" Agbonma asked still looking shocked." They ran away as soon as they got wind that their father had been caught. No one knows their whereabouts up till now," she concluded shaking her head. "But was he a thief?" Agbonma asked looking surprised, her mouth wide open. "Story has it that he took to thieving when things began to hurt him badly. Hunger must have been behind it." Agbonma went on, shaking her head.

At this point, Violet resumed her cooking. "There is no justification for a thief. War or no war. Once one had thieved, he becomes a thief, "she muttered again, and tried to revive the fire again. She thanked God that none of her children was a thief. "Well, where would they inherit the trait? Neither I nor Tasie thieves," she mumbled, and suddenly remembered Gordon.

Gordon was her last child. Unfortunately he died a few months after the death of his father Tasie, at the age of two years. At this point her mind began to stray faster than she could control. Soon, she began to reflect on the circumstances that led into naming him Gordon. "I wish God had saved that boy," she mused, shaking her head.

Her husband had worked with the Pepsi-Cola before the war began. He worked under a young white man called Gordon. Gordon was tall and slender. He was about seven feet tall. His nose was long and pointed, making his nostrils somewhat narrow. In spite of his looks, Gordon was polite and kind. He tried to relate very well with all that worked under him.

Tasie liked him very much. As if to say that he knew that Tasie liked him, he loved Tasie very well too. He placed

Tasie above his colleagues and invested a high level of trust on him. This gave rise to envy among Tasie's fellow workers. But neither he nor Tasie seemed to care.

As a result of Gordon's good characters and Tasie's love for him, Tasie decided to give one of his children that name. Luckily, Violet was expectant at that time, and in due time, she gave birth to a bouncing baby boy.

"That is not all," she mused. One of Tasie's friends down at Onitsha was a successful lawyer and solicitor. He was also very tall. He probably was only a few inches shorter than Gordon, but he was ebony black. His name was Ibezimako. Tasie equally loved his friend Ibezimako. Based on this, he also gave his son the name Ibezimako. This was to be his middle name. That was how their baby boy got his first and middle names. Unfortunately, he did not live long.

Violet sighed. "Life has not been kind to me at all," she sighed again and shook her head, mopping her eyes as she did. "I don't know why Gordon did not survive," she sighed, remembering how it all happened.

Gordon had suddenly begun to loose weight. His complexion also began to change for the worse. He soon became pale. "This boy is sick with malaria, Edna had said to me on one of her numerous visits to us after the death of Tasie. That had confirmed my observation," Violet had remembered. Her memory had further charged up, showing her the picture of what Gordon looked like a few weeks before he eventually died.

Soon too, his legs began to swell up, beginning from his laps downwards. His cheeks also got swollen up, glaringly. He soon began to loose his appetite. And in the state of not eating enough from the little food that was offered to him, his tummy continued to go up. He became restless. He also cried often as the baby that he was.

"Add enough salt to his food," some people advised. "Although salt was scarce at that time, I had made frantic efforts to get salt because of my boy." "He needs more good things in his food," one man had said to me while we were praying for the boy at the local church near our house. "What he is suffering from is called kwashiorkor," the man had said matter-of-factly. "Where do I get the good things?" I had wondered. I came to realize afterwards that the man inferred things like fish, meat and so on. "Then give him lizard flesh if you can't get meat," the man had said.

Thereafter, I had sent some big boys in our village to help catch some lizards for me. That was when I realized how wicked life could be. The numerous lizards that pestered us around suddenly disappeared. It had become an uphill task to see one around.

"What about rats?" I asked our pastor a few days later. "Rat's flesh is good, very good," he had said to me. "If you can get lizard or rat and cook regularly for him, he'll be okay," he added and bade me goodbye as I rose to leave.

We made frantic efforts but made little success in getting either lizards or rats or both. "Take it easy, my husband's wife," Betsy had said to me. Lizards and rats are no longer commonplace these days. The reason is that many families are out to get them for their little children in place of meat and milk. People kill them in droves these days, that's the reason why the surviving ones disappeared," she had added.

Chapter Nine

However, Violet continued in her effort to provide food and shelter for the rest of the family.

"Providence", they say, "has a way of providing for the weak and needy." This explains why God had given to the family of Tasie and Violet, the gift called Osita. With the benefit of age, Violets level of reasoning was clearly ahead of Osita's own. So when it mattered, she would come up with a bright idea of what to do and how to go about, doing it. Nonetheless, she was grateful to God for giving her Osita, who had become a source of joy to her. Despite the unpalatable nature of these ideas of hers, Osita was always there to help make them a huge success. In addition to this, this little boy of hers, at times, brought up very sensible suggestions that were not akin to his tender age. His own suggestions were usually very great, too. "Mama," Osita once advise his mother "Don't attend all the meetings scheduled on Sundays. Ask for permission to be absent occasionally so that you could rest yourself on such days for a stronger you, the following week." There were times when she was torn between her own ideas, and those of this bundle of succor of hers.

And so, when it became apparent that the continued increase in the cost of a hip of the uncracked palm kernel, had outstripped their little capital, the family had found herself at crossroads, financially. This began to weigh heavily on Violet. Her mind began to oscilate around the problem, making a complete movement around it just like a fan. "Where would she get the extra amount of money that is needed to augment the little capital that she had at hand, or what other business could she delve into, now?" she pondered in her mind The more she thought over this, the more worried she became. This challenge began to reflect on her face.

Violet's face was naturally smooth and bright. Her demeanour was also naturally an easy-going one. As a result of this, she was easily provoked to a smile, except of course, each time she remembered the death of her dear husband and the resultant hardship into which she had been plunged.

This was one of such times. Her face had become furlong and somewhat emaciated. That was not all. More wrinkles had begun to appear on her face. This had resulted in making her face look more stress stricken. Osita did not like this. He looked her over and shook his head. "Mama, what matter is it that is eating you up these days?" he asked, his gaze fixed on his mother, even as his own face now looked worried. For a reply, his mother raised her head up, took a glance at him, and tried to put on a smile. "You look perturbed and down cast," he said further, his eyes moving down to her feet and up again as if he was trying to scan her, a slight frown on his face. "'Osy nwam', you asked that question as if you no longer live in this house with me," she replied, her voice low and nervous, her face wearing a half-baked smile. "But the fact that I live in the same house with you as my mother, does not guarantee that I must know what you have in your mind unless you say it out," Osita stressed, his gaze still fixed on his mother. Violet looked at him and tried to smile again. "Yes I was right, mama. I can only know what is in your mind when you say it out," he reiterated, gesturing with his hands, his eyebrows slightly moved up. His mother regarded him with amusement. "Will you give me the money if I tell you what the problem is?" she tried to joke, her smile suddenly turned somewhat bright and natural. "Well," Osita replied, his face expressionless. "If I do not have the money to offer today, I certainly will get it tomorrow but I can at least share the problem with you, now if you wouldn't mind telling me what the problem is," adding "two heads they say, are better than one."

As he spoke, he jokingly made a mouth to her, and reached out his hands and tried to shake her own hands as if they were comrades. Violet's face promptly brightened up as she forced herself to smile. "My friend, Betsy, was really right when she named you 'His mother's husband'. That is exactly what you are," she tried to tease him. "I do not have another mother, that is the reason why I take care of the only one I have," Osita replied, trying to smile, his eyes hooded. Violet smiled back at him, her own smile broad and firm. What her son just said had immensely impressed her. She could not conceal her gladness. So she drew closer to him and caressed his head. "God will certainly give you children who will really love and care for you as well. I mean children who will equally be concerned over your own concerns."

Moments later she lowered herself and began to peep under her bed. "Are you looking for a bench?" Osita asked, as if he knew that that was what she was looking for. But before his mother could open her mouth to answer, he had bent over and also peeped under the bed. He found a bench, reached his hand and brought it out. “Thank you, son,” she grinned and promptly took it from his hand.

As soon as his mother sat down, Osita bent down again and peeped under the bed. And finding another bench there, he pulled it out, and sat opposite his mother, after trying to dust it with his palm. Osita had barely sat down when his mother raised up the issue at hand.

“Osy nwam,” she began, adjusting her bench for a better sittng comfort. “I am yet to find a solution to the problem that we have at hand.” “Is it about the extra money needed for the palm kernel business?” Osita asked, fixing a glance at her. “That is exactly what I mean, or is there any other business that you think we can delve into?” she replied, looking curiously at him. “There is really nothing to worry about that one, mama. We shall follow the matter wisely,” he said, exhibiting a kind of confidence that baffled his mother. “There lies the issue,” she tried to interrupt. “Wait a minute mama, let me round off. I do not think that we should actually give up the palm kernel business just for that reason.” And as if he had just remembered something, he hesitated. “Mama,” he called, leaning forward, his eyes fixed on his mother, “this is what I think we shall do. We will not stop the palm kernel business. We shall persevere. ‘Quitters’, they say, ‘do not win’. But winners, on the other hand, do not quit. Mama, we are winners and so we shall not quit, we shall rather expand our horizon.”

As he spoke, Osita’s optimism began to affect his mother. Soon, she began to nod her head. And in what seemed like a magic, the previously downcast looking woman soon began to brighten up. Soon also, a genuine smile appeared on her face. But as if she suddenly remembered a thing, the smile suddenly vanished. Her face turned expressionless. She leaned back, hesitated and opened her mouth to speak. No word however, came out. She swallowed a lump, her face looking despondent.

"So how shall we cope under the prevailing price up thrust?" she asked, drawing her bench even closer to her son, her eyes fixed intently on him. "Yes mama, the upthrust in price could be an instrument in the hands of God to cause us to take an insight into the larger world and divercify our handiwork," he said, his eyes fixed on his mother.

Unknown to Violet, Osita had made enquiries about his cousins' line of business. He did not stop at that. He had also made arrangements to join them.

"Mama," he continued, "we shall buy the quantity of palm kernel which our money can afford. You could go on with that business while I join Chidomam and others in their own line of business," he said, still fixing a glance at his mother. And so they were still brainstorming when Chidomam's voice came up, piercing through the air.

"O-ti-si-ti-ta, O-ti-si-ti-ta", she called, interrupting the flow of their discussion. Osita strained his ears to hear properly. Chidomam called again. "O-ti-si-ti-ta...." But before she could complete another round of the call, Osita answered. "Y-e-s, Dana dana m," Osita had called back. And as he answered, he ran to the kitchen, picked a broken plastic bucket and a dull-faced matchet, which he had gathered for that purpose and ran out to meet Chidomam and the others, waving his right hand at his mother, while clutching the broken plastic bucket in his left armpit.

'Otisitita' is a play-style of calling Osita. Chidomam and the others used that perculiar language while in the presence of the adults, to prevent them from understanding what they were trying to say. In this case, they added the alphabet 't' in between each two laters in each word, in each statement they made.

Violet was taken by surprise. But she had no objection to the developement. All that she cared for was what to do to sustain the family's business as long as it was a genuine endeavour. This one was genuine, and so she did not mind.

Osita was still trying to catch up with Chidomam when her voice came up again. "Did you say you were going with us?" she asked, and without waiting for an answer, she went ahead and announced that they were at the verge of leaving. This prompted Osita to hurry up.

Osita was wearing a pair of white shorts and a straight cut flowing gown that served as shirt which according to his mother, is called 'jumpa'. The shirt and shorts were of the same material. They were however not brilliant white. Osita cherished the dress. He would always remember the day his mother bought the cloth. She had gone to the market specifically to buy a simple dress for Osita, since he had outgrown most of his dresses. Unfortunately, the money she had at hand could not buy any ready made dress. And so she had bought him what other mothers buy for their young children. She had bought two empty sacks of cooking salt and had hired the services of the local tailor at the Afor Obodoma market square. His name was Danqua.

Fortunately, the dress had become ready within a few days after the cloth had reached the tailor's desk.

Each time Osita wore the shirt and the shorts, he received compliments from people. They praised the handiwork of the tailor. And so Osita liked to wear the dress.

As he put the dress on today, he was sure that he was going to break new grounds. But what he did not know was that every business had its intricacies.

But by the time he caught up with his cousins, they had moved somewhat far away from home. "'Nwankpanaka nne ya' His mother's pet," Nduka joked. All had laughed. "'Inujuola ara afor'? Have you had your fill of your mother's breast milk?" Chibunka had taken his turn. "'Agam ahu nu otu isi epio ohia taa' I'll be watching you to see how you'll fare in the farms and bushes today." This was Charity speaking.

Charity's house was only a stone throw from the respective houses of the others. She was the only one that was not a bonafide child of the larger Dimaku family. She was infact, born in the next kindred from the others. They all however related as brothers and sisters.

Before long, the humorous train had arrived at an ideal spot. "Let's take our starting point here" Chidomam suggested, her tone firm, though, as if trying to issue a command. "But we were in this bush yesterday," Charity tried to point out looking at no one in particular. "Yes" others chorused as if so arranged, "but for a different objective."

Osita had come to understand that they actually came there the previous day. They came to search for mushroom. But today they are searching for oil bean seed or 'ugba'.

Suddenly, Chidomam gave out a shout. "'Ugbam'," she announced, bent down and picked an oil bean seed and dropped it into the broken plastic bucket which she was carrying. "'Ugba m kwanu, Ugbam ozo'" shouted Chibunka, who also bent down and picked two oil bean seeds, spread side by side, each other, in front of him. Every now and then, someone gave out a shout, indicating he had picked one. One after another, they went on picking the seeds and depositing same in the container they were each carrying. At sun set, when they were ready to go home, they had each collected substantial quantities, Osita's own however, being the least.

This was the first time he had embarked on an expedition of this nature. He had not learnt the intricacies of the deal yet. For instance, while he had moved ahead, looking down for the seeds, the others had in addition to doing so, walked briskly towards any nearby oil bean tree, and searched, thoroughly at the foot of the tree, beating down the shrubs with the edge of the matchet they are bearing in their hand. Nonetheless, his colleagues really praised him, asserting that he had relatively done very well.

The oil bean seed is an important ingredient in the making of salad, African salad if you like. When boiled and sliced, it could be used in cooking soup. It is as delicious, to eat as it is highly esteemed in Africa.

This was Chidomam, Nduka and the others' way of contributing to the economic wellbeing of their families. It was cultural. The upkeep of the entire family did not have to be left in the hands of their parents only. The children offered a helping hand. Although this was true with the children living with their parents in the villages only, it had a lot of merits. First, it reduced the incidence of the family's economic work load on the parents. Furthermore, it helped in the provision of variety in the family menu. For instance, if the children of a family got rodents like rats or crickets, the family would have a choice in the soup to cook. This culture also impacts directly on the children's psyche, in that it acts as a stepping stone in building a child into a prospective industrious father or mother as the case may be. It also helped to inculcate into a child, a lifestyle of the discipline of giving and sharing which is not inherent in a child.

"Please, let's move fast," Charity suggested, suddenly to no one in particular, though. "Did you say to move fast?" Osita querried. "Y-e-s," Charity demanded, frowning. "What should I have said?" "Please let's move quickly" Osita tried to correct, feeling superior. "Did you think you are more intelligent than I?" she asked, betraying a measure of displeasure. "Before we fled down to the village, due to the war, I was in primary one in Onitsha," Osita boasted. "You are not the only one who was in school before the disturbances," Chidoma tried to protest. "I too, was in school" "So was I," Chibunka claimed, his face expressionless. "Even me," Nduka took his turn.

As a matter of fact, virtually all of these children were in school before the disturbances. For over a year into the war, Osita and his cousins, both far and near have had their education suspended. "Would they remain out of school for as long as the war ravaged?" Osita wondered. This is a million dollar question. Only God can answer that, at the time being. Another golden question cropped up in his mind. His teacher, back at Onitsha, had told him that the country was made up of three major tribes. Now his young mind had reflected upon the names of the tribes. Suddenly he remembered Taiwo. Taiwo was one of the most brilliant boys in his class. He and Taiwo had become friends after they challenged each other on who beats the other in the last test which they held in mathematics, while in primary one. Now is Taiwo also out of school because of the war? "God please don't let him overtake me," thought Osita "out of circumstances that are not due to my own fault." This apprehension took the better part of him for the day.

As Chidomam, Osita and the rest chatted home, they made movements in dual directions.

They moved in dual directions. They principally moved forward in a bid to get home. But they also made backward movements.

This happened, when one of them happened to bump into a strange object, and called at the others who would readily run back to have a glimpse at what it was. And this happened many times, over.

However, by the time they got nearer home, they discovered that someone had been calling to their name, one after the other. "Go and call them. Tell them to come back and help in the kitchen," Chidomam's elder brother, Ugwum, had said. "Wait," "I think I heard your name, Chidoma," Chibunka said, fixing a glance at Chidomam, his mouth wide open. And as if the caller sensed that they were straining their ears in order to hear clearer, Edu started again "Ch-i-d-o m-a-m-o, C-h-i-d-o-m-a-m-o o ooo, C-h-i d-o-o-m-a-m-o o." Each time she tried to call, Edu, tried to manipulate her voice in a way that helped her achieve a high pitched sound.

"O-o-o-o-h, replied Chidoma. And thereafter, they noisily began to run to their respective houses.

"Good evening mama", Osita greeted with a smile. "I have had a tremendous experience today." But Violet was not really happy at that moment. She therefore did not readily respond to his greetings. Osita realized this and so tried to probe into his mother's demeanour. "Are you alright, mama?" he asked, trying to sit down beside his mother, who was trying to make fire for the supper. "I was beginning to wonder what had held you back in the farms till this time" Violet said, hissing, her face deeply frowned. "I'm very sorry, mama. That means, if we go again tomorrow, I wll insist we start coming home on time." Her son assured her. "That would be better," she said heaving a sigh of relief. But did you say that you would be going out there again tomorrow'? Violet asked, absent mindedly. "Do you know what?", Osita began again, his face brightening up as he felt a sense of importance build up in him. "Just like the palm kernel business, Mama, this one is an everyday affair," he took time to explain.

When the mother and son had examined the content of the plastic bucket in the son's hand, they were no longer in doubt, whether the later, would go out again, the following day or not. "Mama," Osita began again, holding one of the seeds in his right hand, his full gaze focused on his mother. "They call this 'ugba', it could be used in..." he tried to teach his mother but was cut short by her. "Keep your breath my son, I know the value of what you brought home. It is just great" she had rather enthused. And by the time we'll have about three times, this quantity, coupled with what I can make out of the palm kernel deal, I'll bet you that our menu would change for the better," Violet assured him, her heart bubbling with hope, hope that their prospect of surviving was growing.

Later that night, Osita had a long dream. He had seen his mother standing and looking stranded at the bank of 'Okatankwo'.

'Okatankwo' is a stream at the other side of the Obodoma village. They say it traverses many villages in the neighbourhood. And that it is a seasonal affair. That means that it dries up every dry season between the months of December and April. But 'collects' again in the rainy seasons. The volume comes up fullest in the months of September and October. Many a child had drowned in this stream, at this period of the year. Parents have not failed therefore, to drum into the ears of their children the need to desist from swimming in the Okotankwo at this period. "Please 'Nnadim,'" Violet would plead, "do not join others in swimming during this season. Rather than swim in the stream, collect water from it, but come home and take a hot bath."

The reason behind this is that Osita and his brothers and sisters were used to going to the stream. It is the main source of water supply to the villagers. There are times when the bank of the stream becomes very crowded. So crowded, that one would have difficulty, trying to fetch water from the stream. Children would be spread all over the stream swimming and playing. In that case, no part of the water would be calm and settled. This is where the problem in trying to fetch water lay. Fetching water from the spot, where someone was bathing was tantamount to collecting dirty water. So, the general thing was to deep one's vessel into the spots, where nobody was bathing. To an average villager any water collected at a spot where no one is bathing was considered pure and therefore safe for drinking.

"The colour of this water looks so good, Nneka," her father, Odogwu remarked,"I hope you didn't fetch it on the last Eke market day?" "Papa what's wrong with water fetched on Eke market days?" Nneka asked, trying to answer a question with another one, her mouth wide open. "I didn't mean any water fetched on Eke market days, I was particularizing on the last Eke market day when almost all the children in Obodoma were said to have converged at the stream as if they were asked to gather and take a bath simultaneously," Odogwu replied, holding a calabash cupful of water in his left hand.

Nevertheless, during the months already mentioned, as risky periods, the picture changed. Fewer number of people, especially those who are truly sure of their ability to swim do so at that time. Nonetheless it still remained risky, swimming at that period of the year.

Instinctively, Osita was startled when he saw his mother standing at the bank of the stream that morning. He was the one who fetched water for the family's need. So he wondered what his mother could be doing in the stream. Although he was not happy seeing his mother at the stream, he had nonetheless helped her fetch the water. His first impulse was to also help place the bucket full of water on her head. But at a second thought, he reasoned it was improper to allow his mother carry water in his own presence. Therefore, he had placed the bucket full of water on his own head, and they left for home.

Shortly after, he woke up only to discover that all was a mere dream. This made him feel better. He wondered what on earth could make his mother want to go to 'Okatankwo'. Could it be that he had not been living up to his mother's expectation… "What can this mean?" he wondered.

He was still pondering over this when he dosed off again. But no sooner had he slept off, than he went into another dream.

The second dream was worlds apart from the first one. In his second dream, he was holding a questionnaire exercise with one of his former class mates, called Abraham. "When did our country become a republic?" He asked looking at Abraham. "First October 1960," came the reply. "You failed it". He had tried to correct, his face, expressionless. But the latter continued to argue, insisting he was right. However, after a prolonged argument, Abraham had finally succumbed. "Now tell me, what is the correct answer?" he asked, fixing a glance at Osita. Osita later corrected his friend, and let him know that 1960 was Independence Day. The very next statement made by Abraham had made Osita's blood run cold. "Primary two 'A'?" "Did you say primary two 'A'," asked Osita, with a husky voice. "Yes, I'm in primary two 'A'," reiterated Abraham. "Next year, I shall be in primary three 'A'. That's how our school is run," Abraham tried to narrate. But for an answer, Osita had inadvertently given out a shout that woke his mother up from sleep. "Son, what's amiss?" his mother cried, shaking him into consciousness. Several days later, Osita had unavoidably kept wondering whether Abraham had really continued schooling while he, on this side of the world had remained indefinitely out of school. "God! he had mumbled "what a life, what a bitter taste of war." In a moody state of mind, he brooded over the fact that he had left the township where he was living a good life, and here he was in this village having no choice, than to eat the kind of food he could not have eaten, were his father alive. And worse still his friends who were less brilliant in class than he, continued getting education, while he went on languishing here in the village, "What a bitter taste of war." He lamented.

Chapter Ten

Umuehiri, like every other village had her own population density. She, like any of those communities, was experiencing food shortage, too. Unfortunately, indegenes of Obakwa, Amanlu, Achalu, Umueleagu, Umuediome, to mention only a few, got compelled to converge at Umuehiri. This gave rise to a population density that was more or less, explosive. Food situation became what could be termed 'food outage', government's policy on food and crops, not withstanding.

Government had enacted a decree, making it legal for every citizen to harvest and use any farm product anywhere in the land. This was done probably in consideration of the uncountable refugees spread across the country, who no longer had access to their own bonafide farmlands. They had fled their own villages and by so doing, had left their own farmlands behind. But they had to eat anyway.

Ordinarily, food is the number one necessity of life. Unfortunately, things had changed. Food had been thrust up to the height where the masses could no longer get it.

"Rather than remain here and die out of hunger," Theresa said, holding Chidinma and Kelechi in her bossom, "consider going to Umualaoji and see if food is being shared in that food centre."

Theresa is the wife of the youthful Odili. She is also the mother of both Chidinma and Kelechi.

As she instructed her children to go to the food centre, her mind raced straight to that same issue. Each time she gets close to her first daughter, Chidinma, her mind tends to move towards the same issue ..... Chidinma's striking resemblance to her husband, Odili, who is also the father of the child, Chidinma and her sister, Kelechi. "Mama, will you go with us?" Chidinma, asked thereby breaking the flow of her mother's thoughts, her gaze fixed on her mother's stress-stricken face. "There's no point going with you since no one would serve you if I am with you. You need not be told that it is an affair for the children." Theresa had replied, trying hard to avoid the child's gaze. "Please mama," Kelechi, the younger of the children pleaded, "take us to the place." Theresa opened her mouth to decline the plea but was cut short by her first daughter. "Mama," she had begun, "you can wait for us at a distance if you do not want to come close." And as she spoke, her eyes appeared puffy. Unknown to the children, their mother's three months old pregnancy made her less agile than she used to be. That was the reason why she was trying to find an excuse upon which she would opt out of getting up from the bench, how much more moving out with them. At that moment Theresa felt like fumbling the little girl's mouth as it reminded her of her husband's own mouth. She however, instinctively stopped short of doing that. Lately, she had begun to experience a great deal of foreboding or is it a mere feeling about her husband which she could not explain? “God,” she mumbled, “I wish Odili would come home one of these days, and stay with us even for a few days”. As she mused over this, a few drops of tears strolled down her cheeks but found their way to the ground. She hastly mopped her cheeks with the back of her hands. “Mama why are you crying?” Kelechi asked, her eyes fixed on her mother, her lips slightly parted. “Mama are you really crying or, did Kelechi not observe very well?” “Don’t mind Kelechi,” she tried to deny, turning her face the other way in order to hide her wet eyes away from the probing eyes of her children. “But I saw tears on her cheeks,” Kelechi tried to stress, fixing a gaze on her mother, trying hard to ascertain that tears were still hanging on her mother’s cheeks.

Unknown to Theresa and her children, their beloved husband and father who was conscripted into the army, a couple of weeks earlier, did not survive his first appearance as a soldier at the war front. His tall, muscular body got bullet- ridden on the very first day he was deployed into the war front.

“So children,” Theresa found her voice and said, “since you insist that I should bear you on my back, and take you to the food centre, go and get your food bowls so we can get going.”

“’Abughi m onye’ red cross n’achughuari odu okporoko, ogaghi ewuta m ma ndi army jide ha’ I am not a member of the Red Cross Society, who go all out in search of the tail of stockfish. I shall not be perturbed if the soldiers conscript them into army.” That was the song that was right in the air, at the time that Theresa and her children arrived at the food centre. It was one of numerous songs sang every day at the many food centres spread across the land. What she saw at the food centre nauseated her to the marrow. That was not her first time of coming in contact with sick children even during the war, though. She however could not make out the reason why she felt the way she is feeling now. Shortly, however, it dawned on her that she could guess the reason for it. "This is probably the first time that I have had to stay long and close to a child who is suffering from this kind of disease," she mumbled, nodding her head in nostalgia. "Mama, is it me?" Chidinma asked, trying to hold her mother's hand in her own hands. "'Tufia'," she retorted, spitting out, "it could't be you, my dear." Even while at home, Theresa could not help visualizing the ugly looks of children of various ages and sizes as she saw them gathered in their hundreds at the food centre. Pathetically, almost all of these children looked awful. A look at them revealed various odd appearances. One readily discovers that most of them give the impression of having their eyes pushed back into their eye sockets. Conspicuously, too are those whose tummy got out of proportion with the rest of their body. This is apparently in contrast to their buttocks which so got diminished that they appeared to be devoid of it in the first place. Equally noticeable were those whose limbs were bloated at the lower end, but unappealingly, diminished at the upper end adjoining the buttocks. "Medically speaking," she mumbled, and at the same time grimacing, "most of these children are visibly suffering from kwashiorkor." "Mama, whom are you referring to," Chidinma asked, slanting a glance at her mother, while also busy, trying to mope up her food bowl with her palm. "I was talking to myself," she replied, still grimacing. "How come you're talking to yourself?" Chidinma querried, chuckling.

Usually, the centres were schools, either secondary or primary schools, closed down at the outbreak of the war, 'for security reasons'. Each of the buildings that had corrugated iron sheets for roofs were camouflaged with palm fronds.

Suddenly, while Theresa was absorbed in watching the children as they struggled for position, with the attendant sobs and outright shouts of crying, a set of members of the Red Cross society emerged from one of the school blocks. She was to notice later, that they successively came in in pairs. Each pair carried a basin full of corn meal which they managed and shared among the children as they lined up in queues. "Sit down all of you," one of them ordered, her face expressionless. "If you do not sit down," we shall not share this food," her colleague said in support of the first speaker, taking position beside her, too. While Theresa watched, this order sparked off a reaction that was better seen than heard. Those that where strong began to outsmart the weaker ones, by usurping the positions originally occupied by the latter. As a result of this, more sobs and cries rose to mountainous levels. Theresa's horror increased when she noticed a little girl who was by her own assessment about seven years old, who looked sick and weak, but was trying to carry another sick looking girl who probably is her younger sister as they tried to join the queue. She felt like going up there to help the children out, but quickly remembered that the Red Cross sisters, as they were referred to, would frown at her appearance at the field. Her displeasure evaporated when one of the Red Cross members hurried down and not only helped the struggling little girls, but also put some food into their respective plates. As she watched on, she noticed a tall but thin girl of about ten years of age, running towards her direction. Suddenly, the girl swerved and faced a set of children who were more or less of her own age. And as soon as she reached them, she began to yell. "Ngozi, Chisara, em, em, em, did you see Emenike?" As she tried to speak, she panted helplessly. "We did not see him," they chorused. "What about him?" one of the girls demanded. "Emenike and Obii are lucky. Emenike's own plate is impressively filled up with food," she answered, her eyes roaming around as she panted. "What about you, have you gotten your own share?" she asked, fixing a glance at her friends, her lips wide apart. "No, we have not gotten any ration," one of her friends answered, adding, "they said to sit down here in the queue." "There's no point waiting any longer. Father said that food has finished," she said, turning her back as she made the last statement, and made to move.

This incident flashed a memory into Theresa's mind. She remembered the disappointment which she felt recently at this same food centre. She, in company of her younger sister, Ogemdi, had arrived the place at twelve o' clock noon day, much earlier than the normal time of four o' clock in the evening, and so had made it earlier than everybody else. Ogemdi had convinced her to accompany her to the food centre, while the children stayed back at the hut, optimistic that they would succeed in getting food. Finding a spread under the mango tree near the door leading into the office that served as school's bursar's office which now served as store to the Red cross, Ogemdi had placed her bowl at the foot of the mango tree and climbed up the tree.

"Who on earth kept this plate here?" one of the Red cross sisters asked, her eyes darting here and there, her mouth wide open, her face deeply contorted. Ogemdi could not trust the Red Cross sister. She was not sure of her motive for demanding for whoever owned the plate. For that reason, she kept mute and remained hidden in the foliage of the tree. But when the sister raised her right leg, poised to kick the plate out of that place, Ogemdi quickly opened her mouth and spoke. "Sister it's me," she answered, and quickly began to emerge from the tree top. "Then take it away from here," the sister snapped, still frowning. That singular encounter had been Ogemdi's saving grace. She had taken advantage of that to remind the sister incessantly, how she had met her even before other people began to arrive. That was how they eventually got served.

A couple of days after, Ogemdi and her self had repeated that strategy. They actually arrived earlier than every other pesrson. "Eventually, after a couple of hours," Theresa recounted, "I noticed a movement among the crowd that was not there initially," instinctively, she looked yonder and seeing that Ogemdi was appropriately positioned, she had felt relaxed. Shortly, however, she remembered her children back home. "How would Chidinma cope with Kelechi's antagonism for hunger?" she pondered, hissing. Although the war had made her children learn to do without food, "was there no limit to what a child could do? Was a child not a child after all?" This thought precipitated discomfort in her mind. However the feeling was pacified when she remembered the food she would bring home for them. "After all," she thought, "the presence of food these days could earn one worship." As she pondered in her mind, she inadvertently stole a glance at the queue where Ogemdi was positioned. Fortunately, the long queue was diminishing and this gladdened her heart. "God please let them share this thing with dispatch so one can leave here shortly from now," she mumbled. Occasionally, she glanced around the vicinity. "This is a good place to be," she mused, noticing the looks of the place for the first time, adding, "Father Rowland made a great choice in picking this place in replacement to the former food centre. She could remember vividly, all that transpired, giving rise to transferring the food centre from its former base. St. Columba's Catholic School compound had been the venue all along. But there had been an air raid at the former food centre, resulting in its relocation to St. John's Catholic School.

She could see it all in her mind's eyes. It was as if it took place only yesterday. Many children were gathered as usual at the food centre to receive free food. The Red Cross Sisters were at the verge of serving the food when a jet bomber emerged from oblivion and had flown so low above the centre that its occupants were seen by some people.

A great stampede had ensued. This is because most aircrafts flying above the horizon those days were either jet fighters or jet bombers.

"Take cover, take cover," the Rev. Father in charge of the church as well as the food centre began to shout. Spontaneously, the children began to scamper for safety, falling head over heels as they tried to do so. And as if to confirm their fears, the aircraft suddenly began to reel out bombs from the rear end of the vessel. "Gbim, gbim-gbim, gbim, gbim, gbim, gbim," came the sound of the explosives. Distress cries filled the air. Parents and their older children began to run to the centre, crying and yelling as they did. "Chinekem o o, Chinekemoo, Kelechi nwam oo, John nwam." On the other hand, and as if so arranged, the children began to yell and call on their parents. "Papamoo, Mamaoo," and their elder sisters and brothers, some of who were at home, or the ones that brought them to the food centre. "Dee John o-o, Dee Hillary o-o."

As God would have it, the bombs followed the air craft a distance away before exploding. At the wake of the explosion, a large and deep pit was discovered a few yards away from the premises.

"I saw the pilot and his crew members," a boy tried to announce, sweating and emerging from his hiding place and at the same time trying to demonstrate what he saw with his hands. "I saw them too," another boy also tried to announce, his head and entire body dirty with sand.

"God had performed a great miracle for us today," said Gaius, the chaplain, but to no one in particular. "Yes, yes," chorused the people around. These were those who had seen their own children. There were others who had not seen their own. These ones had continued to roam aimlessly round the the premises, shouting the names of their children. The children who had not seen their bigger sisters or brothers also began to cry miserably roaming round the premises looking for them. It was indeed a pathetic scene.

That night many people remained awake until the early hours of the following day. The story of the air raid was what kept them awake. "I think the pilot was scared, so scared that he flew away in a hurry," Nnadozie began, thoughtfully. "Well, you may be right," Chidi replied, his eyes fixed on Nnadozie, "but my own view is that he ran out of supplies, so he had to move on without risking his life by wasting more time." "The two of you are entitled to your opinion," Gaius said, shifting glances from Nnadozie to Chidi. "But I think that God is behind it all. God influenced his mind, turning it away from the children. Otherwise, if he had his way, he would have hovered over and over again, and that would have been disastrous," he stressed, grimacing. "Yes, my husband is right," Gaius' wife said, trying to shift her bench closer to her husband, her lips, slightly parted.

The following morning news about the demise of two among the children that went to the food centre that fateful day spread like harmattan fire.

"Oh my God, my God," Gaius lamented, shaking his head, his face lowered. "They must have been stepped upon in the stampede, yesterday," he concluded, his face deeply grimaced. "But someone said that their demise was as a result of a severe shock," Anurue pointed out, fixing his eyes on Gaius. "If shock was behind it, why didn't the children die that yesterday? Why did they have to wait till early this morning?" Emmanuel, demanded, taking a hard look at Anurue.

Much later that same day, the villagers gathered under Gaius' supervision and covered the corrugated iron roofs of the school blocks which roofs were not yet covered, using palm fronds.

"This place is large," Theresa mused, as she glanced around the compound.

The church building is positioned at the centre of the compound. Pitanga Cherry shrubs lined up beautifully at strategic positions. At specific points, the cherry shrubs were arranged to form a circle. At such spots, some economic tree stood impressively at the centre. Yet, along the drive ways and walk ways, these shrubs adorned both the right and left hand sides, leaving an impression of an expert's arrangement. The floor itself was well scalped, done in such a way that at the end of each rain no water ever collects at the compound. Furthermore, green grasses also adorn specific portions. There was a lawn tennis pitch at the right hand side of the Parish headquarters' building. This building houses the Irish Reverend Father, the head of the parish, Father Rowland. Except for the over growth of the trees, cherry shrubs and grasses, this premises looked so much like the European quarters in the big cities of Enugu and Lagos. The war had however, made difficult, the up keep of the premises. Looking over to the opposite direction, one notices a not-very-large football field, just across the main road leading to the village. The building which walls are installed only half way, serve as the convent school for primaries one to three only. Pupils pass out here, after their last examinations in primary three. They are however, expected to proceed into the bigger schools to continue from where they had stopped.

Suddenly, a noise filtered into Theresa's ears, breaking the flow of her thought. Consequently, she glanced at the direction of the noise. She could however, not make a meaning out of the noise. But as she looked on, she noticed a figure making its way towards her. At first, she could not place the figure. Moments later, as the figure drew closer to her, the obvious dawned on her. "What's the matter with you?" she heard her own voice yell, her eyes propping out, as she finally recognized the figure, as it walked dejectedly closer to her. “They started sharing food from the other end, and before long, they announced that food had finished.” That was Ogemdi, as she tried to explain, as soon as she got close to Theresa, her face downcast.

Chapter Eleven

"Anu m'enyou okuwo, Anu m'enyuo okuwo." A voice sounded from the remote end of the school block. "Anu menyou oku woo," Nsogbu's father persevered in his shout. "Anu menyou oku woo," this time, a different voice that was actually mimicking Nsogbu's father followed.

Nsogbu, Mkpagbu and their parents were among the refugees who encamped at Umuehiri Refugee camp. At the early stages of the camping, his fellow refugees especially those ones from the eastern part of the country would mimic this man's dialect. His dialect which was more or less a glorified language of one of the tribes in the eastern part of the country should have been "'Menyu o nu oku, menyuo oku,' put the lights or fire out." At nights, when aircrafts fly past, doing so at high altitudes, their presence could only be detected by their faint sound and different coloured lights. Some men would begin to yell, warning inmates to put lights off. Papa Nsogbu was sure to be one of the voices. Virtually every refugee at the L.A refugee camp at Umuehiri knew him very well. Many knew him simply as 'Anu menyouoku woo'. Others knew him as the father to a strange looking set of two girls; Nsogbu and Nkpagbu.

Although the former is older than the latter, they share a striking resemblance to each other. This made it difficult to differentiate one from another. A stranger at the camp would assume that they were a set of twins. Both are exceptionally tall. Perhaps too tall for the girls that they are. From a closer view, one notices that their legs are strangely too long for their trunk. Their respective heads also appear to get out of proportion with the rest of their bodies. This makes their heads look rather too tiny for their neck and the rest of their body trunks. Often times, they not only moved together, they also strictly kept to themselves. While they played around or moved out of the camp, scores of eyes were wont to follow them. Speculation had it that they were deaf and dumb. However, whether this was true or not, remained unclear to many uptill the time of dispersion. One of Osita's many older cousins, Mary, once said that Nsogbu, meaning trouble and her younger sister Nkpagbu meaning persecution, moved about like elephants. "How do you mean, sister?" asked Osita's younger sister, Ijeoma. And for an answer, Mary told them the characteristic movements of elephants as she knew it.

"Elephants do not turn sideways once in motion. They rather move ahead, facing the front without turning towards the right or the left," she had said, looking at no one in particular. "Brave hunters," she had continued, "take advantage of this behavior of elephants, and fell them like trees, in spite of their awe-inspiring sizes. A hunter would steal under a moving elephant, and start cutting the flesh while the animal was still moving. "Serious," Ijeoma remarked, adjusting her sitting position, "you mean they would keep moving in spite of the pains?" she asked in apparent amazement.

"Yes," Mary replied casually, but went on with her story. "Trouble will only precipitate if the hunter is unable to avert the animal's huge limps." She went on, this time, fixing a glance at Ijeoma, as if the story was meant for her ears only "But if on the other hand, he is not careful enough to do so and the huge animal steps on him, its heavy weight will most certainly crush him." Mary gestured, clapped both hands and grimaced as if she had just witnessed a scene of that nature. Ijeoma sat directly opposite Mary. And so, when she suddenly thrust her hand while trying to demonstrate, Ijeoma involuntarily, tried to dodge her face. Ijeoma's reflex action amused the rest of the people sitting with her. "On the other hand", Mary went on, thereby cutting short the laughter that was in the air, "if he is experienced enough, he could go on and on, and cut the live animal's flesh until it loses consciousness, falls down, and dies." Continuing, Mary recounted that elephants move about in herds, and slowly, too. All that the experienced hunter has to do therefore is to target the last one on the queue.

This of course, is one of those stories, adults tell to their younger ones, some of which are untrue. When such young persons grow older, they reminiscent over some of these stories and place them into real or feeble stories, as the case may be.

Another story was told Osita, his younger sister, Ijeoma and some other little children of Osita's age. The story was long and baffling. But there were two or three issues that caught Osita's interets, most. The issues bordered on cultures of the Western world and the Jewish town of Jerusalem.

Mary said that the cultures of the white man offer priority attention to the ladies over their male counterparts. This sounded both strange and amazing to the children. To support Mary's story, Dee Sunday, gave instances that helped to substantiate the story. "For instance," he said, "in a public gathering, ladies are offered seats before their male counterparts." He went further to say that it was not considered awkward for women to actually make the first moves in marriage proposals, directly or indirectly. This also sounded very strange to Osita and the other listeners. "That makes a case for ladies', first?" Osita asked, his lips wide apart. "Yes, ladies first," he said matter-of-factly. This was a total reverse of what had been handed over to Osita as a way of life. Severally, down here at home Osita recollected, "I have heard that, next to age, the male gender or man has to be given priority attention over the women." He could remember some of the family meetings held in the family hall or 'Obuma'. Wives and children would go all out to get chairs or benches for the sitting comforts of their husbands and fathers. Subsequently, the women would perch around. Two or three of them, could share a chair or any sitting device that was available. Furthermore, right in his home, Osita remembered how his mother would serve his father's bath water and food, before taking her own later. Moreover, one did not have to live a hundred years in this part of the world before one realizes that families with more of male children, are considered luckier than the ones having more of girls.

Another issue that had baffled Osita's mind highly was the issue of Jerusalem being existent here on this earth. "'Echem na Jerusalem no n' eligwe' I thought that Jerusalem existed in the heavens?" Osita asked, conspicuously baffled. For the first time, Osita and his sister had come to realize that those societies that are commonly mentioned in the Christian religious book, the bible, actually existed on this earth. Such places include Israel, Egypt, Jerusalem, Jericho and so many others.

In furtherance of the gist, Dee Sunday, was about to tell the children another story when suddenly, another stampede arose in the camp. He seemed to have sensed it earlier than Osita and his other listeners. So before the latter could comprehend what was going on, Dee Sunday, along with other young men living in the camp had run into the nearby bush to hide away from the searching eyes of the soldiers who visited refugee camps, day after another in search of able bodied young men. Any young man caught in this exercise was given a quick military training after which he is sent into the war front. Needless to say that, some of them do not return alive.

Often, some soldiers invaded not only the refugee camps, they stormed the villages as well. They searched for teenage boys. Among the teenagers caught, the lucky ones were later allowed to go home based on one reason or the other, while the unlucky ones were however recruited into the army. This resulted in young boys and men in the refugee camp, staying always at alert. Alert, not only in case of any sight of an aircraft, in the air, but also against the conscripting soldiers' invasion. The women and the children got displeased when the men were not in the camp.

The importance of the presence of these young men, in the camp, cannot be quantified. To cite an instance, when the air raiders came threatening, and they did so often, they were the ones that had courage to stand and direct other people on what to do and how to it, too. They did so by way of shouting on top of their voices; "Don't run, don't run, don't run, take cover, take cover." Or "stand still, stand still, stand still, don't move." Generally speaking, the directives they dished out, depended on the situation on ground. "Take for instance," one of the army officers, once, while addressing members of the public said; "if the plane is still very far away, a standing still posture could pay off better because every standing object would appear to the pilot and his crew members as a tree. But if the plane had gotten close already, it would make more sense, to take cover." "What is take cover?" Osita asked, looking at the young army officer. "That is a brilliant question" the man had replied. "Taking cover means lying on ones belly and remaining so until situations changed for better," the army officer took time to explain. There were also times when they advised folks, to jump into the bunkers which they dug at various strategic positions in the bush.

Bunkers are dug like mini swimming pools, but they are rather rectangular in shape, and without water. They are not meant to be very deep. The reason is to allow persons taking refuge inside it, to be able to watch the level ground above, while on his feet. This will in turn, make him know when situations demand him to come out and run away, into safety.

Life in the refugee camp is devoid of comfort. Each family is allotted to a portion of space inside the school block. All allotments are equal. No consideration was made regarding the size of the family. Families that were fewer in numbers therefore 'enjoyed' more space than the larger ones. The separating devices between one family and the other, was the school benches, and desks, and of course, the black boards, as the case may be. So to create a complete privacy, women of the families concerned, used their wrappers to seal up, or cover all openings. This was to checkmate prying eyes. Right within that allotted space, the families' belongings, the beds, which consisted of mats or blankets, and the likes, are spread out only at nights.

Furthermore, it did not matter whether the school had functional toilet facilities. The reason is that both sides of the road close to the school compound, were always full of defeacates of various 'ages'.

One early morning, Osita and his younger sister Ijeoma, woke up from sleep. To their dismay, they found out that they could not open their eyes. "Mama, mama, mama," Ijeoma cried, worried at her inability to open her eyes "My eyes, I can't open them." Her mother took some water in a small basin, dipped a piece of cloth into it and used the wet piece of cloth to soak out the white mash that glued her eye lids together. It was later discovered that many other inmates of the camp have had the same experience. For several weeks later, the red eye or 'Apollo twelve' as the ailment was known, continued to ravage the camp. Suggestions of a possible cure arose from various sources. Some suggested the use of salt solutions. Others said it was sugar solution. Yet, some people still suggested the use of human urine. Nevertheless, the ailment seemed to take its toll before vanishing. However, of all the crude medications suggested above, only the last one was practicable, because both sugar and salt were practically unavailable at this period in time.

The 'L.A' school had a moderate church building that is not far away from the school. The church is obviously a Catholic church. The premises served as a food centre, but operated only on the designated days. Among all the centres that Osita had visited for food, this was the most orderly.

Based on the good reports about this centre, Osita's mother, Violet allowed not only Osita, but Ijeoma too, to walk down to the centre for food. "'Ekene m Maria juputara nagracia ...,'" one of the Red Cross sisters would begin, "'Maria di aso, nne nke chukwu, riobara ayi ndi njo, aririo...,'" the children would chorus. This creed would be repeated several times over. At times the sister would add some additional that are supposedly, not part of the main creed but these are actually added, in order to add more 'flavour' to the main creed. But for a reply, the children were expected to repeat a particular response. Often, only those from catholic backgrounds would get the right response. Their counterparts who are non-Catholics would fail to get it right. "No, no, no," the sister would frown. "Listen to me..., 'Ekene m Maria'...., now say that," she sister would correct. And for as long as they failed to give her the right response, the learning continued. This was however, to the discomfort of the children. As they recited this, Osita would remember the songs they used to sing at the other less disciplined centres. Not that he preferred those centers. But the songs out there, contrasted favourably against the recitation that was going on here. In his mind he would begin to sing one of the tunes that held sway in those centers. "'Unu choro imata ndi n'eri nri,' kwashiorkor, 'Unu choro imata ndi n'eri nri,' kwashiorkor? Do you want to know who monopolizes the anti-kwashiokor food?" "'Onyechege,' number one, 'Dianyi', number two, Jessi number three, 'bu ndi n'eri ya." They would answer the question themselves, by mentioning the names of the people who they believed were behind the short fall in the supply of what the caritas magnanimously gave to them.

Chapter Twelve

"Charlie, Ekenna, 'buru nu akankpo. Gi n'eti, gi n'ata, gi n'enye nna gi', Charlie, Ekenna, please pick up the stone and start cracking the palm kernel. Do justice to the palm kernel, crack as much as you can, eat your fill and give to your father so I can equally eat." "Papa" asked Charlie, "shall we fill a cup?" "Yes" replied his father, "make it two full cups," he had said, his stress-stricken face expressionless.

That was a headmaster of the first grade. His children had been used to showing respect to their father, so they would pick up the palm kernel cracker and go to work.

The palm kernel cracker is not a machine as one is prone to think. In the days of our fathers, every home had one or more. It consists of the heavy trunk of a felled tree. It must be a mature tree. When felled, the trunk is cut into various sizes. It is cut in the size that would serve the user a comfortable sitting position, if he is trying to carve a palm kernel cracker. Finally, the wood is allowed to dry and harden more. Additionally, a hard stone is cut to the size that the human palm can conveniently carry without undue weight incident on the hand. By the time the objects are really hardened, one has a ready device to crack the palm kernel.

So Charlie and Ekenna would get to their duty posts as directed by their father, Okponku. By the time they got through with the work, they had eaten a good quantity of palm kernel. That served as the family's breakfast. It is a known fact that palm kernel is a hard nut. When chewed and swallowed, the oil and the cake offer no roughage. So, in the morning of the next day, members of Okponku family found it difficult to open their respective bowls.

The Okponku family was not alone in this fate. Every family was involved. Palm kernel became the most common food. It does not offer the satisfaction that food gives. It only succeeds in depositing something into the stomach.

Out there, one could see some men doing the cracking all by themselves. Among this group are those whose children were all grown up and probably joined the army or married out in the case of the women.

"'Gwam, gwam, gwam ihe Eze jiri raa ntu,' who can tell me the object that led a man who is no less than the King, himself to taste ashes?"

In Africa, it is a common phenomenon for a family to gather in a room or 'obuma,' after the days business. This took place usually at nights. At this time the family will have had a good supper. This included foods like garri or fufu with soup. If available, these heavy foods are preferred early in the mornings or late in the evenings. The reason is obvious. The night is long. It is so long that it requires a heavy food to carry one althrough its length. If one takes a light food, one finds it difficult to relax and sleep well. The morning is another time that requires heavy eating. This is because one may not be fortunate enough to have another meal later in the day.

Now after supper, the father of the house would be seated on his easy-chair, or 'izu chia,' as it is wont to be pronounced. His wife would sit beside him. Then the children would take their own respective seats, usually at the centre of the stage. Naturally children are prone to fear. And so acting on this impulse, they try as much as possible to avert the outer spaces. Many times the youngest and the one after him tend to squeeze themselves either at the middle of the stage or close to their father or mother. "Chidinma shift for me," Nkeiru would complain, trying to squeeze in herself even before Chidinma makes a move to grant her demand. "Papa, Nkeiru smells of soup. Tell her to go and wash her hands better," Chidinma pointed out, a frown on her face. "Nkeiru," their father, Ejike, called, his voice rising, "go now and wash your hands and mouth very well before joining this gathering, did you hear me?" And without bothering to give an answer, Nkeiru would run into the house and hurriedly do as she was told to do.

Sometimes the story in the air would be awe-inspiring. In that case, Nkeiru would require some one to escort her into the house. Ejike would understand the child's feeling and ask someone to accompany her into the house. "I want to sit here. John, please shift for me," Nneka also complained. "John, please shift for your younger sister," Ejike ordered, glancing at John, and momentarily stopping the gist. This family gathering, usually gives rise to either fable stories, or riddles, as the one above. It is usually a cherished experience for children born into such families. Sometimes children of a family in the neighbourhood, sensing such a sitting, would sneak into the gathering when they think they would not be found out. This is, however, in contrast to others who come out openly and ask for permission before they joined. "'Ndewo Dee Ejike, please can I join you?" Ikechukwu, the son of Amanda Ikeogu, who lives next to Emenike's house, pleaded. "You may sit down and make yourself at home, son," Emenike replied, gesturing Ikechukwu to sit down.

Children learn a lot from such oral hand over stories. This is because, in addition to hearing how the tortoise, for instance, got his shells, fathers sometimes told what happened in real life, in his ancestral lineage.

However, the riddle above was not thrown up for the purpose of fun. Hunger was behind it. Dee Eze had sighted some of the oil palm seeds picked from a nearby farm and this had aroused in him a strong desire for food. But because there was no food in the house, he had strongly longed for the oil palm seed, hoping to at least use it to have something deposited into his stomach. His wife who had caught the 'joke' promptly called on the children. "Mgbechi, mgbechi," she called, adjusting her voice into a higher pitch so that Mgbechi who was not in the room at that time would hear her. "Yes mama", Nkechi answered, her face dull and furlonge. "What is amiss?" Nkechi's mother, Lucy asked, her eyes locking on Nkechi's own eyes. "Are you hungry or sick?" Of course, Mgbechi did not reply. As a matter of fact, she did no need to answer. On her own side, her mother was not really expecting any answer. Everyone was always hungry at any given time. And she was no exemption. There was not enough food to eat at any giving time. People were only eating every little thing that was available as food. This made them to eat at any time. There was little or no solid food within reach and those little things that were available did not bring the satisfaction that solid food offers. Those little things however, offered momentary relief from hunger.

Thereafter, Mgbechi had occupied a portion facing the already existing fire. While she was getting around to roasting the palmseeds, a question cropped up in her mind and she casually asked her mother, "Mama, what are you cooking?" "Mgbechi, I'm cooking your head. Mgbechi, I said I'm cooking your head." Her mother retorted. Mgbechi, who had grown lean, out of non-ending, 'no food' circumstances, could say nothing more. She rather tried to 'fold her legs' after two drops of tears had appeared on her cheeks and had found their way to the grand. "Yes, that's what you'll always do," her mother snapped, her voice rising, adding, "tell me, is there any other thing you'll do, other than what you're doing now. Cry Mgbechi, I say cry," her mother continued, "Throughout this Umueze Village, you are the only girl that has not eaten any food today." Mgbechi still held herself together.

Meanwhile, Dee Eze who had gone into his room awaiting the oil palm seeds' arrival had overheard his wife shouting at the girl. Unlike Mgbechi his last child, Dee Eze could not hold himself. He had let out sobs that rent his heart. Tears, hot tears had flowed down his cheeks without enough energy on his side to restrain them. His mind could only blame him for his inability to fend for his family. But was he really to blame?" A voice asked from within him. His mind raced back to the pre-war times. Dee Eze was one of the leading board members of one of the equally leading soap manufacturing companies in the country. As a consultant, his wide experience had earned him the name,

'Ahitophel'. New intakes into the company had thought that his real name was Ahitophel. Once, the Chairman of the company, Sir Doughlas, had asked a driver to go and pick Dee Eze from the airport. The driver who was a new intake into the company, had approached Dee Eze, addressing him as Sir Ahitophel. This had given Dee Eze, whose full name is Eze.O.Eze, a bad impression of the driver. He had considered that driver onwards, as an insubordinate fellow and had rejected him as his official chauffeur.

Chapter Thirteen

"Return the car keys to the 'AD'", Dee Eze had said, his face deeply furrowed, and quickly added "I'm not traveling again". He had later picked another driver from among the company's many drivers to travel with.

'AD' is the abbreviation for Administrative Manager. The name of the 'AD' is Mr. Johnson Cooker. He is tall and fair in complexion. He is however, a very stern man. He and Dee Eze had not been in the best of terms. Although he worked under Dee Eze, he resented Dee Eze. The resentment arose when Dee Eze, as the Managing Director, transferred him to the eastern part of the country. Mr Cooker had petitioned London claiming that he was unduly transferred. The authorities in London had reversed the transfer. Dee Eze was later to discover that Mr. Cooker had a friend who was well connected to London. Ever since that incident, Mr. Cooker had never accorded Dee Eze his full respect as his senior officer. And so Dee Eze had chosen to ignore Mr. Cooker's insurbodination to him. He therefore chose not to get himself directly involved with Mr. Cooker in this matter, or any matter, whatsoever. So, to avoid a direct comunication with Mr Cooker, he rather insisted that the driver should return the keys to Mr Cooker, by himself, and tell him that he had rejected him as his official chauffeur.

Dee Eze also remembered the fat cheques which the company's accountant had lodged into his bank account each time he travelled officially. He remembered also that he made an average of four travels each month. This had left his main salary untouched unless a capital intensive project cropped up. Dee Eze remembered how he had made his beautiful wife and children very comfortable. He had always been a man of the family. "Afterall," he thought, "had his 404 saloon car not been packed at his garage in his house at Marina, Lagos? While at Lagos, he had left the car to his wife and rather used his official car. Furthermore, he had provided adequately for his family so much that they had no reason whatsoever, to grumble or complain about lack of food or any good thing of life, before the advent of the war. Now, here he was, unable to help his little daughter who had cried in his own presence, for hunger.

Dee Eze was not alone in this predicament, however, he was rather lucky because he not only survived the war, but when he went back to Lagos, after the war, God's providence accorded him the grace to get reinstated into his pre-war position, thereby getting his family rejuvenated.

Dee Jerome also lived with his family in Lagos. His house was not far away from where Dee Eze lived. Being cousins, they had been cordial with each other. According to each of them however, they had not been seeing much of each other while in Lagos. Their sure means of comunication had been the telephone. Each of them had been so busy that it had been very difficult for any one of them to visit the other. The other point of meeting with each other would have heen at the village meeting grounds, on the meeting days. But that was not to be. Dee Jerome's business of clearing and forwarding had kept him even busier than Dee Eze. He would ply all the nooks and crannies of Lagos as story had it, either negotiating or trying to reach his clientele, one after another. Story had it that to be able to meet up with his numerous travels in and out of Lagos, Dee Jerome had bought several cars. "Several cars?" Osita and Emma had asked, simultateously. "Yes, several cars," Obinna echoed, his right hand buried in his trousers' pocket, his face beaming with smile, his mind puffed up. "In Lagos," he continued, "there are so many cars that there would be traffic chaos, if the government had not intervened. "To avert this situation," he went on, "government had introduced what they called the 'even and odd number system.' This implies a separate day for cars and other vehicles bearing even numbers from the day meant for the ones bearing odd numbers. Any vehicle plying the streets or roads must ascertain therefore that it was doing so on the day that was appropriate for the number on its plate. Dee Jerome therefore had to own many cars to meet up with his own use, the family's own use, as well as the company's own use".

However, all these had been in the past, now. To say that the same Dee Jerome has now been pauperized to grass roots level is to say the least. He lives in a one room apartment with his family of six, four children, his beautiful wife and himself. Most mornings, he picked up his matchet, sharpened it and lazily walked up to the farms. He would cut any thing that caught his fancy-palm fronds, fire woods or any things of that sort. Once, he had tried to climb the palm tree and cut down a ripen oil palm seed bunch. But his wife had raised a great alarm and that had attracted some people at the farm, since it was not faraway from their home. This had nonetheless, greatly embarrassed Dee Jerome. “When did you learn the art of climbing a palm tree? Who gave you an ‘efe’ or do you not know that palm trees are not climbed bare handedly?” his father-in-law had hurled at him, a series of questions without waiting for him to give an answer to any one of them, before he asked another one. “Now let me tell you,” the elderly man had begun again, his face, contorted, his eyes hooded, “a man does not have to loose his life at the same place where he lost his belongings.” The elderly man had told him many stories bordering on the unpredictabilities of life, gesticulating as he spoke. “Many heroes in life have lost it all when they lost their life,” he had continued, adding, “this is in contrast to as many as have patiently followed the path of the gradual processes of life. Have you forgotten that the patient dog eats the fattest bone?” he finally querried, looking askance at his son-in-law. “Papa,” Dee Jerome finally found his voice, his face looking sober reflective as he spoke. “I have heard all that you said. Let me now promise you that I will not try to climb a palm tree again. “Good.” asserted the elderly man, “climbing a palm tree without an ‘efe’ is another name for committing suicide.” In conclusion, Dee Eleme, for that is the old man’s name, had recommitted the welfare of his daughter and her children into the hands of his son-in-law.

At home, Dee Jerome continued his normal business of cutting and processing of palm fronds into brooms. In the course of trying to cut some of the bunches of the palm fruits, some of the fruits disengage themselves and fall at the foot of the mother tree. He picked these ones, and deposited them into the dirty and worn out leather bag hanging on his left shoulder. Some of the oil palm fruits looked fresh, while others were not so fresh. The fresh ones among them, he cleaned with his hands and ate, one after another, as he moved along. This way, he served himself with the breakfast.

"Gracie," he called out to his wife, as soon as he got home, "please check at the back of the door leading to the kitchen, you will find five bundles of brooms that I kept there. Check equally for a small basin full of oil palm fruits, which I also kept there. Select the ones you'll need, and sell the rest, along side the brooms," he enthused, feelling happy that he had provided for the familly's up keep for uptill the next market day which would come up in the next eight days.

"Jay," his wife called on him when she came back from the market. "I saw Monica, Dee Eze's wife, at the market today. She said that Dee Eze is indisposed. Have you seen him lately?" "In that case," replied Dee Jerom, exhaling deeply, his voice, shaky with anxiety,"I think I should go and see him this evening. I have not seen him lately".

Families, friends and well wishers, did not feel comfortable if any one among them took ill. This was irrespective of how slight the ailment was. The reason is that the war had made food and drugs out of the reach of the people. So, a slight ailment could degenerate into a very serious health problem.

At Dee Eze's house, the two erstwhile wealthy men had talked about life in the good old days and the frustration that is currently eating people up here. "Ehe, least I forget, have you heard that Sam is dead?" Eze asked, fixing a glance at Jerome, and at the same time shaking his head in painful mourn for the departed hero. "Which Sam?" Jerome asked, leaning forward, his eyes propping out, his lips parted, his ears, tingling. "The Sam Ltd of course," Eze grimaced, his head lowered, his hands borne at the back of his own head. "My God," Jerome yelled, lowering his own head too, as if in agreement. In that split second, a series of negative thoughts flashed through his mind. "Suppose he becomes the next person to die? How does it feel to be dead?" While he pondered over this, his mind reflected back to when he saw Sam last. There was actually, nothing to suggest that the man would soon die. "Truly speaking, Sam looked so emaciated that he looked so much like the shadow of himself. But that is not peculiar to him," Jerome mused and grimaced. "Everybody in this part of the world looks emaciated," he mumbled, his head still held down. Moments later, he found his voice, opened his mouth and spoke. "God please stop this war soon before everybody dies of hunger and frustration."

Two days later, precisely on a Tuesday, the two friends left for Amazari. They left very early in the morning before daylight. One of the reasons was to try as much as possible to beat the soldiers who mount at check points trying to catch soldiers who run away from the war fronts. Another group of people that the soldiers looked out for, were the 'able bodied men,' as the soldiers would refer to them, who had refused to join the army. Further reasons why they left so early bordered on the distance. The war had made life upside down. Bicycle owners are considerd rich, now. Unfortunately, neither Jerome nor Eze belonged to this class now. So they had to cover the long distance from Umuehiri to Amazari, the refugee camp of the Sam Ltd and his widow, a distance of over twelve kilometers on foot and barefooted. Early mornings are characterized with cool weather. That was the type of weather which they considered would offer them a shield from the direct scorch of the sunshine later in the day. In addition to this, the weather was sure to allow them to step on cool soil as against the hotness of the sandy soil that encapsulated the area.

Soon they arrived at the refugee camp of the widow of the late Sam Ltd. Soon too, they came face to face with late Sam's widow. "Chei, 'ndi enyi dim,' oh my late husband's friend," Sam's widow, cried, her left hand on her head, her right hand busy, trying to hold her almost loose wrapper in place. "Sam has killed me," she lamented and burst into an emotional round of weeping. "What really happened, madam?" Jerome asked, leaning forward, his voice choky, his eyes fixed on their hostess, his lips slightly parted. And as if acting in unison, Eze dragged the short stem of a felled tree offered him for a seat near the woman, sat down opposite her, and also leaned forward facing her, his attention completely focused on her, his own lips also parted. The question seemed to have helped to stop the weeping as the woman had lazily mopped her eyes and nostrils, using a loosed end of the ragged wrapper that covered her body from shoulders to her feet. "Sam," she began, "had complained of fever and weakness that fateful early morning. Shortly later, he indicated an urge to open his bowels. This was habitual with him. It did not matter whether he ate any food or not, the previous night. He was sure to open his bowels each morning. And in order to really open his bowels well, he was served with a chewing stick, some water to wash his mouth and a good quantity to drink. Sam passed stool, came in here, but urgently began to demand for food. The demand was so urgent that we had to hastely get some tapioca for him." As the woman made the last statement, she broke down again and began to weep. Jerome and Eze were later to hear that their friend collapsed and gave off the ghost before the tapioca was served. "Just like that?" entoned a down caste looking Eze, as he gently tapped his right foot on the floor, gnashing his teeth in the same vein. "Life, they say is a walking shadow, now I know how true it is," Jerome paraphrased, shaking his head as he spoke.

Chapter Fourteen

One morning, Osita and his younger sister, Ijeoma, went to the food centre at the outskirt of the Umuehiri village, not very far away from the refugee camp. It was a popular one. Children converged at this ground from various communities around Umuehiri.

There had been a rumour that a special food package had been arranged for children by caritas, by ten o'clock that morning. Osita did not know the full meaning of caritas. He only knew that it is a catholic mission organization worldwide.

Rumours were the order of the day during the war times. For instance, the sound of shooting was always in the air. They were of various dimensions. This was perhaps because the guns used were of different makes and sizes. While the sounds of many were heavy, others were relatively light.

However, they brought apprehension to the people. The proximity of the gun shots determined the magnitude of apprehension among the people of that village. When they sounded near the inhabitants of that place naturally 'stood on their toes'. Under such situations the people began to gather some of their personal effects. Things like dresses, mats, pillows, plates and other cooking utensils only, for a possible flight away from the disturbed village.

Thankfully, however, there were times when the gun shots which had previously sounded nearby, began to sound remotely, or ceased completely for an appreciable period of time.

At such times, rumour mongers would be handy to tell the masses what brought about the change. "Our own army came up hard against the army of the other side, and forced them to a retreat."

This information usually evoked jubilation among the masses of this side. People would throng the streets with happy tales of how it happened.

Unfortunately, the versions differed greatly. Another version of the rumour could crop up. This would tell the populace that the gods of the town or village where the retreat was enforced were responsible for the retreat. "They had inflicted unbearable injuries on the invading soldiers and forced them to a retreat".

This version usually massaged the ego of the inhabitants of the village in question.

The sun rose up the sky early that morning. This made it a little difficult to determine what time of the day that they got at the food centre.

However, when they got to the place, not many people had gathered there. This was unlike what obtained usually. "We came rather too late, Osita," Ijeoma observed, glancing at her brother, her hands clutching two little bowls, one in her left hand, the other in her right hand. "This is strange," Osita remarked, glancing around the school premises that was the food centre, his lips slightly parted. "But how could they have rounded off so early today?" Ijeoma asked, her eyes now following her brother's own gaze.

"I told you to hurry up. If you had hurried up, we would have arrived early enough to get our own ration," Osita blamed her, a frown on his face. "I did not waste any time after you told me to get ready. I only asked mama to give me my plates and she promptly found them and handed them over to me," Ijeoma tried to protest, her face also frowned.

They were still deliberating on this issue when some other children who were somewhat bigger than they arrived. They were five in number. They exchanged glances as if that was premeditated. As if they were not satisfied with the number of children they saw too, one of them, precisely, the only boy among them lazing walked up to Osita, his eyes roaming round the whole place. "Are they no longer sharing the ration, today?" he asked as soon as he got about two yards away from where Osita and his sister were standing, his eyes fixed on Osita's own eyes. "We arrived here only a few minutes ago. We are about as surprised to see this semi empty place as you are," Osita tried to explain, glancing back at the boy. Soon another set of children came up. And before long a sizeable crowed had formed. It was however, in Osita's estimation, not more than a quarter of what gathered at the centre, ordinarily. Nothing meaningful was happening. Some children took to roaming around the premises. Others sat in groups chatting as if they were so organized. Osita and his sister sat down on their own, though. They had stayed for quite a long time, before a man came out from one of the school blocks. He was tall and robust. When Osita and the others noticed him, they rose on their feet expecting to have him arrange everybody in queues as was usual. They recognized him as a member of the Red Cross Society. Not that they knew him facially, though. They rather thought so because of his looks. Only the Red Cross members looked that good at the time. They were however disappointed when the man came nearer Osita and his sister and greeted them with a mockery. He said something that bordered on information having overtaken the first one. This one was as funny as it was incredible. "The war has ended and you all are here bearing plates," the man said and promptly walked quickly away. It was as if the children did not understand him. They all stood their looking confused.

Soon some of the children began to leave. As they lazily walked out of the place, they jeered along the way. "The war has ended, the war has ended," they refrained. They were however not saying it in harmony. It all sounded like a mere noise.

When news or a rumour started making the rounds that the caritas and their agents organized a special package for the children, Osita had taken his little sister along, on that particular day. This was so that the ration would become bigger. "After all," he mused, "have we not been stared at, on the face, by this severe hardship and hunger? A trend which the national food policy had been unable to control"

Government had legalized the act of harvesting food crops from any available farm land, irrespective of who owned the farm. As a result of this policy, people began to comb the nearby farm lands in search of what to harvest and eat.

Food itself had become a luxury. The sight of a person, eating solid food like garri, evoked envy from the person next to him.

Osita looked at the jeering children and smiled. He had remembered something. He remembered the story which his mother told him not quite long ago. His mother said that the event took place when they were little girls.

They had been told that the Queen was visiting the country. She was going to come in an aeroplane. This had piqued the interests of those of them who were young children at that time. They had imagined an aeroplane landing in their village play ground and a white woman alighting from the aeroplane and shaking hands with them, one after another. "Will she really come to our village?" mama had asked. "Yes, why not?" mama's father had answered and quickly added, "Is this community not part of the empire? With an aeroplane," he had continued, "one could easily tour round the whole world in a matter of a few hours. So she would be able to tour round the empire, including this village. This is to get a first hand information about the welfare of the people of the villages that make up the empire." "Papa what is empire?" mama had asked. Her father had hesitated a little, but had come up with an answer a few seconds later. "An empire is a collection of localities or local governments under one central government." "And please what is localities?" she had asked further. "You ask too many questions, my daughter. I do not know how to explain this to you," he had replied, but quickly added, "Suffice it to hear that our village is an example of a locality." At this junction, my grandmother had tried to make an input. "Violet," she had called, pronouncing Violet as Vailate, "when you get to the sunday school lesson tomorrow, don't forget to ask your teacher to tell you the meaning of locality, did you hear me?" But before mama could open her mouth to say 'yes', her father came up again, this time feeling somewhat irritated. "Does her sunday school teacher know better than me? Well, I don't blame you. A prophet is least regarded in his home stead," he said, frowning. "That is not what I said," my grandmother had tried to protest. "That is the implication of what you just said, woman," grandfather had replied, his voice rising, his eyes flashed at grandmother as if he was trying to perforate her face. "When you open your mouth to speak, you do not think before you go on and talk," he quickly added, fuming, and rising from the bench he sat on, he dragged himself into the hut, leaving mama and grandmother on their own.

After a brief pause, Osita had asked her mother the reason why grandmother had asked her to meet her sunday school teacher instead of her school teacher, for the meaning of locality. "There were very few schools in those days," she began, "people were opposed to going to school. It was considered a thing for slaves and stubborn children. Stubbon children were sent to school so that they would be disciplined in school. Good children were not sent to school. This was to prevent the 'good children' from being flogged."

"What about you, mama? Did you go to school?" as he asked this question, Osita averted his mother's eyes. This he did out of sheer pity for his mother. He already knew that she didn't go to scool. "No my son," Violet said, "that premitive trend overlapped into our own time, too." "So mama," Osita said, trying to change the subject matter. "What about the Queen's visit, did it hold?" "Yes my son, it did hold." Violet now began to tell her son how they had seen an aeroplane in the sky, and had begun to run after it, expecting it to land in their village playground. But it didn't. They had followed on until they lost sight of it. That was when they came to realize how very far away they had followed the aeroplane, covering a distance of seven kilometers. They had dejectedly trekked back home only to hear that their village was not among the areas mapped out for her to visit. "It was a highly disappointing adventure," she had summed up, smiling.

Soon after the story, Violet lazily walked out into the ground allocatted to her for cooking at the refugee camp. It was at the verandah of the school block which housed her family and many other refugee families. She already had in place three pieces of block which served as tripod stand for her cooking. She therefore picked her old pot, poured out some water into it and placed it on the fire which she made with some dry leaves and dry fibre extracted from palm fruits. "What do you want to cook, mama?" Osita asked, fixing a glance at his mother. "Soup, I want to cook some soup," she said, her face expressionless. "And you are using water?" Osita demanded, his lips wide apart, his eyes fixed on her. "Y-e-s," she slowly answered, smiling, "what's wrong with that?" "Do they cook soup using water?" he asked further, a surprised look on his face. "Everything is cooked with water, except, of course if you want to fry the stuff," Violet explained, still smiling.

Osita was going to express in words how surprised he was to hear that soup was cooked with water, when the voices of the jeering children brought him back to his sences. He began to wonder if these children would go on and jeer along the road until they covered a very long distance without knowing it. He was thinking along this line when he felt a hand touch his shoulder. It was Ijeoma's hand. "Others are leaving, let's equally leave," Ijeoma suggested. If not for his sister, Osita was not prepared to leave the place at that moment. He wanted to stay until they were compelled to start sharing the special gift from Caritas. He thought it must be a trick to lure people away from the centre and then share the package with only a handful of children who were prepared to persevere.

Back at the camp, people were gathering up their personal effects, consisting mainly of ragged dresses and wrappers, and of course, cooking utensils.

Chapter Fifteen

"Thank God you two are here now," Violet chuckled. "Now come up and help out as much as you can, everyone's leaving the camp, we must not be left on our own" she said further, directing Osita to where to start. She had hardly pronounced the last word when a voice came from behind. "'Nwunye dim', my husband's wife, you are still packing up, but am through with mine," the voice said. Violet looked towards the direction of the voice and saw the person. It was Edna. "My husband's wife," she began, "the children I told you about arrived here about five minutes ago. Wthout wasting any time we're trying to hurry up," Violet replied, her eyes still on her children. Edna stood nearby and watched her friend do her packing up. "Won't that kettle fall off from there?" She asked trying to make an input. "Yes, you're right, my husband's wife. I'll use this rope to tie it up in with the basket's handle," Violet tried explaining, pointing at a twine she had cut a few minutes earlier, before packing up the kitchen knife. "Okay, that makes sense, now," Edna replied. Soon an aeroplane appeared up in the horizon. The size of the vessel showed that it was flying at a very high altitude. But while the aeroplane moved along, it seemed that the sound rather followed behind, but from a pronounced distance. "An aeroplane, again?" Edna mumbled, slanting a glance at the moving object as if a direct look at it would expose her to the dangers which aero planes had purportedly become associated with. "I thought they said the war had ended. God please let this information be true after all," she prayed, silently. Violet did not say amen as she expected. Edna quickly turned her head and faced her. "Woman," she called, slanting a glance at her companion, "I hope you're still there." "My sister, please never mind me. I wouldn't claim that I didn't hear you. I was rather wondering how my other children are faring, wherever they are now," Violet answered, sighing. "You mean Lawrence and Henrick?" her companion asked, stealing a glance at a gmelina tree standing nearby. Her gaze was in reaction to a faint sound produced as a result of a lizard's body coming in contact with dry leaves, spread randomly on the ground, as the rodent tried to move along. Funny enough, the faint sound was produced by the rodent as it tried to run away from Edna's gaze. Edna had been frightened instead. That was not strange. The reason was that the incessant sounds of gun shots with the attendant sounds of flying bullets, in addition to the daily scenes of death had eroded, the people's peace of mind. Every sound or noise in the air, irrespective of the magnitude, was capable of jolting any Dick or Harry to his marrow. It did not matter whether the noise emanated from a human being or animal. As a result of this, Edna had fixed a slanted glance at the source of the noise even while she was still conversing with her friend, Violet.

"Yes, who else?" Violet replied, grimacing. "Suppose they arrive home before us, "Edna enthused, giggling. "I pray that happens. And if it does, my mouth here would be at a loss for what to say and how to thank God enough. "Violet replied, touching her lip with her index finger. "What would you give him?" Edna asked, smiling. "You're talking in rhetorics, my sister, but I'm being serious. However, with my extreme emaciated looks, would he even accept me?" she asked. Thus the two women went on and engaged themselves in chatting.

And finally, the two families set out en route to their marital homes.

"Which way do we follow?" Violet inquired, stretching her body. "The road bisecting 'Afor-Nguzo' market square is ideal?" Edna suggested, locking eyes with Violet.

Edna lived with her family at Onitsha, before the war began. Her husband, Paul, had been in good terms with Tasie, Violet's husband. The two families have since been close to each other. Edna however was more familiar with the roads to and from Obodoma than Violet. It was based on this reason that Violet sought for Edna's own opinion.

"Agreed, the road through 'AfoNguzo' market is short, but is it not lonely?" Violet asked, fixing a glance at Edna. "It used to be lonely before the war began, but no longer so these days," Edna replied.

As the journey progressed they passed a lot of people by, most of who were coming from the opposite direction. While they moved on, they noticed that the faces of the people coming from the opposite direction showed some sign of happiness and relief. "We're on our way home," some of them announced, "that seemingly un-ending war has finally come to an end." Edna grinned, her heart enthusiastic to seeing home at last.

"Mama, I'm tired," Iheanyi said, suddenly, apparently reluctant to move any further. "I'm hungry," Victor, added, his face, deeply frowned, his hands somewhat raised as he tried to stretch his body. "These children, you don't seem to understand what's going on. Is it not a stone throw from home now? Can't you exercise a little more patience?" replied their mother, Edna, not willing to stop.

Iheanyi is the last child of Edna and her late husband, Paul, while Victor is the next to the last child, and interestingly they are about the same ages with Ijeoma and Osita, respectively.

So, when, both Iheanyi and Victor exhibited tiredness, Ijeoma and Osita had sympathized with them naturally, by brandishing same feelings. This prompted the two families to finding a convenient resting place, at the foot of a huge tree, right inside the market square, sat down there and rested awhile.

Edna produced a water-proof bag carefully placed at a corner in the basin she was carrying. She also brought out a bowl imbedded at the centre of the basin. Before long, she had presented a bowl full of tapioca to her children. Typical of African culture, she was washing the remaining tapioca, which she meant to pass over to Osita and Ijeoma, when coincidentally, Violet had just presented also a quantity of tapioca to her own children and was getting around to presenting the remainder to her friend's children. "I was rather going to pass over to your own children the one I have in my hand, now." She asserted, holding back the loose end of her wrapper. "A coincidence then," Edna chuckled, and the two women laughed over the issue. The adults having now discovered that the food they prepared for the children's launch were same delicacy, withdrew each, the one for the friend's children.

Soon the launch was over and the journey resumed after gulping down, a large amount of water. "'Ugbo rijuo afo, ya ekwe njem' When the train or any vessel is properly fuelled, the journey becomes certain," Violet said as she finally lifted the basin and balanced it unto her head. "In this case 'nwunye dim' not all 'ugbo' have been sufficiently fuelled," Edna said, trying to force herself to smile. "Yes," Violet said, trying to also smile, adding "the children are by implication, more important than you and I." "Humn" Edna said, seemingly having nothing more to say.

As if in agreement, the two friendly women trekked the remaining part of the journey mostly in silence. Only the children spoke a little and at wide intervals. It had become obvious that everyone of them had gotten worn out. Even the children, who had all along moved somewhat swiftly in front, had started lagging behind. Their mothers had now taken the lead. They would however, walk up to a remarkable distance, only to have to stop, after finding out that the children were not coming closely enough. At that point they would beckon on them to hurry up. In an effort to suit the children, they would tell them that they were close to home. "Hurry up children, come to the front we are getting close to our home." It was very pertinent to have the children in front. This was so that the elders could keep an eye over them.

Thank goodness, they didn't have to walk a lot further, before they arrived home. The two families therefore, happily parted ways at the entrance of the home compound of Violet Tasie.

Chapter Sixteen

"Victor, Iheanyi, bye, bye," chorused Osita and his little sister, Ijeoma. "Thank you, Osita and Ijeoma, 'Noro nu nkeoma" replied Victor, and his younger brother, Iheanyi. "'Noro nu nkeoma' take good care of yourself, my husband's wife," and quickly added, "do remember to visit us subsequently, at your convenient times. We would be very glad to have you around us, at least occasionally," Violet said, waving cheerfully at her friend and her children. "Yes, I'll make out time again to come over and spend some time with you, one of these days. Meanwhile it's been nice being in your company," Edna replied, waving happily too at the family that had made the long trek back home. Her own matrimonial home, which is actually, not far away from her friend's own, now seemed a million miles, away. Slanting a glance at her children, she increased her strides. Momentarily, she could find little or nothing any more to talk over with the children. Her mind had suddenly developed an immense longing to seeing home again, after a long absence. As she increased her pace, her children equally increased their own pace. It was as if they were trying to compete with her. That was actually, not the point. The point is that they had also, suddenly remembered home and had begun to feel a longing to get home, too.

"What could have become of her little hut?" Edna mused, inadvertently increasing her stride. "Suppose…?" She did not want her mind to move in that direction and so had cut the thought short by declining from pronouncing the word. However, the thought stubbornly flashed through her mind like lightening, moments later. "Suppose, she gets home, and finds out that the mud which formed her house's walls, had collapsed? God," she muttered "please don't let this be true." Suddenly, she remembered Ndawi's mother's hut. Someone had told Edna and herself that Ndawi's mother's hut collapsed before the villagers returned from the refugee camps. A bomb had exploded in their compound while everyone was away at the refugee camps. All the three huts in the compound had collapsed including Ndawi's mother's own and those of her husband's wives.

"Thank God that no one was in the huts. They probably would have been buried alive," Edna had replied, shaking her head as slightly as the load she was carrying on her head allowed her. "Yes thank God that no lives were lost," Violet had added trying to also shake her own head, but quickly asked her own question. "What would she and her husband's wives do now that everyone is going back home?"

"I heard that Ndawi's mother is planning to take her children to her place of birth. She intends to live permanently among her own people," their informant had said, adjusting the basin that she expertly balanced on her head. "What about her husband?" Edna asked standing momentarily at a spot trying to wait for her informant who was lagging behind due to the heavy load that she was carrying on her head. “My husband’s wife,” the woman said, “please let us move on, this world has become something else, it is a wicked world, she concluded, sighing.” “’Ima nke anyi g’anu, is there any other serious matter?” Edna tried to probe. The woman hesitated, but sighed. Moments later, as if she had made up her mind to tell, she sighed again, and said. “About three moons ago, rumour began to spread, behind Ndawi’s mother, though, that her husband had died at the war front. And as if to confirm the rumor, no one had heard about him since that time,” the woman had said, and sighed. Silence followed. “’E wo, ije uwa’, how awful,” Violet said and shook her head, sighing as she did. “Is Ndawi her only daughter?” Edna asked, trying to fix a glance at the woman. “She is not only her first daughter, she is her only child,” the woman, tried to explain, exhaling deeply.

As Edna moved on, the premonition that her hut might be among several other ones that had collapsed, quickened her pace. For the first time since they left the camp earlier in the day, the thought that she might have to pass the night outside, as a result of not having a place to stay, had hit her mind like a thunder bolt. She could no longer exercise patience in trying to keep pace with the kids. Suddenly too, she felt a pressure to urinate. “Children,” she cried, “you certainly can trace your way home from here, so come along as I hurry home to urinate.” Having thus said, she hurried home. Once she got within focus range, she flashed her eye lense towards their hut. Luckily, the hut was intact. Only weeds growing randomly, throughout the compound and around, had made the difference. At the sight of this, Edna had heaved a sigh of relief “’Chineke, Imena’ God thank you," She had muttered to herself, and heaved a sigh of relief, for the second time. At this juncture, the urge to urinate, suddenly disappeared. Presumably too, her blood pressure, which had abruptly shot up, though unconsciously to her, would have begun to normalize. At this point, she turned to see the children. But they were not within eye focus. This made her to regret ever leaving them behind, in that lonely village. "God," she heard her own voice mutter, "please protect these children and forgive me for leaving them on their own in this lonely place." And in that confused state of mind, she walked out of the house's premises and looked along the path through which she came back. She could not find them. "God, these children have killed me, they're still nowhere to be found," she mumbled, and moved further along the path. As she moved along the lonely pathway, fear began to toture her mind. She however, was no longer sure whether she was scared for her own safety or the kids. "Do I call on their names at the top of my voice, or what?" she mused. In spite of the efforts she made trying to restrict herself, she still felt like shouting their names and actually made to do that, but practically could not just go on, as she felt a lump in her throat. Her displeasure, increased, when she went back home to relieve herself of the load she was carrying, but discovered that she could not bring the basin down without a helping hand. So she made a move to go back the second time and check the boys, but met them at the entrance to the compound. "You're here, at last, she said" heaving another sigh of relief and at the same time, making a sign of the cross on her forehead. "The whole place is bushy," Victor more or less shouted. "Don't be silly," his mother retorted. "We're the only people around here now, so we need not expose our presence to the world, at least for the night," she summed up, rather in hushed tones. This statement was later to hunt Victor's young mind, tormenting it with fear. "Mama," he found his voice, unable to hide his fears any longer, "shall we sleep in this house all alone?" "Never mind, son," his mother had replied, "we'll come up with a plan later," she assured him, "meanwhile let's prepare some food for the night."

Thankfully, Edna still had a good quantity of tapioca left in the water proof bag which she brought home from the camp. She also had enough pepper and potash in her can. Luckily too, there was also a little oil remaining. Her greatest source of happiness, that evening, was that the pack of matches which she bought, at the cost of one pound, the previous week, was still remaining.

To make the matches last longer, she had used dry palm fronds in collecting, and making fire, while at the refugee camp. She remembered what pain it cost her to pay for the pack of matches at the price she bought it. Although she desperately needed one, her fancy was to exchange some of the salt which her first son, Ben, a member of the Red Cross Society, had brought home for a few packs of matches. But to her dismay, the only person whose matches were remaining in full packs had declined a barter trade.

Chapter Seventeen

"No my husband's wife," the woman had insisted. "I have some salt in the house and as a matter of fact, I intend to sell in cash," Edna tried as much as she could to make the woman change her mind but could not achieve that. And as if to make matters worse for her, the few others, who also sold matches, refused to sell to her, either in packs or in barter. They preferred to sell in counted bunches. "It is more profitable to sell in sticks, my husband's wife," the woman sitting next to her had said. "So" she went on, "these few bunches that are remaining are supposed to fetch all the food types and their respective condiments that I need." In such cases, the market women would package the matches in sticks of five pieces or ten pieces, as the case may be. And by the time they sold off the bunches of five sticks each as well as the others, they would have gotten some cash to buy food items, including garri pepper, salt and so on at reasonable prices. All these food items would have been gotten through the sale of a single pack of matches.

That was how Edna had been compelled to pay a whooping one pound, to buy a pack of matches. She also remembered how she was bitterly cheated by the woman whose own market stall was next to hers. This woman, whose name was, Clarice, sold garri alongside other food items. When Clarice and herself, bargained for trade by exchange, the woman had also had an upper hand in the bargain. The reason is that Victor and Iheanyi, had complained of eating corn meal monotonously, lately. "Mama, please let's eat something else other than corn meal, this night," they had said in unison. So she had decided to exchange some corn mill with garri. This was to enable her to provide her children with a little variety. The last encounter with the person whose garri was still remaining, was one she would not forget in a hurry. Just like the matches' seller, the woman whose garri, she exchanged with corn mill, probably realized that she desperately needed the garri and so had insisted on her own terms of the exchange, without any compromise.

That was one of the banes of buying and selling during the war. The quantum of money in circulation was probably very high. Whereas the goods, mostly food items, were relatively very small. This had devalued the money, for that reason, it was not uncommon for a buyer to spend a large sum of money and yet end up getting a little in return. Under this situation, one supplemented one's purchasing power with trade by batter.

Edna, was still going through her remaining food items, so as to assemble the ones she would use that night, when one of her sisters-in-law and children arrived. "Mama Betsy, you're welcome home. Uzoho, it's good to see you again," she heard her own children say. She was not sure however, whether her mind was playing a trick on her. As she made to peep through the door leading to the kitchen, Iheanyi came into the kitchen and confirmed the arrival of the family. "'Betsy nnem', my sister Betsy," Edna heard her own voice cry impulsively, and at the same time, inadvertently jumped out of the kitchen, and both women embraced each other. "You're just coming behind us," she explained panting, and moments later, she helped Betsy to bring her load down. Edna was moving towards Uzoho, when suddenly, she realized that tears were hanging on Betsy's cheeks. "Is anything the matter Betsy?" She asked, her eyes boring on Betsy's own eyes. At that moment however, no answer seemed to be on the way. Worse still, rather than giving out an answer, more tears flowed down Betsy's cheeks. "Please talk to your sister, Betsy, is…is anything the matter?" Edna stuttered, gasping and at the same time, roving her eyes inquiringly, from Betsy to Ozo, in an attempt to find out what really was going on. It was at this juncture, that the two women burst into emotional cry. Betsy had briefly opened up, still clinging to her friend and sister in law as if she used her body to support her own body fraim. "Was he involved in an accident?" Edna asked further.

"One afternoon," Betsy began, I had managed to get some cassava tubers which I peeled into fine tapioca strands, when my husband spotted some, which he identified as 'oburu'orie, a-cassava specie that could be boiled and eaten as yam. Actually I made a move to cross check the pieces of cassava but was barred from doing so, by an inner feeling which I could not and still cannot explain" she had said, adding, "Clearly, Eluchie had been very hungry and could no longer conceal the fact. My sister, hours after my husband had eaten the cassava, he started complaining of stomach ache. And before long, my husband had started groaning. Unfortunately by the time we collected some oil palm fruits, since we had no fresh oil, Eluchie could not open his mouth any longer, to eat the fruits." "Stop hei… stop, don't tell me anymore," Edna's voice range in the air and they both swung into another round of emotion-laden cry. A few 'umunna' who had so far returned from exile, gathered and pacified the crying women, "It is strange that a thing of this magnitude took place but we were not informed." Edna tried to protest later. While some of the 'umunna' who had gathered in the compound had admitted receiving information to that effect, others had brandished a glaring surprise to the issue. "We weren't informed at all," Nkem confessed. "Neither were we," Dee Anto had said, spreading both hands out in a bid to support his claim. 'Anto' is short form of Anthony. Children of their clan had become so used to calling him Dee Anto, that many of them had become confused when someone else addressed him as 'Dee Anthony'.

Chapter Eighteen

"My husband's wife, I think I must leave you now to go. You have done noble by coming to stay all this while, with us" Violet said, beaming with smiles. "I might as well thank you for the great hosting, you've accorded me' returned Edna. "Please receive me the way you see me," the former said again. "I must in that case confess that you are a great hostess indeed," remarked Edna, giggling. "'Ehe', thank God I didn't forget, have you heard that Betsy lost her husband, a few days before the war ended?" Edna asked, glancing at Violet. "Which of them?" Violet demanded. "Betsy Iruka is the one I mean." Edna emphatically stated. "You mean your own Betsy, your husband's wife?" Violet asked a glaring surprise on her face." She hesitated, her eyes flashed as if that would make her understand her friend better. She opened her mouth, but closed it almost immediately as if she could not find the right words to use. And as if she waited for Violet to express her emotional feeling first, Edna answered her question in the affirmative. "That's the one," she had admitted. And without waiting to get more information from Edna, Violet had hauled more questions at her friend; "When, Ha..., how... what happened to him?" she stuttered.

The two women were still talking, about the death of Betsy's husband, when a group of soldiers in army uniform pulled an old army land rover and stopped beside them.

Edna was the first to notice them. As the open army land rover pulled up a couple of meters from they were standing, she had involuntarily turned towards the direction of the vehicle. Her eyes suddenly met with those of one of the soldiers standing at the rear side of the vehicle, his hands clutching firmly at one of the cross bars in the land rover. This had sent shivers down her spine. She quickly diverted her own eyes and tried hard to stop her eyes from looking in that direction. Unfortunatelyy, in spite of the efforts she made, her eyes tended to stray towards the parked vehicle. This tendency added up to the emotion of fear now building up in her. She could no longer take total control of her eyes. She began to steal glances at them, her heart pounding increasingly harder agaist her ribs. She summarily stood on her toes.

Violet had equally heard the sound of the army vehicle as it pulled up not quite far away from them. But she did not feel like looking up at the vehicle. There were very few vehicles plying the roads at the time. Most of them were army vehicles. She had therefore assumed that they were on security patrol. But when she noticed that her friend was no longer responding to her questions, but had rather diverted her attention sideways, she quickly turned her face towards the direction of her attention. To her horror, she sighted the stern looking faces of some of the soldiers. Her horror increased when she noticed that they were looking at both her friend and herself. At that moment, her heart suddenly jumped into her stomach. She quickly looked away. At that same instance, fear gripped her like a pair of pincers. She hesitated and began to slant glances at them, her heart pounding heavily against her chest cavity. As the seconds trickled by and she could not determine their fate, she began to wish that the earth could just open up and swallow them up.

The soldiers on the other hand fixed a glance that seemed as if it could see through the women's respective bodies. But shortly after, as if induced by an unseen force, they drove off as unannounced as they had pulled up, their vehicle throwing up immense dust as it sped off unto the untared road. The two friends looked at each other in apprehension. They could not etermine whether the soldiers would come back again, or not. They had better leave that place before the soldiers changed their minds and come back for them. And so as if pre-planned they exchanged glances a second time. Edna was the first to find her voice. "My sister, it is time you went back," she opined, adding "I think, Priscilla is the one I see in front, let me run and catch up with her, so that both of us can go home together."

She began to run after Priscilla. As she ran, she held the lower end of the worn out wrapper which she was putting on. This was to offer her legs enough allowance for wider strides in the course of her running. Although she did not run fast, the scarf that she was wearing on her head tumbled and fell of. As if she felt it just before it did, she quickly held out her hands in the bid to catch it in mid air. But it was already too late. It soon landed on the ground. She quickly stopped, turned round and picked it and went on this time, however, she stopped running. She had begun to feel exhuausted. She rather began to walk. She walked as fast as her legs could carry her, holding the scarf in her right hand. And after a short while, she caught up with her, feeling exhausted and panting. "I thought you were going to the market, Priscilla, why did you go back or did you forget anything?" she asked, her mouth wide open as she tried to augment the volume of air she could inhale through her nostrils with the one she got through her mouth. "Not really, my sister. I saw those soldiers and remembered their escapades lately, that's the reason why I retraced my step, 'Ike mu na nnama ahaghi'" Priscilla replied, ending her answer with a proverb meaning that she would not equate her strength with a cow's strength. Priscilla had gone on to tell Edna how the main road, had become a trap for the young women and girls, using it. The soldiers, according to her, would ply that road a thousand and one times, looking for young ladies to take by force, or 'commander', as they termed it. This had become their stock in trade. So, ladies, had tried as much as possible, to avert that route. "Initially", she went on, "the ladies whom they accosted, had excused themselves by simply expressing their marital status. "'Ejim nwan'aka', I am a nursing mother," they would declare and that would expressly guarantee their freedom. But lately, they had started turning down, such excuses. So the safe way now is to avoid meeting with them entirely. When the hunter learns to shoot without missing, the birds learn to fly without perching," she said, adding, "I saw them from afar and hid myself into that bush." She said, pointing at a nearby bush. "To be on the safe ground," Priscilla began again "I'll pass through the Umuchima road, even though it is longer." "If that is the case, which ever road you're using, my sister, I'll go with you," replied a scared Edna.

"In that case too, we'll go together and commiserate with Adanna and her husband first, because, that's where I was headed to, before I saw those soldiers." Priscilla explained. "Is anything the matter with their family?" Edna asked, her blood pressure shooting up a bit as her heart skipped a beat "Their first son did not return from the army." Priscilla explained. "'Chei, Adanna, my husband's wife please accept my sympathy," Edna lamented, as if Adanna were there with her.

When the war was on, it sufficed the people to hear that a young man had joined the army. There were no further questions about their welfare because, most of them were seldom home. But with the war so ended, those whose sons were yet to return till date are visited and commiserated with, one after another. Actually, nothing can be more obvious than that the young men in question are dead. Unfortunately, there are many families so affected. Some families unfortunately lost more than one young man. How terrible! Most pathetic are those families who lost their only son.

The truth about wars, including this one, is that it is always a bad wind that does nobody, any good. There is hardly any home that did not get a share of the loses associated with it. The ones that did not lose their father, either lost one or more children. Landed properties were either lost here in the village, or in the townships. Virtually, every family lost either in human or material resources. This is most unfortunate. "Well, people have to be sure, before they conclude that those who did not return immediately were actually dead," opined Edna. "How do you mean?" demanded Priscilla, as she adjusted the wrapper on her waist.

Edna had gone ahead to tell the story they heard some two weeks earlier. Two young men, of not more than twenty two years old, each, were spotted in a bush not far away from Amazara. Once, they had positioned themselves in such a way that bared the villagers from entering their farm land. A group of little boys and girls, who went into the farm land to fetch firewood were chased back by these two young men. Luckily, one of the children happened to be a son of the local chief in one of the villages. The chief was very confused when he heard that the boys were wearing the flag because that was the symbol of the army uniform. The chief who was himself, a soldier while the war lasted, had picked about five of his subjects, who were equally former soldiers and made for the forest. As the chief and his men got near the bush, a voice suddenly shouted at them… "Who goes there?" the unsuspecting chief, being both scared and confused but adequately trained and competent as a soldier had involuntary replied. "Friend of the country." "Oku", shouted the voice, "Mmiri," replied the chief. Having passed the test the chief and his men were allowed into the forest, and they had met with these two handsome, young men. "We will not surrender to them, not after I've lost my father and mother". One of them said, explaining that an air raid had struck and that had resulted in the killing of both of his parents, and many other people, at a town called Obinize. They were nonetheless later convinced to remove their uniforms, and change into civilian dress, at the house of the chief.

"This is very serious" concluded Priscilla. "Yes it is," admitted Edna "and the men were very lucky to have escaped the prying eyes of these bloody soldiers". "Could that be the reason, behind our own local chief assembling young men into a down to earth combing of our farm fields last week?" Priscilla asked.

As a matter of fact, the village local governing council had organized a comb of all uninhabited farm fields in and around the village a few days earlier. The search rather revealed hidden guns, and other types of light ammunition, believed to have been hidden by the home going former soldiers. Along with the ammunitions, were army uniforms.

"Talking about who lost what, my husband's wife, I did not hear you talk about any woman lost to the war." Edna tried to reflect. "Does it mean that only men and children were vulnerable at the war?" "How can you say that?" Priscilla queried. "I was not saying it, I was rather asking a question?" corrected Edna. "We're saying the same thing, my sister," Priscilla tried to argue, "Did you not hear about Joyce's recent death at child birth?" Priscilla began again, pronouncing 'Joyce' as 'Joicy.' "Which of them?" demanded Edna, rather panicky. "The one from Obiudo," Priscilla replied. "I think she was staying with you, at the same refugee camp?" "'Chineke m… O, Chinekem o'…" Edna began to lament. "Please stop raising your voice, it is over three months now since the ugly incident took place," Priscilla interjected, "Come, who told you, or are you sure of what you've just said?" Edna querried, stuttering. "One of these days," suggested Priscilla, "we should go and commiserate with her husband, most people have done so, we must not be left out.

Chapter Ninteen

"Joyce experienced labour late, one afternoon, when most women were hardly back from the farms. As usual, most of them had gone to search for leftover cassava tubers. Others had either gone to pick oil palm fruits, or palm kernel. The few men around could not really help her. There were no hospitals or maternity homes around where she could be rushed to, and by the time the men succeeded in getting one or two women, who came to cut the placenta, the woman was said to be already lying in her own pool of blood and had become very weak as a result of hemorrhage. Actually she could have needed blood infusion under normal circumstances in a hospital. Unfortunately, while they were still making their little efforts, the poor woman gave up the ghost," Priscilla narrated, grimacing at the same time.

For many seconds, or rather minutes later, the two women walked side by side each other in silence. It was as if, a moment of silence was declared. Undoubtedly, they were each, reflecting on something beyond their comprehension. Edna for one, was immensely absorbed in thoughts and had as a matter of fact become very emotional and had all of a sudden too, began to mumble. She did not stop at that, nonetheless. Every now and then, she would not only shake her head but would also produce an awkward sound by snapping her fingers. "What a wicked world this is," she mused, barely managing to keep pace with her companion, who, having heard the news of the ugly incident weeks earlier, had brandished a more controlled stance. There is no gain saying here that she was more affected than her friend. A close look at her would show clearly her efforts in trying to control her emotion, unfortunately however, her efforts could not really hide it. Occasionally still, one would hear her hiss and mope her eyes with the back of her hands. To say that she was visibly shaken could pass for an understatement.

Apparently, she was hearing the news for the first time, and this had given rise to her reflecting back in 1964, when she gave birth to her last child, Chima. She could remember how the nurses on duty had run helter skelter, in a bid to procure blood for her infusion. She remembered vividly too, how frantically they tried to get the Doctor. As she visualized this incident, two emotion provoking facts swept through her mind "if those appropriate medical and frantic efforts were not made, she, perhaps, would have also been dead by now. Conversely, if such treatments accorded her were also available for Joyce, she probably would still be alive today." At the thought of the possibility of her first fear, her blood ran cold. "What a thin gap between life and death?" she had pondered and grimaced. And apparently with a deep sense of loss, Edna started recounting, the gains or otherwise associated with the war.

Furthermore, while Priscilla listened, Edna started enumerating the ugly effects of the war. Top on the list according to her opinion, was the up thrust in the number of widows, precipitated by the war. Although many men had died at the various refugee camps during the war, it had now been discovered that perhaps ten times over that number had died in the war fronts proper, both thereby sum up to reducing terribly, the number of men.

"Why on earth, was this war fought in the first place?" Edna querried, directing the question however to no one in particular. "It takes two to tango, however, says an adage." And so Priscilla had taken the question upon herself as if it were directed to her and had answered the question by herself. "I wonder, my husband's wife," she had replied, gesticulating with her hands thrust up towards the high heavens. "Couldn't the powers that be have applied a less confrontational approach to settle their political differences in the first place?" Edna asked, this time expecting an answer, having directed the question to her companion, Priscilla. "You know as well as I do that neither you nor I can actually do justice to that question," Priscilla answered, "only our leaders can." "Are you in any way of the opinion that only the societal leaders can incite wars?" Edna querried, slanting a glance at Priscilla. The two women had however, acknowledged that the society would have been better off, if the war was averted. "What with the obvious loses and destructions," Priscilla pointed out. "What with the hardship and pains that trailed the war?" She added, mumbling. "I didn't hear your last statement," my husband's wife, Edna said, "did you talk of the magnitude of deaths?" Although Priscilla did not highlight the issue of death in her last point, she had taken advantage of her friend's mention of the issue. "Yes," she had cried adding, "death of both the young and the old." Continuing, she began to recount, "children's education have been delayed by at least three years. So were the wedding dates of marriageable young men, against their women counterparts. This puts the chances of unmarried ladies, on the high side. Consequent upon this will be higher rate of prostitution, and single motherhood. Yes, when the young men, who should marry the young ladies and girls die in droves, the result is that the number of marriageable girls would exceed by far the number of the surviving men," Betsty pointed out.

"Furthermore, with the discovery of those hidden guns and other light ammunitions, the society, is definitely put at a high risk," she continued. "Please tell me, how does the discovered guns put the society at a risk?" Edna asked, fixing a gaze at Priscilla. "Simple!" cried Priscilla. "Remember that the war that absorbed the young men as a sort of employment opportunity, and means of livelihood has ended, for better, though," she said. "Now doesn't it occur to you," she went on, "that these same young men that are now unengaged, might pick these same guns that have been given to them in a platter of gold, as a means of livelihood?" Edna challenged.

"Certainly, the war had come and gone. But the 'bitter tastes' hardly died with the war," the two women chorused. The women acknowledged also, that severe hunger which is a strong precipitate of the war turned some people into thieves. Ordinarily, most people who turned thieves during the war could not have been so behaved at all. Discovery has also been made on why more of those men conscripted into the army died as against those who joined, voluntarily. The latter passed through a more systematic and rigorous training, while the conscripted ones were rather given a 'mock' training.

Chapter Twenty

Schools, primary, secondary, and tertiary institutions of learning remained closed, for as long as the war lasted. "Now that the conflict is over, parents and guardians, are advised to return their children and wards to school…" came the radio announcement.

Osita was registered into primary two, even though his mother had wanted him to repeat primary one. "I'm afraid, madam, we cannot register any more pupils in primary one. You did not bring him early enough. I'm afraid there are virtually no more chances in primary one, now," asserted Mr. Onyeocha, the headmaster. "Let's get him registered into primary two. If he passes the primary two examinations, when they come, he goes ahead with the rest of the pupils, as they would catch up with him and that would balance the equation," continued the headmaster. The matter was thus settled.

Thus, Osita saw himself in primary two. As a matter of fact, most schools, especially those in the rural areas, had become explosive in population. Villages had accommodated both families who originally spent their lives in the village alongside those, who previously lived in the urban towns. So, as it stands now the schools in these villages had no option than to accommodate all the surviving children of the many families currently living in the villages. Consequently, the schools became unimaginably densely populated. Comparatively, there were only a handful number of schools in existence in these rural areas. For this reason, there was no limit to the number of pupils admitted into any school. The classroom registration followed suit. Only primary one was barred from admitting more than a stipulated number. And it seemed the order came as an afterthought, as the conventional number of pupils in a class had been exceeded.

The name of this school was Obodoma Group School. But now that government had taken over all schools in the federation, its name had been changed to Obodoma Community School. However, only the name was changed, the dilapidated state in which the war reduced it, still obtained. This includes broken parches from which emanated such pets as jiggers.

Jiggers are tiny beings that find their way into human feet. When they come in contact with human beings, especially children, they lodge in their feet and live there for as long as they are not discovered. While there, they sustain themselves by sucking the blood of their hosts. Parents, who are not careful enough, hardly discover the presence of these pests in the feet of their children on time. This results in the distorting of the natural shape of the child's feet and thereby altering the way he walks. But when discovered, the jigger is removed from the host's foot as a swollen white mass, with a tiny black head.

Furthermore, there were no chairs or any sitting device in the classrooms. In place of chairs and desks, each school provided the classrooms with trunks of palm trees, cut to the required sizes, often between ten and twelve feet long. The trunks are arranged and used as chairs while the pupil's both knees knocked together, provided the services of the table or desk. Each class could boasts of as many as over eighty pupils. The roofs over some of the classrooms, had holes that allowed water leakages into the classrooms on rainy days. The walls posed an ugly sight, too. There were equally, broken patches here and there. These patches were mostly perforations, made by flying bullets while the war was going on. The paints on the walls leave nothing to write home about. The windows and door shutters were virtually absent.

Some classes had two teachers in attendance. This was however, not for the reasons of comfort or luxury. The reason rather was that some of the classroom blocks were so dilapidated that they had lost their usefulness during the rainy seasons. In such cases, students from classes that fell within such blocks were merged with the ones that were not so bad. Finding themselves in such a situation, the teachers concerned were therefore charged with the planning of their duties on a routine that best suited them.

When one entered a classroom of about sixty to eighty students, one finds out that each student wore whatever colour of dress that was available to him. The dresses were not only of assorted colours, they were sewn also in various styles. The reason for the absence of school uniform was not far fetched. The war had ended only recently, and every family was poor. Parents found it very difficult to provide food for their children. One can imagine how much more difficult it would be to provide dresses which is a lot more tasking responsibility. For this reason, no school authorities did mention the issue of school uniform to the children. An so, for many months or perhaps years after the re-opening of the schools, school children all over the area attended school, wearing whatever their parents could afford in terms of dresses. The issue of food and drug naturally demanded to be held paramount over that of school uniform. Interestingly too, even after the introduction of school uniform, it took what could have been upwards of another one year before all the pupils were able to pay and collect their own uniforms respectively. That was the level of poverty in the land. And within this period, it seemed that no child was really put out of school or reprimanded for inability to pay for the uniform. No one blamed the children. Poverty and hunger were boldly written upon all faces including the headmaster's and teachers' own faces.

Obviously, a first timer, entering the school premises was offensively greeted by an embodiment of a state of disrepair. First, the roofs of many classroom blocks were torn while their roofs were missing at intermittent portions. There were others too whose roofing sheets and other specific parts, had caved in along with the wooden rafters. In addition to the condition of the roofs, the blocks of some of these buildings had also collapsed.

Osita was rather lucky. His classroom of primary two 'A' was among the most 'comfortable' ones. His teacher, Mrs. Constance Ajaero, was a quiet and kind woman. She belonged to that rare class of teachers who took their pupil's interest seriously. Her method of teaching was down to earth. So were her characters too. Her pupils could ask as many questions as they wished, without her getting irritated. One morning, she came into the class, holding a cane in her hand, quite unlike her. As usual, the class monitor made a slight sound, using his two hands. And in unison, the whole class rose up, and greeted her "Good morning madam," with the girls, genuflecting. "Good morning children," she responded, raising her cane up. "Today is Friday," she had begun, "we shall take our first week-end test in both Mathematics and English language, now." This was followed by an uneasy calm. The pupils exchanged glances. This was to be their very first test and so apprehension took over their respective faces. And as they were each pondering over what shape the test would take, none of them could speak out. Only murmurs could be heard from the background. Moments later, however, broke the jinx and spoke out. "Now," she continued, "I want every one of you to tear a pair of sheets of papers from one of your notebooks like this one." As she spoke she demonstrated by showing a pair of sheets picked from the centre of a book. "Now write your name and date at the right hand side of the top of the paper, and start writing along with me, is that clear?" she asked, raising her voice higher as emphasis on the phrase,'start writing along with me' in addition to doing so as she pronounced the last three words. "Madam, are we to write?" Chukwudi, one of the pupils, sitting at the rear of the class, asked. This generated a subdued murmur among the pupils. "No noise, no side-talks, shouted the teacher, who was later to be secretly called "is that clear?" by the pupils. "As for you, what is that your name?" she demanded. "Chukwudi, Chukwudi Ajoku, replied the boy, looking both confused and askance at the rest of the class. "Chukwudi, Chukwudi Ajoku," reechoed the woman "the time for the test would soon be over, so you may continue to look at me, without writing, if that's what you want," she grinned, but went on writing out the questions on the blackboard.

Chapter Twenty One

By the time the twenty-five questioned objective English language test was over, the bell for the day's short-break had rung. And as soon as the bell sounded, Mrs. Ajaero stopped the test. "Pencils up!" she shouted, raising her right hand up while clutching the cane with her left hand. "Pass your papers here right away…If I catch you writing any further, I'll give you six strokes of this cane," she said with an air of finality, this time, raising the cane up while her eyes roamed the nooks and crannies of the classroom. As the pupils dropped their papers respectively on her desk, she continued to roam the classroom with her eyes in a bid to ascertain that no pupils flouted her 'stop writing' order. A few minutes later, when she had become satisfied with the whole show, she took the floor again. "Go back to your seats," she ordered "and get ready for the next test." At an occasion like this one, Mrs. Ajero would habitually not want to deploy the services of the class monitor. She would rather do everything by herself. Following this policy therefore, she picked the class duster and began to mope the blackboard. Soon she was done with that. "Now children," she said, "tear out a pair of sheets of papers as you did in the first instance and as usual, start writing along with me, is that clear?" "Yes madam," the class chorused, and a faint noise ensued as the pupils got around to start writng.

While the pupils of primary two 'A' were busy writing their tests, those of other classes were outside, observing their short-break. Some of them however, inwardly wished they belonged to Mrs. Ajero's class. Before long, windows of the primary two 'A' classroom became crowded with pupils of other classes who had gathered there to have a glimpse at their colleagues in Mrs Ajero's class. "I don't want any one of you to stand by those windows any more..." Mrs. Ajaero said, frowning. She amazingly had hardly completed the statement, when one of the pupils who stood outside, involuntarily shouted "Is that clear?" This was followed by a subdued laughter. "Come here you," she retorted.

After that test, almost all the classes now imbibed the routine of holding a test every Friday, especially the last Fridays in the month.

The very next Monday, school activities took off as normal, Mr. Gideon Achonu, the school games master, took the day's opening session. He organized the whole classes to a match past around the school mini-sports field. As they matched on, the pupil's sang one of their common matching songs, "Today is bright...is bright and fair..." "Stop, stop, stop!" shouted Mr. Achonu, on top of his voice, backing the command up with a wave of his hand. "It is wrong to sing 'today' is bright", he corrected, "it rather is 'THE DAY' is bright, is bright and fair... Now start again", he commanded. When they resumed, there were still some of the pupils whose tongues slipped and they ended up with "today is bright…". "If you don't get it right, no lessons today until you all master it." He retorted. This was repeated a few more times before he got satisfied.

After the morning devotion, which was capped up with a prayer, said by Mr. Achonu himself, the gathering dispersed into their respect classes.

The last Friday's tests had brought an air of uneasiness among the pupils in primary two 'A'. The pupils had been made to stand on their toes' all through the weekend. "Monitor, please go to the staff room, and call 'is that clear', Austin joked.

Austin Amadi was a popular pupil, in the school, both in the junior primary and senior primary sections.

Within the short period of the resumption of schools, Austin had distinguished himself as a gifted football player. Story has it that, he also played while in primary one, before the war started. As a matter of fact, all his brothers who happened to be older than him were good football players too. This had earned not only Austin, but all the Amadi brothers, both in this school and in the secondary school which is situated only across the road, some honor. Austin though not every brilliant, had made up for that with the leather prowess. So, the class monitor, who ordinarily would have threatened to report him to the class teacher, for name calling, merely warned him. "Madam is at a meeting with the entire school's teaching, as well as non-teaching staff."

A few minutes later, Mrs. Ajaero entered the class. "Good morning madam," the class rose and greeted, following the monitor's signal. "Good morning children," returned the teacher. "Did you have a nice weekend?" she humorously asked. Some pupils replied by merely saying 'yes' while others merely opened their mouth, without knowing how to respond. "I expect each and every one of you to say 'yes, thank you madam'," she retorted, adding, "However, I advise every one of you to read your books very well, from now onwards, so that you can cope with this class. But if I discover any one who is not performing up to expectation. I shall recommend the fellow to the headmaster for demotion, is that clear?" she demanded, slightly pulling at her own ears with both hands. "Yes madam," chorused the pupils, with a subdued murmur as they took their respective seats. "Meanwhile," she continued, "come out here and take your answer scripts as you hear your name, is that clear?" And as the children came out, one after another as they heard their names, MrsAjaero handed over to each one of them, his answer scripts, but deliberately held back some of them. "Who is Nkeiru, Nkeiru Onuma?" She questioned, a conspicuous frown on her face. "I am, madam," Nkeiru answered, and moved out from her seat, dragging her feet, as she walked towards her teacher.

At this juncture, the teacher read out most of the answers the girl had written against the Friday's test, all of which were objective questions. "Nkeiru, you did not do well at all," the teacher said, her face apparently contorted. "I scored you twenty-five percent in English Language." She went on, but added, "You did not perform well in Mathematics either. Remember my advice which can as well serve as a warning, and read your books henceforth," she summed up, with an air of finality. "Gabriel Onyeji," the teacher started again as she picked another pair of answer scripts. "Yes madam," Gabriel answered, his heart skipping a beat. "Let me save my time and breath by calling only to your names," MrsAjero said, lowering her voice as her strength reduced. "If you hear your name, come out and take your paper, but bear in mind that you failed woefully." And within a short while, she had called to a few other names of the pupils who failed her tests and handed over to them, their respective answer scripts.

"Now stop whatever you are doing and pay attention here," continued the teacher, bringing up her cane. Moments later she spread out into the air, a pair of answer scripts, one of which was in mathematics and the other, for the English language.

Osita Tasie was one of the smallest members of the class. This had prompted the teacher to allocate him a seat among other pupils of his size, in the front row.

So when the teacher raised the scripts alongside the cane, Osita having recognized the handwriting on the script, had been jolted to the marrow. "God, what is going on?" he mused to himself. But by the time the teacher had gone only half way in praising the brilliant performance of whoever owned the scripts, everybody knew the fellow had done very well, including Osita himself.

"Osita Tasie," she called, an expressionless disposition on her face. "Yes madam," calmly answered the boy, strolling towards the teacher. "Your papers," she said, handing him over the scripts. "The headmaster saw your scripts, and he is very impressed with them," she said, adding, "he made a suggestion, which I'm afraid, I shall abide with. Class now listen," she began again, "following the headmaster's instruction, as from today, Osita Tasie becomes the new 'monitor' of the class, while Jude assists him," she concluded, keeping back her cane on the desk. She tried as much as she could to explain that it was not a calculated attempt to demote Jude, after all, he was not doing badly as a class monitor. But this is in keeping with trying to appreciate hardworks among the youth and thereby challenging others to work hard, too.

Chapter Twenty Two

Osita's uncle, Ezekwem, was about the only enlightened man in the family. Based on this ground, every member of the extended Ojiugo family had entrusted their money unto him for the transaction including Violet, Osita's mother. "Nnam Ochie," Violet had said to Ezekwem, "here is the little amount of money which I saved. Please help me change it into the new currency for an easier up keep of your siblings." Having said this, Violet handed over to Ezekwem, the bundle of notes of the currency, carefully wrapped up in a clean, but faded piece of white cloth. "How much is the the money?" Ezekwem asked, fixing a glance at Violet and at the time, reaching out to receive the pakage with his right hand. "One hundred and fifty thousand pounds," Violet answered, her eyes also fixed at her brother-in-law's own eyes. As she rose to leave, Violet's heart began to beat somewhat hard against her ribs. She began to imagine how a lot easier life would be like, when she would have received the twenty pounds of currency, all to herself. "God, this is certainly going to make life a lot more meaningful to us, I mean the kids and myself," she mumbled and slanted a glance up to the heavenlies. In her mind's eyes, she could visualize herself buying a large quantity of palm kernel at a swoop, thereby reducing the cost of transport which had always been her problem as she had had to buy in little quantities. She had discovered lately, that the amount of transport fare which she paid each time she conveyed the little quantity of palm kernel which she had been able to buy, due to lack of funds, equaled the amount she would pay if she were able to buy in large quantities. "This has negatively affected my overhead cost, needless to say that it reduces my profit margin," she hissed and shook her head. Based on this fact, Violet had always looked forward to the day when she would raise a substancial amount of money as capital to change the status quo. She was however, disappointed when the money she received from Ezekwem was only a token fraction of what she expected to get from him. Her dream of boosting her business with additional twenty pounds of the new currency, received a great blow. "Osie nwam', she complained with tears, see what your mother received. I blame your uncle for this. If I knew he would lump everyone's money together as he claimed to have done, I would not have produced my own at the time I did." As she spoke, she tried to mope up her eyes and nostrils with one end of her worn out wrapper that she was wearing. "I've come to understand that what one wants from this life may not reach the one at the first efforts." Osita answered, trying to cheer his mother up, adding, "it takes perseverance to get to ones destination, so mama let us hold this for now, by God's grace, we will get what we want." "You are a bundle of consolation to me, my son," Violet managed and spoke again, her eyes red as she tried hard to cheer herself up, and at the same time, pulled her bench closer to her son's own bench, "I wonder what I would have been if I stopped child bearing before I had you." Thus mother and child sat close to each other and began to brainstorm on how to move the family's sustenance forward. "If this money were close to two pounds, I would not bother so much. But as it is now, less than one pound as against the twenty pounds that it should have been, I feel very sick about it," Violet spoke out again, being the first to find her voice after a long silence. "In that case mama," Osita responded, turning towards his mother, "we're now working on how to raise another two pounds to complement the one at hand." "You talk like you could enter the room now and just bring out the money," Violet joked, an awkward smilse on her face. Thus the thought of what to do to improve the fortunes of the family posed a great challenge to Osita and his mother. "If bad comes to worse," Violet opined, "I shall have no option than to sell off this 'iron' bed," she said, pointing at the ten springs vono bed spread at the other end of the room.

The bed which is commonly referred to among the Tasie family as 'iron' bed, was bought at the very beginning of the war, for the sleeping comfort of the family. "Yes mama," Osita chuckled, "that is a very good idea, you can sell it off and add the proceeds to the little capital at hand," adding "we could make use of this bamboo bed upon which you and I are sitting now."

When the war was on, many families lacked solid food to eat. They simply ate what little things that was available. Although they were not satisfied at any rate, they rather became used to it and so they seemingly retired themselves to fate. But when on the other hand the war ended, the challenges of beginning normal life afresh, posed a grossly greater challenge, than the war itself. The situation was no longer one of tasting some 'food' today, and expecting death tomorrow. The scenario became one of a long struggle for survival. As natural as life itself, there was varying financial muscle struggling it out in the open markets. Naturally too, those who were lucky enough to obtain the federal government's subvention of twenty pounds, had great advantage over those who were not able to access it. To a lot of people, life during the war times was rather easier except perhaps, for the death associated with the war. As far as this group of people are concerned, one could just pick a handful of oil palm seeds, sell them in the market and earn money that counted in pounds in the old currency. In the same vein, one could crack a handful of palm kernel, take it to the market and earn at least a pound too. Although this was actually true with the old money, it was far from being true with the new currency. As a matter of fact, the new currency representing the new pounds was scarce and so was in very high demand. Many families as it were, sold some of their properties in order to be empowered with the new currency. Incidentally, within the period that the federal government allowed before the final date for the exchange, both old and the new currencies existed alongside each other, thus tagging each commodity in the market with two prices. Buyers and sellers in the market were therefore faced with the stress of haggling the prices of almost every commodity in dual currencies. And as if there was an agreement to that effect, everybody wanted something of good value with the new currency. Conversely, the old currency was relegated to buying only the common food items. Consequently, the new currency bought goods at relatively cheap prices, while the old one did so at very exhorbitant prices.

"How much is that he goat?" "Oh it's you my brother John. How is your family?" enquired Nkemakolam. "We are doing well for as long as life is still in us," replied Mr Eze. John Nkemakolam and Stephen Eze come from the same kindred of Umuezem. Both worship at the Holy Trinity Church, Umuezem. Besides, they also serve as church wardens at the same church. Once, the Rev Canon in charge of the church remarked that the two gentle men struck him like they were of the same parents. "No Sir," was the gentle but firm reply by Stephen. "We're only from the same kindred. However Sir, you're not the only person that has made that remark," Stephen added with a grin. "Ah, so some other people do see you the way I see you?" asked the Rev gentleman. "In that case please don't blame me for that mistake, for you really look alike, I dare say."

After the pleasantries, John repeated his enquiry. "I was asking after that goat," he said, pointing at one of the goats in Stephens's herb. "Which one?" asked Stephen, trying to follow the direction of the movement of John's hand. "That black male, the one that has the longer horn," John directed, nodding his head as he comfirmed the one that met his fancy. "Well, give me one pound, ten shillings, in the new currency," Stephen replied, fixing a gaze at his customer. "How much, on the other hand, shall I pay in the old currency?" asked John, looking enquiringly at the seller. "Well I decided against selling in the old currency, but because it's you, my brother, I'll demand only twenty five pounds," said Stephen with a grin, even though he made the statement with an air of finalty.

The power of the new currency was not limited to the markets only. Special events like marriages were also affected positively or otherwise, depending on whether the bridegroom could perform the marriage rites in either of the currencies. "'Esi moo, Esi moo, Esi moo…ima na arum achoghi nsogbu, gaghariba choba size gi. O n'aso gi inu nwagbogho, I ga akwuni kwa ego ohuru." That was one of the major songs sang at the traditional betrothal of Esther, the first daughter of 'Ozo' and 'Lolo' Ibe. 'Esi', or Esther for real, is the pretty daughter of a very prominent man in the Obodoma clan. Shortly after the war, a man whose name was Akaraka, had come to the family of Ozo Ibe, indicating his intention to marry the young and pretty Esther. Akaraka, though short, was about the richest man in the whole village and probably beyond. He was known to own the first and perhaps, the only land transport fleet of buses at that time in the vicinity. In addition to being short, age had began to tell on Akaraka. This had become evident in the traces of wrinkles gradually rearing its ugly face on Akaraka's own face. Without doubt, he was one of those young men who were delayed in life as a result of the war. "I will not marry that old man," Esther had said in her natural soft spokenness, and began to sob, fearing that she would be forced to marry the man. "Why are you crying," her mother scolded her. "Stop crying, I will talk to your father later. True, the war had made us hungry, but that is not to say that I will give my only daughter to a man she does not actually want to marry." Lolo Ibe had consoled her daughter. And a few months later, Esther got married to young, but not so rich, Uchenna. That was the day 'Esi moo' was first sung in Obodoma. Akaraka happily left Esther Ibe for Adaku, the first daughter of 'Nze' and 'Lolo' Nwaka. Adaku Nwaka and Esther Ibe were class mates before the war began. However, the former, had always been adjudged by many people in the village, as being more beautiful than the later. Adaku and many other girls like her, whose husbands could brandish the power of the new currency, during their marriage rites and the wedding ceremony, were termed lucky. Their parents too, were likewise envied by their peers. In such marriages, the age of the bridegroom as against the age of the bride, does not really matter. How the girl feels about him is also totally inconsequential, as long as the man could dish out the new currency.

"I'm serious mama," Osita said, still chuckling. "You can sell the 'iron' bed. I assure you that I will make do with this bamboo bed." "Can you really manage the bamboo bed?" Violet asked, looking enquiringly at her son. "Remember that it is both stiff and hard, and so nothing close to the comfort that the 'iron' bed could offer," Violet added, her eyes still fixed at her son. "Mama," Osita called, let us get money first, we can always get comfort subsequently. "On the very next day therefore, Violet knocked at the door of her late husband's elder brother, Michael, just before the man left home for the day's business. "Nnam Ochie," she began shortly after greetings. "Our people say that the house fly that has nobody to advise it aright, ends up in the grave with a corpse." She shared her son's opinion, concerning their bed with the man, and finally sort his advice on the same matter. "That is the reason why I came to you, this early morning so that I will get a superior counsel," she had summed up. "Thank you my 'oriaku'," the man had said, adding, "since we married you into this family, you have not given me nor any body else, any reason to regret ever bringing you into this family. It is my utter regret that my brother did not live long to really consummate this marriage," the man had replied, reaching out to make use of the chewing stick he had in his mouth. In furtherance of the discussion, Michael had confirmed to Violet the truth that a lot of families had sold some of their belongings in order to raise capital. "Since the children you gave me are still very young, I do support that you raise money, regardless of whether it entails selling off that 'iron bed' to enable you take off along side other people, this is because he that is not as good looking as his peers, remains unhappy," he summed up.

Chapter Twenty Three

It was supposed to be the break period, not the short break though, but the long one. All the pupils in the junior primary section were gathered in the schools mini foot-ball field, and were made to face the school's main block.

The school, the Obodoma Group School compound, was bisected by the church building, the Mary Trinity Church, Obodoma. This had hitherto, created two almost equal segments of itself. One segment comprising, the classes of primary one, two and three, otherwise called the junior primary section, and the other segment, consisting of primary four, five and six on the other hand and is known as the senior primary section.

"It is my pleasure," began the headmaster of the school, Mr. Onyeocha, giggling, even as his eyes roamed from one end of the gathering to the other, "to announce to you the results of the term, ending today, but before I do that," he continued, this time, shifting a bit away from his original position, "can we clap for ourselves for being present here today?" He enthused. "Now ready go?" "kwam, kwam, kwa, kwa, kwa kwam," sounded the clap ovation, with the children giggling alongside the rest of the staff members of the school. "Again," shouted the headmaster, his face beaming with smile. "kwam kwam kwa, kwa, kwa kwam. "For our teachers who teach and guide us, every day, can we give them three healthy shouts of hurray, ready … hip, hip, hip." As he gave out the command this time around, he humorously raised his right leg alongside his right hand up. This was ostensibly in a bid to pique the children's interest. "Hurray," came a thunderous happy reply by the children. Now as the children shouted on top of their respective voices, the headmaster and some members of the staff tried to protect their eardrums by inserting a finger into each of the ears. This was to control the frequency of the sound reaching their earsdrums. On the other hand, the children acting on their natural impulse to adventure, saw in this exercise a sure avenue not only for their respectine enjoyment, but one to compete among themselves, on who outshouts the other. Of particular interest are those that had jumped up in the bid to really outshout their peers, but unfortunately had missed their balance and so had tumbled and finally crashed on the field. Fortunately, the presence of one of the female teachers who had voluntarily positioned herself close to that spot saved the situation. "Some of you shouted 'hurrah'," the headmaster pointed out, "whereas the headmaster wants to hear a clear pronounciation of the word 'hurray'. "Can we do that now? – Hip, hip, hip," he shouted, this time tilting his voice to produce a higher pitch. And in response, the pupils gave another thunderous shout of 'Huurray'. This was followed by a calm that so contrasted with the shouts of a few minutes ago that if a pin had fallen down on the pitch, only the cushion effect of the grass, could have prevented it from being heard.

"Now," the headmaster began again, apparently reminiscenting fulfillment, "if you hear your name, please come out here for your gift." As he made the last statement, he transferred the scripts he held in his right hand over to the left hand and thereafter, used his right hand to adjust his reading glasses which he had all along tilted downwards to rest on his nostrils. Next, in what seemed to be an additional act of comporting himself further for a tasking job, the headmaster also adjusted the leather belt he wore on his waist before delving into the announcement of the results.

Now as the man stood before the entire school, holding scripts in one of his hands and his long cane in the other one, Osita's heart began to beat hard against his ribs. He felt like sitting down on the grass, but quickly remembered that the headmaster was standing only a few yards away from where he was and so he knew he could not do so there. He put his hands upon his head and down again. Suddenly he started feeling feverish, so feverish, that his body responded by shivering. "Are you alright?" the boy standing behind him asked? Lowering his voice by way of lowering his head as he spoke. "Yes I'm fine," he replied, trying hard to hold himself together even as he lowered his head while speaking. This was to hide away from being detected, the inevitable movement of his mouth, while he spoke. "But you're shivering," the boy stressed on. "But I'm fine," Osita insisted, trying harder to hold himself up firmer.

"No noise there," shouted one of the teachers, looking towards Osita's direction. Osita did not hear the first name called by the headmaster. He only saw a boy of about eight years of age, go out to meet the headmaster. As he looked on, he saw the headmaster offer the boy a good handshake, and thereafter, he directed him to his assistant, who was standing beside him. The assistant headmaster, on the other hand gave the boy both a pencil and an exercise book. "Clap, clap for him," shouted the boy's class teacher, pronouncing the word 'clap' with emphasis. This teacher happened to be the one who gave the previous 'stop-the-noise' order."

Every body, including Osita, knew this teacher very well. He was both humorous and stern. To some people in the school, this man is known by his nickname – 'Sir, Umu-infant'. Others preferred to call him by the real name, Sir Gnela. Whether one called his name as Sir Gnela, or Sir Umu-infant, however, any pupil of this school irrespective of the length of time the pupil had spent in the school, was sure to show the inquirer the man's whereabout, without delay.

Sir Gnela hails from one of the villages in the neighbourhood of Obodoma. And he does not hide his identity, especially when it bordered on his place of birth. He spoke his dialect so perfectly, that one wondered whether he would be able to speak any other language in the world. One day, two boys from the senior primary section came to one of Mr. Gnela's friends, with the intention of determining, the real nativity of the man. "He's from Owerri," replied the man, can't you hear his heavy accent or dialect?" the man explained, wondering why a person from this part of the world would not be able to place Sir Gnela's dialect. "I told you, Nnamdi, but you wouldn't believe me," Obinna Ohagwa said frowning. "But, the way he spells his surname, implies that he is not really Igbo," argued Nnamdi Onyedi. This argument was said to have gotten to Mr. Gnela's hearing, and he had taken time one morning, to clear the air before the gathering of the whole school. That was on a Thursday.

The Obodoma Group school observed what she termed 'moral instructions' every last Thursdays of the month. During the moral instructions, pupils were taught on the precepts of the Christians' religious book, Holy Bible, especially as it pertains to human relationships. No particular teacher has the monopoly of teaching the subject. Teachers are rather assigned to hold it in turns. This made it possible that each of the teachers had an opportunity to hold the whole school at a swoop.

Furthermore, it was not an assignment for the academic teachers only, the school principal and his vice equally took their own turns. Was it not in one of such periods that the principal taught the school on one of the schools most cherished and most popular subject matter which he captioned 'Jekuru Danda', meaning 'consult the ant'. Expantiating on this lesson, the principal had quoted some portions of the Christian religious book, the Holy bible to back his facts up. He had advised his pupils to emulate the ant, who according to him laboured hard to gather in the dry seasons, what they ate in the rainy seasons. Next, he had pointed out to the pupils, that the ants also work in full collaboration with one another, thereby making the work load lighter on each of them. The virtue of oneness which constitutes the underlying factor behind the success of the ants 'kingdom', the principal urged the pupils to imbibe.

This lesson had imprinted a far reaching monument in the minds of the pupils. As a result of this lesson, the pupils had been spurred to work harder, both in their academic pursuit and in manual labour. Any pupil, who thereafter exhibited any sign of laziness in the school, was shouted upon by his peers, to 'jekuru danda'. The lesson had further popularized the headmaster, Mr. Onyealocha.

CHAPTER TWENTY FOUR

Furthermore, it was at a moral instruction period that Sir Emma Iroulo taught the school about the story of Macbeth. That was Osita's first time of hearing the story about Macbeth. "Having told you about the evils that are inherent in someone being overtly ambitious. I'll back my lesson up with the story of Macbeth," Sir Emma asserted. Osita and his peers both school and class mates had been all ears as Sir Emma told his story. "Hail Macbeth, hail to thee, Thane of Glamis," continued the teacher, who was not only telling the story now on how the witches met with Macbeth and Banquo, but was equally demonstrating the actions of the witches, like he were present at the scene of the event. "Sir, can I ask a question?" Osita inquired. Without an iota of doubt, his interest had been piqued by this ongoing story. Suddenly, he remembered having heard about a subject known as literature in English from one of his cousins back home. "Frankly speaking," he mused "if this is what the subject known as literature looks like, I think I have certainly began to feel an impulse of love for it alongside other literary works. Moments later, as the story progressed, he took a decision. "Literature, whether in English or any other language, shall be my vocation," he mumbled, without actually knowing how far reaching that decision would turn out to be. As he spoke he leaned back a little and stole a glance towards heaven, the supposed throne of God. "Master Tasie, what on earth are you doing, looking up at the ceiling?" querried Sir Iroulo, fixing a glance at Osita. Osita opened his mouth to explain himself, but the teacher quickly asked him another question. "You asked a question, right?" But before Osita could answer even the last question, the man quickly added again, "for now, no, I'll allow time for questions, later," and continued the story. "Shortly after," he continued, "the same witches reappeared before Macbeth and Banquo, and greeted them once again. "Hail Macbeth," they had said, "Hail to thee, Thane of Cawdor." "This was the witches' second greetings to Macbeth," he said, his face expressionless. He went further to narrate what transpired between the witches as a party in one hand and Macbeth and Banquo as another party on the other hand. At this juncture, Osita raised his hand again for question. "Ok," said the teacher, "Master Tasie, what is your question?" "Sir, after the witches had so greeted Macbeth, how did they greet his companion, Banquo?" asked Osita. "According to the book, no greetings were recorded to have been accorded Banquo. Remember this is an imaginary story of what happened somewhere, so while relating the story, one should not fail to stop where the story teller stopped," replied the teacher. "Sir, please tell us the meaning of 'imaginary'," asked Nnamdi.

It was also on the platform of the moral instruction that Sir Gnela unveiled the puzzle that enveloped both the meaning and the spelling of his surname. "My grandparents," he had begun, "had a lone son." As he told his story, he gesticulated so much with his hands, his face full of smiles, that the hall became charged with noise, especially among the big boys at the rear. "They so got fed up with the intimidation with which their peers treated them that they decided to do something about it. "What did they do about it?" someone asked from the background, thereby generating a subdued round of laughter. "What's the cause of the laughter," demanded Sir Gnela, feigning surprise. At that juncture, Obinna Iwuoha raised up a finger. "Yes Master Iwuoha, what's the question?" "Sir, please tell us what your grandparents did to annul the intimidation," "'Unu wu umu' infant, you're all infants," he giggled, adding "if you lend me your ears, I'll let you know." As he made the last statement, Sir Gnela made thumbs up sign, as a sign of solidarity with the children. This was greeted with a loud ovation among the pupils. While some of them shouted 'Sir Gnela', others chose to shout 'Sir Umu infant'. This was very typical of Mr Gnela, he could be both humorous and stern depending on the situation on ground. When situations demanded seriousness, he could scare even the biggest and the most defiant boy in the school. But he could be jovial too, when in a lighter mood.

"My grandfather not only decided, but actually gave as many as seven wives to his only son." Having so said, he cheered the pupils, "Umu infant kwenu." And for an answer, the whole school yelled a most thunderous shout of "E eyi," with the attendant expressions of merry. Nonetheless, before he rounded off, Mr Gnela had made clear, the African culture whereby the esteem of any family revolve largely on the number of children, especially boys, that the family could boast of. "So the seven wives married to my grandfather, swelled the family with additional fifty children," he announced amid laughter, adding, "it might interest you to know that two out of these women, gave birth to twelve children each." This also erupted an atmosphere of prolonged laughter and jokes. "Finally," shouted the man, defying the noise, "these two women were celebrated with the slaughter of a goat for each of them."

"Having rounded off the results of primary one as a whole," announced the headmaster, "we'll now delve into primary two."

"The first person I have on my list in Primary two is Master Osita Tasie," announced the headmaster. Osita had heard his name in a dream, at least that was how it appeared to him. And so he did not answer to the call.

"Are you not Osita Tasie?" the girl beside him had shaken him. "Osita Tasie," repeated the headmaster, who was at the verge of calling the next name, when Osita casually walked out and headed towards the headmaster. "Are you Master Osita Tasie?" asked the headmaster, visibly impressed. "Yes Sir," returned the boy, along with some voices of the pupils in his class. "Listen, listen, listen, announced the headmaster. "No noise," shouted Mr. Gnela. "The boy standing here before me has impressed not only the headmaster. But the whole teaching staff of this school, said the headmaster waiting for silence to take place.

This was very typical of the headmaster. At times he did not use the pronoun 'I' or 'me' while making reference to himself. He would rather address himself as the headmaster.

"This boy was brought to the headmaster by his mother," the headmaster began "who wanted him to be registered in primary one. But because there were no vacancies in primary one at the time they came, he was instead admitted into primary two. This is very impressive, ladies and gentlemen and of course, the kids standing here also." "Based on this," continued the headmaster "the school has decided to give this angel, a double portion of what is given to others who topped their respective classes." Amidst cheers and applause, therefore, Osita was given two 'HB' pencils and two 'Olympic Games' exercise books after a hand shake by both the headmaster and his vice.

"Do we really have hands that can clap?" demanded Mr. Gnela. This had evoked a celebration of applause. Nevertheless, while the applause was going on, the whole staff of the school was asked by the headmaster to take their turn each, and have a hand shake with this boy. "This was to really appreciate greatness," explained the headmaster.

Chapter Twenty Five

"Oh worship the King of Glorious above ... Oh gratefully sing His love and His care..." "On behalf of the entire staff of this great school..." the headmaster, Mr Onyeocha, hereafter took the floor, holding a sheet of paper in his left hand, and a cane in his right hand while his reading glasses, although on his face, hung carelessly upon his nostrils, leaving an impression of the headmaster not actually making use of it, "the headmaster welcomes every one of you back to school for the new academic year. We thank God for keeping us all through the last holidays, and finally converging all of us here in good health," continued he. "Next, the headmaster, on behalf of himself and his family, equally welcomes all the members of the staff of this blessed school. It is the expectation of this school headmaster, that the support and cooperation accorded him by all and sundry last year, shall be maintained or even improved upon, this year," continued the headmaster, making his welcome back speech, segment by segment.

Having rounded off the first segment of his new academic year welcome speech, the headmaster delved into the next rung of the speech which largely bordered on some changes that had been effected. "For the smoother running of the school," he had said, lowering his voice as he red out the last phrase. "Top on the list of the changes," he had continued after a pause, his face expressionless, but occasionally raised up to face his audience and moments later lowered over the write up "is the path bisecting the netball field upon which the axe of change had fallen, getting it permanently closed, henceforth. Anybody, walking across that pitch shall have committed an offence against the school," he stressed, pronouncing the words 'committed' and 'offence' with a glaring emphasis that sent shivers down the spines of most pupils. "Which field did he mention?" asked a voice at the background, as the inquirer shifted his glance from one pupil to the other. And as if the question had aroused an air of uncertainty, an air of murmuring had sprung up, nonetheless in hushed tones. "What is the noise all about?" the headmaster querried, looking askance. "Ssssh," began a member of the teaching staff, but was cut short as the headmaster's voice over ran his own. "The fellow, shall be reported to the school's games master, Mr. Achonunwa, for appropriate reprimanding," he had read out, turning his face towards the position occupied by his staff members, as he tried to locate his vice. And as if in agreement, the vice headmaster nodded her head in solidarity. "Next," he went on after the sign, "the act of trying to pluck down ripened mangoes and other fruits from their mother trees by the pupils, through any means has been banned. As a result of that, anybody caught trying to pluck down any mangoes or any other type of fruits through whatever method, should be reported to the second headmaster, for disciplinary measures. We must all be disciplined." He had asserted.

The man had gone on and on to read out the new changes that would hold sway in the new academic year. However, the most far reaching was the introduction of school fees into the school system by the federal government. Following this directive, Osita and every child in his class was to pay the sum of one pound, six shillings and eight pence each term, totaling to three pounds, twenty shillings for one academic year.

"Finally, having accomplished that duty, the headmaster must point out a mispronunciation he observed while you were singing from the hymn book, earlier this morning. "That word is pa-vi-lion," he corrected, trying to pronounce the word with emphasis, and thereafter, explained the meaning of the word. As if he expected any questions, the headmaster stood there for a couple of minutes after the address, allowing his eyes to roam round the hall. Shortly later, he came back in the air and concluded the outing thus, "meanwhile, have a nice day". After the speech, an uncomfortable silence pervaded the hall. It was as if a moment of silence was called. Most of the pupils who had come to school in high spirits as they were used to do, had their spirits hopelessly dampened.

"Now, go to your respective classes, children," Mrs. Nlemchukwu commanded in her capacity as the vice headmaster of the school, having officiated at the morning devotion, which doubled as both the beginning of the day, as well as the year.

Inside the classrooms, pupils sat down quietly. The usual morning exchange of pleasantries among the pupils that generated noise in every class, before the arrival of their teacher evaporated into thin air, owing to the announcement.

They found little or nothing at all worthwhile to discuss. Rather than the normal easy going disposition that is characteristic with children, most of these ones wore furlong and downcast faces. Only a few could still muster energy to say one thing or the other. "I… I love education," Nnanna, stuttered, being the first person in Osita's class to find his voice, thereby breaking the uneasy silence that perverted the classroom, "but my elder brother who could pay my school fees died in the war front, that means that I may discontinue," and as he said this, looking at nobody in particular, his eyes turned misty, and as if that would offer him a measure of consolation, he lowered his head and got it leaned upon his desk. Shortly later, he dosed off. Nnanna is sleeping this early morning, Collins joked raising his voice in order to wake the sleeping one. He was at the verge of shaking Nnanna into consciousness, when about three or four voices lambasted him almost in unison. "Leave the poor boy alone, Collins Aku," one of the voices sounded out overlapping the others. Seconds later, Uchenna, whose voice overlapped the other ones in checkmating Collins from disturbing Nnanna, turned solemn and withdrawn. He tried the much he could, but could not relieve himself in sleep. Rather than take solace as Nnanna did, his perturbed mind pictured the situation that held sway at home. "When would the school fees reign take of?" he found himself pondering. "Is it this or next year? If next year, what is the guarantee that his widowed mother could shoulder his school fees alongside his siblings' own. If on the other hand it takes off later this year, what would he do? "I know what to do," he had said, inadvertently speaking out to the hearing of all and sundry. Consequently, many heads had turned towards him. Little did he know however, that some of his classmates had taken the same decision as he had taken. Interestingly, Uchenna and his likes withdrew from school henceforth having decided to learn a trade. "The earlier one starts off, the better," Uchenna had told his parents.

The pupils were not acting in isolation. Teachers themselves were equally affected. Unlike the pupils, this was not the first time this information was getting to them. They had sat together with the headmaster in the series of meetings summoned by the later, over the issue. They knew that the policy would result in many parents and guardians withdrawing their children and wards from the school. "How can the government do this to parents, now?" queried Mr. Achilo. And as if complimenting Mr. Achilo's contribution, Miss Udensi added, "only one year after the war that severely impoverished our people." Miss Udensi has a reputation for chewing gums almost every time, except probably at the time when she was sleeping. She is among the few ladies in this school that are yet to get married. So typical of her, she was chewing gums while making her own contribution, and although not all the teachers present heard her clearly, no one took the pains to ask her to repeat herself. Afterall was this the first time she spoke without people wishing that she repeated herself? Additionally, the events of the day, do not they carry more than enough challenges already, so why would any one add more burdens to himself? "Africa is a very backward continent," Mrs. Achilo said hissing, and at the same time shaking her head, but quickly added, "in the advanced economies the free education introduced at the end of the war would remain in place for at least five solid years." "This government has not acted fairly," Mr. Joe Ekeoma pointed out as he joined the band wagon, and added, "If they had allowed a three year grace period, that would have somewhat allowed the wounds of the war to heal better."

Furthermore, this situation discouraged the teachers from entering their respective classes. "I was looking for you, Sir Joe," said Sir Gnela, jokingly. "And where did you check me?" Mr. Joe casually asked. "In your class of course, aren't you supposed to be teaching Civic now?" Sir Gnela asked further. "Well, I'm no longer in the mood. I'm dispirited as a matter of truth," replied Sir Joe. The latter opened up his anxiety by telling his colleagues that he had four children by his wife, in addition to two younger ones by his parents, who look up to him for financial support. He expressed anxiety over the source of funds for the huge responsibility. "How much is my salary?" he demanded, looking at no one in particular, and as if he expected any replies, paused briefly before continuing. He pointed out that the war made him loose lucrative job with a British firm that was into oil drilling. "If not for the war," he said, his voice rising now, I'd still be working with them and my fortunes would not be the same with what it is at the moment, Sir Joe narrated, rather unhappily.

The clock on the primary three C teachers table continued it's 'thick, thock, thick, thock…" movement. So were the lesson periods.

"Mama, good afternoon," Osita greeted as he entered the house back from school. "Welcome back, and how was the day?" replied Violet, looking straight into her son's eyes. "Your face looks dull my boy, were you flogged in the school?

I'm sure you did not leave home late in the morning, so you can't tell me you were late to school today. Or are you very hungry?" Violet continued to probe into her son's mind, to unravel the reason behind his low-spiritedness.

Chapter Twenty Six

And with a hiss, Osita narrated the events of the day. "Mama," he began, but realizing that the urge to weep was putting pressure on him, he tried to pull himself together, wishing he could hide the information away from his mother, because he already knew what impact it would have on her. Violet, however was not the type that could easily be swayed. She looked at her son, expecting him to tell her whatever the matter was. But when he seemed to have declined from going on, the woman pressed on. "Yes?" she asked, anxiously looking at the boy's face. She knew something must be wrong somewhere. Her bundle of joy had hardly emitted such high magnitude of melancholy. Truth remained that, she was the one who got low-spirited. And as such times, Osita had been the one that cheered her up. Now that her pillar of happiness had turned depressed, what was she going to do? "You called me, Nnadim?" she demanded, fixing a gaze at him. "So tell me what's eating you up." "Nothing's eating me up, Mama," said the boy, trying to sound manly, "only that I may not go to school again, that's my anxiety." As the boy tells this, two drops of tears appear on his cheeks but quickly find their way to the ground. "Why, what happened?" His mother asked, her voice rising and shaky. “Did you fight or what?” Violet reasoned within herself that her children did not inherit any bad trait, so as far as she was concerned, it was out of place to fear that the boy was caught stealing, or anything of the sort. She remembered how Gordon the white man, with whom Tasie had worked, had always said that their company, the Pepsi Cola, would be better off if every worker were like Tasie. That remark was based on his general conduct. She also remembered in the early days of their marriage, when Tasie was working as a church warden at the Mary Trinity Church Obodoma. Successive Reverend Ministers had come and gone, but each had remarked and extolled the good conducts of her late husband.

“So tell me, what did you do in school today?” she repeated betraying broken heartedness. “Mama, I did not commit any offence, but they said we shall start paying school fees from today.” Osita revealed, his face lowered, his eyes hooded. “School fees?” his mother shouted, her mouth wide open. “Who said so?” she queried lowering her voice now, as if trying to control her own emotions. “Our school headmaster, who else?” He said that’s what the government has decided. But I know we may not be able to afford it. If my father were alive, I’d relax like some of my class mates,” he stressed.

The boy’s last statement had hit the mother like an arrow. She became silent. What on earth could she say? Now she could not tell between her boy’s last statement and the introduction of school fees proper, which one bothered her more. As she pondered what to do, it occurred to her that this was her own turn to cheer the boy up.

"So, is that the reason why you're fussing yourself like this? Who told you we can't afford your school fees?" This, she said to cheer him up, even though she had doubts herself.

Later that evening, both mother and child retired into the bed shortly after supper. But as if on an agreement, each had gone to bed and started weeping.

Osita on his own had remembered that the announcement bordering on introduction of school fees did not seem to perturb some pupils in his class. He began to visualize the class, along with the pupils after the devotion that morning. He could point out pupils like Collins Aku, Iheanyi Okparaji, Maurice Uduma and many others, who were not in any way affected by the announcement. There were also others like Collins Iro, Donald Ahunanya, and Collins Cheta. All of these and perhaps a few more had showed nonchalance to the announcements. To Osita's interpretation, this meant nothing other than the fact that they were sure that they shall pay their school fees come what may, and so continue their education. As he tried to analyze the situation, he could see that all of them had one thing in common, and that was that each of them had his father still alive till date. Also among the other members of the class who showed that they were not happy with the school fees saga, Osita could not see any one of them who seemed to be in his predicament. He still knew some of them who could boast of having elder brothers and sisters who survived the war. He had come to know about this, because most of them were his friends. Based on his relationship with each of them, he had visited their homes one after the other. This was inspite of the fact that he had not in turn taken any one of them to his own home. While at their homes, some of them had produced biscuits and chin chin which were seen last, not only eaten last by Osita in the hay days before the war started.

"Let's eat the biscuits at the school, Iheanyi had suggested, "as for the chin chin, we had better eat here, now." That was a few days ago when Iheanyi Okparaji had taken him to their home during the long break period. Iheanyi had made the statement as a suggestion, but Osita had not felt like bringing up another opinion. "Your suggestion is very good, I have no objection to it," he had responded. The two friends unsealed and ate the chin chin, but had brought the biscuits back to school, and shared among other friends of theirs. But that was after dismissal of school. They could not get back to school on time as they had expected. "Why are you two coming back to school this late?" Mrs. Iwuchukwu had demanded. When they could not offer any meaningful excuses, she had kept them standing for a long time.

"God," Osita mused to himself, "why are some people lucky, while others are not so lucky? Could I be among the unlucky ones in this life?" As he pondered over this, he could feel hot tears drop successively on his pillow. He could not restrain them, rather he had therefore allowed the sleeping dog to lie. But right inside his mind, he rejected being unlucky.

A few minutes later, a million-dollar question struck his already disturbed mind. "Suppose you could not continue schooling on account of inability to pay school fees? God forbid, God will provide," he had retorted.

However, in the innermost depth of his mind, he could visualize a situation where he dropped out of school, for the same purpose. He remembered his earlier vision of being his state's commissioner for education. At the thought of all these, more tears poured on the pillow, unrestrained. So how could that dream be made manifest without getting education? he wondered.

He started wondering what would become of him, his dreams and visions. He had nursed dreams of greatness, time without number just like the biblical Joseph. The dreams had led him into giving the inscriptions of nomenclatures, like Dr., Professor, etc against his name, each time he wrote his name on the few books that his mother was able to buy for him, even as a primary two pupil. Deep in his mind, Osita knew he loved and cherished education, but the thought of not being able to go on and get what he so loved, brought great pains to his mind. Consequently tears, hot tears flowed down his pillow, still unchecked and before long, he dosed off.

Violet, on her own had equally been engrossed in mind-shattering thoughts. Thoughts of how not to fail this boy, but instead prove his fears unfounded. But could she afford to pay a whooping three pounds and twenty shillings for each of the four children of hers, who are at school ages, both primary and secondary school levels? That would make a frightening total of about thirteen pounds a year, she reasoned. "Oh God, where are you?" she sobbed, shedding tears on her own pillows. What on earth does she have on this earth that people could buy?

Fate has a way of being inconsiderate. Rather than forget, her mind reminded her of her son's heart-rending statement. "But I know we may not be able to afford it. If my father lived I'd relax like my friends."

This statement tore her mind in shreds. "Tasie, where are you?" she sobbed, "come here now and hear out your own son."

Early the following morning, Violet left the house without telling Osita or anybody her whereabouts. Later that same morning, her son woke up, swept the back yard premises, swept also the room and the little family parlour and finally, warmed the soup that remained in the pot. Breakfast was one of the 'luxuries' which he had grown up and become used to not expect. Therefore he took a hot bath and hurried to school. While en route to school, he had been on the look out for his mother, who according to his postulation, had attended the very early morning prayer service at the church, which shared the same compound with his school. There were times when they both met on the way, moving however in the opposite directions. While the son was heading to school, the mother on the other hand, would be backing the school and the church, facing home. When he did not meet with her, he had wondered where she could have gone to. However, he pushed the thought aside.

Chapter Twenty Seven

"Thank God you are in the house," an embattled Osita had said, and then gently dropped his school bag on the bamboo bed upon which he sleeps, at the left end of the room. "Welcome home from school," replied his mother. "But how do you mean, by thanking God that I'm in the house?" queried Violet, leaning forward, while fixing a glance at her son. "Where else did you think I'd be?" This question gave rise to unexpected silence. Young Osita had not attached any seriousness to his own question so had least expected his mother's reaction this way. He opened his mouth but could not find the right words to use, so he had quickly closed his mouth. But his mother's prolonged gaze at him made him realize that he must say a thing, at least to explain himself "You know," he began, "when I woke up in the morning and did not see you in the house, I'd thought you'd gone to the church for the usual 'ekpere ututu'. But when I neither met you on your way back, nor met you in the church, I became worried." As the boy spoke, he drew a mark on the floor of the house. He only tried and raised his head up slightly, but quickly lowered it again. "Why?" asked his mother. Why would you get worried because you didn't see me in the house at a particular time?" "I… I…I feared that you probably had run away, leaving us children on our own, on account of the school fees saga," he stuttered, stealing a glance at his mother. As a matter of fact, this statement made Violet feel a chill sweep through her body. She could not understand the reason why her own son could think in that line. Suddenly, she found herself standing on her feet without actually knowing when she got up. "My God," she heard her own voice yell, "how could I do a thing like that? If I leave you, where on earth shall I go, or for whom do I leave you, son?" she had continued, visibly shaken, "I could never bring myself to doing a thing near to that, did you hear me?" And as if she had consulted further with herself, she gently placed her hands on the lad's head, trying to soothe him. "Please do not ever harbour a thought in that line again, my dear," she said soothingly, and after a pause, she added with a forced smile, "for the whole lot of you, constitute the reason why I live, is that clear?" she managed to ask, unable however, to hold back hot tears that had welled up in her tear duct. "Yes mama," Osita answered, raising his head up for a view of his mother's face. As he spoke, he felt his mother's tears move downwards from on top of his head, and tried to mope it up, using his right hand but, could not catch up as his mother's own hands over ran his own hands and moped up his head. "But you know mama," he found his voice and said, his eyes focused on his mother's own, "I did not mean to upset you, it was only an emotional fear, do forgive me, mother," he pleaded, suddenly remembering his teacher in primary two who would always end up asking 'is that clear?' "Son, there is really nothing to forgive, it's good that you expressed that feeling so I would take caution by letting you know my movements henceforth. Now go and call the others, so I can tell you where I went early yesterday's morning," she commanded, withdrawing her hands from on top of the boy's head.

That was when Violet told her children how she had consulted with about three women at the early morning prayers, at the local church, and they had mentioned the names of three philanthropists in the village, who could help her with the schooling of her children. Her plan was to take the last two of her children, Osita and Ijeoma, to go and live with, as well as serve the people and at the same time attend school as the reward for their service to them. The effort had however, not worked out at the moment, the men had respectively asked after their classes. "If the boy had finished primary school, and you were talking about secondary school," said Chief Amadi, "that'll make a difference." On his own part, Chief Ekwebelem had advised Violet to bring the children up beyond primary school level, and thereafter start seeking for help.

"So, as it stands now, we shall continue to work hard and pray to God but certainly, with inner strength, we shall prevail," Violet had said. "Henrick and Roseline shall learn trade while Osita and Ijeoma continue in school," she concluded.

Later in the evening of the same day, Violet had mapped out a plan on how to keep the two younger children of hers in the school, at whatever cost it might be, while the bigger ones find something doing, and be able to help out, when necessary.

"Another Friday is here with us," announced Mrs. Constance Nlemchukwu, Osita's new class teacher. "As should be expected therefore," she continued, "every one of you should pick up your writing sheets, and other writing materials and get ready for a test in English language." While the pupils were busy writing the test, the teacher walked round the class, perhaps observing the behaviours of each of the class members.

"This class is reducing in number, day after day," she observed. "Can any person suggest, or tell us exactly what is going on?" She asked. "Madam, it is the school fees," shouted Collins Ekejiuba. "What about it?" returned the teacher, looking up to fix a glance at him. "Some children will not return back to school again," explained Collins. "Collins," retorted the teacher "your grammar was wrong, now I want you to say it this way, some pupils may no longer come to school."

The school headmaster was running the school on the policy that, in addition to many other details, each teacher was to bring weekly details of the observations, made from the class. The compilations, made known to the school at large by Mrs. Iwuchukwu, the second headmaster, showed that in less than three weeks after the announcement of the introduction of school fees, no less than one hundred and eighteen pupils had withdrawn from school. "This is unhealthy for our society," the woman had said. "Tell your parents," she had continued "and brothers and sisters out there, that education is supreme. Whatever vocation you'd like to undertake in this life, first and foremost get education, it'll help you get to the zenith," she had stressed, folding a sheet of paper she was holding in her hands.

Early the next morning, Violet carried the 'iron' bed upon which her son Osita, usually lay on, to the women who had made an arrangement with somebody else who would buy the bed.

"It's fairly new," she tried to explain to the buyer. "We bought the bed at the very early stage of the war, which had necessitated our leaving the town, following incessant bombing of the town where we lived. There was no gain saying that we needed the bed, so in addition to many other things that we needed, we had bought the bed for my son's sleeping comfort."

And so, Violet had parted with the eight-springs 'vono bed' meant for her son's sleeping convenience.

"So far, so good," announced Mrs. Constance Nlemchukwu. "The results of the last Friday's test are ready now. Some of you did well, while a greater part of the class, I must admit, failed to meet the expected grade," she said. "I am determined nonetheless to brush this class to enviable heights, whether you like it or not. Compulsorily therefore, so long as you remain in this class, you must read your books and make out of yourself, at least, an average student," she went on, her face deeply furrowed. "Now bring out your English textbooks. Where is your own book?" demanded the teacher, when she discovered that only a few had theirs in hand. "How many of you do not have one? raise your hands". She began to take count -one, two, three..., ten..., twenty six, twenty seven, twenty eight..., Jesus Christ, including you, Osita. This is very discouraging," she lamented, stretching the word 'very' with an uncommon emphasis. "Pay attention now," she continued, her face somewhat contorted, probably in line with her innermost feeling which showed how serious the matter was. "We are all aware of the economic situation on ground now, but we must also help ourselves. Tell your parents to buy your books. Any child that reads his books is sure to do well. But how can you read if you do not have the book?" she queried, projecting her hands forward with both palms open, and looking askance at the class.

"Now sit down, let us take the correct answers to the questions borne in the test, together," she said, gesticulating.

Subsequently, both teacher and pupils thrashed out all the questions set at the last Friday's test. "Now, look this way," she started again, betraying a reminiscenting smile. "My happiness is that there are still some among you, who can stand tall and prove to the world that a teacher stands in front of you every day. My regret is that they are very few."

"Osita Tasie," she called. "Yes madam." "Have your answer sheet, please," she said, trying to conceal an emotional feeling that was detectable only in her next question to the lad. "Have you paid your school fees?" she asked.

The next day, while the school at large was gathered for morning devotion, the assistant headmaster strolled quietly into the assembly hall which was actually the classrooms of primaries three 'A' to 'E'. Every sensitive pupil in the school knows that the presence of either the headmaster or his assistant preceded an announcement of a grave matter concerning the school. And so, when the Assistant Headmaster of the great Obodoma Group School took over from the officiating devotionist that morning, all eyes had gotten focused on her, as all ears equally were wrapped up in attention.

Mrs. Iwuchukwu is her name. Speculation had it that she was married to a successful medical practioner, but that was the much that most pupils knew about the man.

This was not common place because the spouses of almost every teacher in the school was known to many of the pupils.

Dark in complexion, with oblong face, the woman who could still pass for a beautiful woman, stepped a little further nearer the pupils, and in her characteristic soft-spokenness, greeted the pupils. "I salute you all, children. We're all aware of the economic condition of our people, as an aftermath of an unfortunate war that has barely gone a while ago. We're equally aware that education has never been a cheap venture, nor will it ever be. So as expensive as education is, we must all brace up for the financial challenges that go with it. In that vein ….."

The woman had gone on to unveil the importance of education in the life of any pupil in this school and future generations. But finally, she had expressed regret on behalf of the school authorities to ask any pupil who was yet to pay the school fees to leave the school premises pending when the fellow paid up. "Please, make the work easier for us by not going into your class if you have not paid. Collect your bag, go and let your parents know that you've been put off school, on account of failure to pay your school fees. Teachers have been directed to flog any offending pupil, good day," she had summed up.

And so from various classes, pupils, boys and girls, had left the school and had all headed to their respective homes. Almost all the roads connecting the school both directly and indirectly, pupils strolled and chatted home. Coincidently, pupils from neighbouring schools, who were equally going to their respective homes on account of same reason, bye-passed one another, some of them moved in groups, others moved individually.

“We’ve been put off school,” Osita said to his mother, his eyes red as crimson.

Chapter Twenty Eight

"Don't worry," stuttered Violet, "you'll attend school tomorrow," she assured. "Mama it's not about going to school tomorrow or not, it's about paying the school fees tomorrow," protested Osita. "We're saying the same thing, son," she said calmly. "I'll give you the money to pay tomorrow," she reassured. "Are you se…serious mum," Osita, also stuttered, but without waiting for an answer, he went ahead to ask "how did you get the money?" "Don't forget that I did not sell the 'iron' bed for nothing," replied the mother, holding each of the little children in her hands, Osita at the right hand, and Ijeoma at the left hand.

The thought of her children going to school the following day with their school fees aroused a feeling of happiness and peace of mind in Violet, who had become withdrawn from her usual self since the death of her husband, few years ago. The peace of mind was to endure very long. This was unfortunately interrupted by the impending school fees for the following term which seemingly, came a short while later.

On the other hand, Osita and his sister, Ijeoma were very elated by the assurance that they were going to remain in school. "Thanks be to God, I'm going to pay my school fees tomorrow," Ijeoma said, giggling. For a reply, Osita told how he had been praying that God might miraculously provide their school fees. And here was he, having received answers to those prayers. Reflecting back, he also remembered occasions when he asked God to intervene in some of his life's complexities and had surprisingly received answers to such prayers. He remembered particularly, some of the questions he had encountered in his primary two examinations, which answers he was not really sure of. But had prayed and God had answered. God had miraculously led him into shading the right answers to the questions. He would never forget the mathematics questions during the exams under review. After shading the answers to the questions he was sure of, he had prayed briefly, but deeply too, asking God for guidance in the choice of the answers to the remaining ones. He was sure that he was not a dull child, but he knew also that he had not completed primary one, before the war started. And immediately after the war, he was compelled by fate to register in primary two, and that had posed a challenge to him.

"I remember clearly too, one Afor-Obodoma market day," said he, "the palm kernel mama had for sale, was not as much as she usually had." He had according to him feared that the sale would result in her buying less garri for the week, and as a result of that they would have to eat soup without garri at some meal times. Such situations did not give lasting satisfaction after eating, and he did not want that to happen. And so he had prayed earnestly, shortly after his mother had left for the market. He was surprised when his mother brought home sufficient garri with soup condiments, telling them how God had granted her a special sale that morning. In addition to all these, Osita remembered that God had surprised him immensely on his first day in the farms, in search of oil bean seeds with his cousins. "I didn't actually know how to search for it. I had no previous experience about it," said he, "but when others announced incessantly, their luck in picking the seeds, I knew I should talk to God. Right there, after a brief but heart-borne prayer, I started bumping into the 'things' and by the time we left for home, my colleagues admitted that they really didn't beat me in the act. So, after the head master's announcement concerning school fees, that morning although I cried, I let God into the matter, and thanks be to Him, my prayers have been answered," giggled Osita.

"Those of you," announced, the Vice headmaster, "who came with their school fees are expected to visit the bursar's office straight from here so that you do not have to report any stolen money to anybody, okay?" "Yes Madam," chorused the pupils. But because, she probably did not get a reply that was as resounding as she had expected, she moved a bit closer to the children.

"I don't think many of you heard me," she said, tilting her movement towards the right, as if motioned to move in that direction. Every step, producing the sound, 'kwoi, kwoi, kwoi'. This sound was as a result of the heels of her shoes coming in direct contact with the cemented, but patched floors. "I repeat, go straight to the bursar's office from here if you have your school fees on you, so as to forestall a loss of the money. Mr. bursar? please can you move forward so that those who do not know you can see you," she pleaded.

"My office," came the bursar's voice "is the fourth door from the headmaster's office. It is easily identifiable, especially with the help of the inscription, 'BURSAR'S OFFICE' at the top of the door. If you're coming to me, make a tap on the door gently, and come in. Do not wait for an answer before you come in, because nobody'll give you one. And as the Vice Headmaster rightly said, do not go to your class first, before coming to my own, as nobody'll entertain any complaints, bordering on the loss of any pupil's school fees, thank you," he concluded, stepping back behind the Vice Headmaster.

Following the announcements, Osita, Ijeoma and many other pupils had thronged the bursar's office right at the close of the morning devotion.

The bursar's office was rightly the fourth from the Headmaster's office, which is right at the beginning of that block, and the very first door. Next to the headmaster's office is the Vice headmaster's office, which is followed by the staff room. And next still, to the staff room, comes the bursar's office. This office is larger than any of the three before it. Prior to this dispensation, it had served as the school's library. The war, no doubt, had gone with the books neatly packed on the shelves in the library. The shelves had been removed, leaving scars of nails probably used in fastening them to the walls. This had rendered the walls rather unsmooth or outrightly rough, if you like.

"Queue up behind these two persons here," announced the bursar, pointing at two girls who leaned upon another set of pupils already seated opposite him. Following this directive, two long queues had been formed, from inside the office, stretching out and projecting well along the corridors and covering the entrance door to the primary five class room adjoining the bursar's office.

"Don't stand in front of that door, give way so that somebody can come in as well as get out of here, using that door. Did you hear me?" ordered Mr. Epuna, who was teaching primary five 'Christian Religious Knowledge', that morning.

Primary five, according to statistics, was not as numerous as primaries four, three and two. So was primary six. Both classes put together, were probably not as numerous as primary one, alone. One of the teachers in the school had once opined that most of the boys who died fighting in the war fronts as soldiers, were those in their lower levels in the secondary school, in addition to those who were supposed to be in primaries four and five currently. This statement may not be far from the truth, following the population indices.

"So, where did I say Goliath was born, class?" asked Mr. Epuna, in continuation of the lesson. As the class remained quiet and seemingly devoid of the answer for several minutes, Osita who was peeping into the class from his position in the queue involuntarily shouted, "Gath." "Yes," said the teacher, "Gath in Philistine." The teacher who had sufficed it to say, "Goliath of Philistine," previously, now seemed to have been reminded to extend the story to a more grass root level, and had therefore, started making it 'Goliath of Gath in Philistine'. "This boy, tell me, who on earth taught you the primary five scheme of work?" queried a primary five boy who incidentally was standing behind Osita in the queue. "We learnt about the nation of Israel versus Philistine in the Church, and you know, one cannot talk about the war between the two countries without mentioning, Goliath," replied Osita, innocent mindedly. This brief drama impressed upon the primary five pupil that this boy definitely would grow up to become one of the people to watch. "You seemingly didn't know this boy," asserted another boy within ear shot. "Large brain is responsible for his inability to grow tall. The size of his brain is so much that it has affected his growth rate." "Nothing is affecting my growth rate," retorted Osita, who does not like people making a jest of him, especially when it concerns his height.

"It's your turn now," said Gemima "please go in quickly, so we may take our respective turns, one is getting bored standing here."

Gemina was ebony black. She was obviously among the many pupils who were delayed by the God damned three year period of war. Tall, dark complexioned, but very well built, she had blossomed into a pretty and mature girl. When she spoke, a stranger is wont to think she is trying to show off her beauty, whereas those who were familiar with her have come to realize that it is her natural way of speaking. When she moved, her gait brandished natural beauty. Story has it that, one of the young male teachers had once made an immoral overture towards the girl, but without success. This had developed an air of antagonism between her and the teacher. The teacher according to the story was said to have asked her to help carry some of his books to his house after school and the innocent girl had obliged him. And as the innocent girl tried to keep the books on the table in the teacher's house the later made the failed move. "Lie for a minute," he had said, pointing at his bed. Obviously, any other teacher who nursed this plan in his mind, must have been discouraged from trying to carry out the plan, because Gemima was said to have personally narrated to her friends in full details, the teacher's unsuccessful move towards her, and the whole school had become saturated with scandal bordering on this. This had earned the teacher the nickname-"lie for a minute." On the other hand, some of the unmarried female teachers had brandished unrestrained dislike to this innocent girl, in a manner that was suggestive of jealousy. Some of them had gone as far as punishing her unjustifiably at the slightest mistake. As a result of this, other pupils find it not comfortable being identified with Gemima. The girls think that they would be unfairly punished if found in company of Gemima whether they commit a punishable offence or not. Others feared that Gemima could constitute a delay to them, if a male teacher had to attend first to her before attending to them, later on. "Gemima, you should be the last to see the bursar, please," pleaded Victor. "'Emenu gi akwapu m na line, nochie, ebe ima ihe'. – You may need to push me out of the queue and take my position, as the wise man that you are," angrily retorted Gemima.

By the time Osita got to his class, 'Christian Religious Knowledge' (CRK), which was top on the class time table, had passed and the second subject, 'Igbo', was on.

"How many of you paid their school fees this morning, asked the teacher, "please raise your hands. One, two ..., six ..., nine ..., twelve, twelve of you. How many altogether have so far paid, raise your hands too" she asked again, gesticulating in line with the order. In all, about twenty two pupils had paid.

While the counting was on, the bell announcing the short break came on air. "Monitor," she said, "please go down there and buy me some banana and groundnuts before you go out for break," asked the teacher.

Although the banana was of a sweet specie, the woman could not enjoy it to the fullness. She was rather engrossed in thoughts. "A class that was as numerous as about sixty two pupils, can now boast of only a little above one third of that number," she reasoned. "Agreed," further thought she, "that another twelve would pay tomorrow, this will only bring the number to about forty two. What then will become of the remaining pupils?" she conjectured, shaking her head in regret. Going by the information reaching her from among the pupils in her class, it is rather unlikely that as many as ten more pupils were returning to school. If that turned out to be true, she will be losing more than twenty pupils from her class alone," she thought, involuntarily hissing, wondering what will become of the future of these children.

She also remembered what the headmaster had said that morning, that her class was ahead of other classes in terms of payment of school fees. "In that case," she mused, upwards of one third of the former population of the school is quitting and this is unhealthy for the society," she concluded, sadly.

Chapter Twenty Nine

Mrs. Nlemchukwu took up the extra-tutorial duty of paying visits to the families of members of her class, especially those who had not paid their school fees. She found out to her horror that about seven out of those children especially the boys had already been given out for apprenticeship into on artisan trade or the other, in less than four weeks after the introduction of school fees. Her survey also revealed that about one, two, no, four girls had been compelled by circumstances to sit at home and await suitors. Following the matter further, she had come to realize that the reason behind the inability of these children to continue in school is three dimensional. First, this is a people who had been impoverished by an avoidable war. "My sister, I do not know how the war affected you, but in my own case," narrated one Jonah, "I lost my job in one of the country's parastatals, where I worked before the war started. You can see that I'm currently jobless. As for Martin my son, I wish I could retain him in school so as to enhance his future. But the truth is that we've not been able to put common food on the table for the kids, I mean my wife and I. So, maybe Martin and his siblings will go back to school in future, God willing, but at the moment, 'ahubem nwa n'afo mkpi' – 'I can't see the he-goat getting pregnant'" the man concluded, with his eyes now turned crisom.

Mrs. Nlemchukwu, who had been too shocked to take her leave, had remained glued to her seat, for minutes nobody spoke, when she finally found her voice she tried to change the emotionally charged atmosphere, she had come up with the story of the recent astronomic findings relating to the current position of the sun. Finally, when she had somewhat succeeded in calming the frayed nerves, she came nearer to Martin, rubbed her hand on his bare head and took her leave after dropping two pieces of coins into the lads palm.

Another reason why Martin and his colleagues could not continue in school was based on the meagre size of the take-off funds of the respective families. Most of the families had acted out of inadequate information. They had handed all the cash in the old currency that they had into the hands of a lone enlightened person. Now when the twenty pounds was shared among the many contributing families, each of them had gotten next to nothing. "Nwunye dim," started Nkechi's mother, before they changed money, I was doing very well in my petty trading." This average heighted but beautiful woman went ahead to tell to the keen ears of Mrs. Nlechukwu, her ordeal during the war and the early post war days. Finally, she and many others among the members of her husband's umunna according to her had handed over to her husband's elder brother, the money for the exchange. "But my heart bled when I was given a few shillings as my own due," she concluded. Perhaps, in the bid to stress her point, she had stood upon her feet, thereby exhibiting a pregnancy that was in advanced stage. "Ever since after that exchange," the money had been spent in the hospitals in form of bills."

Mrs. Nlechukwu did not need to be told a second time that among the reasons why many children of immediate post-war era were not able to pay their way to a secondary education was the untimely death in the war of the bread winners of many of these families.

"Nkechi, would you like to come to school tomorrow?" asked Mrs. Nlemchukwu, her class teacher. For a reply, the girl had passed out some drops of tears, successively, when a pretty face weeps, 'ya arika o na-ere urure' says an Igbo adage. So, Nkechi's sob had attracted more of the teacher's care than mere sympathy. "Obeeakwa," the teacher had called her, "come to school tomorrow, did you hear me?" she demanded. "Yes madam," replied the damsel, trying hard to hold back more tears. In an effort to totally soothe the visibly sobbing Nkechi, the teacher took a few more steps that brought her closer to the former. "Be sure to come on time, otherwise I'll flog you, you know I'm on duty this week," she said, trying hard to put on an expressionless disposition on her face. "But madam," Nkechi replied, "today is Saturday, that means tomorrow will be Sunday." As she spoke, she tried to mope her eyes with the back of her hands, but finding this unsatisfactory, she bent down a bit, picked the right end of her over-sized gown and did justice to that. "Don't do that Nkechi, I mean don't do it again, it's a dirty habit," Mrs. Nlemchukwu corrected, grimacing. And as if she just remembered that she was holding a discussion with Nkechi, added; "Sorry, come to school on Monday, and on time too, is that clear?" Although she had known that the pupils nickname her 'Is that clear?' just like her predecessor, she seldom succeeded in guarding herself against using the phrase. She rather recollected herself after making the 'mistake' just as in this case.

Throughout the night, Nkechi could not blink an eye in sleep. Her case according to her fears had been a settled fate, at least since her father had gone to the city about three times in an effort to regain his employment but is yet to succeed. Her mother who had been the family's breadwinner on the other hand, had not been very agile lately, because of her heavy pregnancy. Since the doctor's report showed that she'll have twin babies, her father had insisted that she stayed at home and help her mother take care of the babies while awaiting suitors since he had no money to pay for school fees. "So why on earth is her teacher asking her to come to school?" she wondered. "Come to think of it," she whispered to herself, "the headmaster is superior to Mrs. Nlemchukwu." Suppose the headmaster finds out that she had not paid her school fees and puts her out of school before the full glare of her peers, would that not tantamount to more shame?" she pondered, more tears.

Originally, Nkechi had nursed the ambition of being a nurse. She loved to dress in immaculate white gown, carry stainless pans, and help take care of sick people. But as it appears, that had ended up a mere fantasy. To cap up to her feelings of despondency is Adaku. Adaku Abia lives next compound to hers. Adaku is still in school. Each time Adaku passes by on her way to school or back, Nkechi would hide away from her sight. Shortly after the school fees drive, Adaku would come home and look for Nkechi. "Nkechy," she would call, for that is what she calls her, "Adanna asked after you. Not only Adanna anyway, Catherine also sends her regards." "Which Catherine?" Nkechi asked, fixing a glance at Adaku. "The one in your class. I do not know her surname." "We have two Catherines in our class," returned Nkechi. "Is she tall and slim?" "Yes, that's her," Adaku said, with her head gesticulating in affirmation. Now they no longer asked after her, perhaps they assume she was no longer coming back to school – tears. The thought of Adaku, Catherine and others remaining in school while she stayed at home had wet Nkechi's eyes more and more, and so regularly that she thought she had better stop any contact with any of them. That is the reason why Nkechi hides herself away on sighting Adaku.

"You have to play along with me, is that clear?" sounded Mrs. Nlechukwu to a nervous Nkechi who had come to school earlier than anybody else. "I want to tell the headmaster that you're my cousin and that you're living with me. That way, you'll be shielded temporally until we're in a better position to pay up," she continued. Nkechi could not make any reply to this. She was scarcely prepared for this kind of meeting. She mopped at her benevolent, mouth ajar, while her eyes seemingly focused beyond the teacher. She only got startled when the woman spoke again. "Anything the matter with you, or don't you like my plan?" "No, y-e-s, yes madam," she stuttered. "What is the meaning of 'no' and 'yes' in this matter?" probed Mrs. Nlemchukwu. "No, I… I like it …" she stuttered further. "Wait," the teacher interjected, "if that is the problem, you may come and live with me, if your parents would not mind. Under that arrangement, I will take the responsibility of paying your school fees," continued Mrs. Nlemchukwu, thinking that the problem was that Nkechi feared that her father may not be able to pay even at the long run.

Finally, Mrs. Nlemchukwu and Nkechi accepted to live together like mother and child. "Now, tell your father this is my little contribution, but if he does not consent, tell me so that I'll know where I stand, is that clear?" the benevolent woman had demanded at the same time, leaving the girl, stunned.

"Dear," for that is how Mrs. Nlechukwu addresses her husband. "I've committed myself and the family by adding more to the responsibility of our family," she said to her husband. "How?" came the voice of Mr. Nlemchukwu, half asleep. "Among the numerous children sent out of school for failure to pay schools fees, I've interest in about two of them, a boy and a girl, there are other intelligent ones among them, but I intend to pick these two only, for scholarship." "How much is involved in the two children?" her husband who had been fully awakened by a talk of this magnitude had asked.

The truth is that Mrs. Nlechukwu did not actually plan to pick two pupils. She mentioned two to pull her husband's legs. She reasoned that if she had made a case for one person, her husband could say 'no' to the move. And the matter would die there. And so, neither wife nor the husband spoke for minutes. But later, he shouted, "No woman, do pick one," I mean only one and be ready to pay the fees from your own salary, Good night," the man said with an air of finality. "Please my husband, let's not talk about whose salary," but her husband did not allow her finish up but shouted, "I said, good night."

The woman knew her husband inside out. She knew he would definitely consent for only one person. She also knew that he had sealed the discussion, having spoken the way he did. Although that given a free hand, she would have picked Martin alongside Nkechi, since he is one of the best brains in her class. Such brains she reasoned were wasted, if not exposed to vast learning. "Men," she thought, "were not soft-hearted beings like women. Otherwise, why would her husband not give scholarship to only two brainy, but poor pupils?" she wondered, shaking her head sadly. "After all, were they not rich?" She mused to herself. "Does she not earn a salary as a graduate teacher, and her husband, not only as a graduate, but the Principal of a secondary school?" she mumbled to herself.

In addition to their salary, the Nlemchukwus are rich. At least they are known to be comfortable. The fact that they are rich is an open secret in and around the village. Villagers misplace the source of the wealth, though. Only members of the nucleus family know that the source was merely providential. A fellow had advised Mr. Nlechukwu against depositing all his old currency notes together with his wife's. The man had told them that no amount of money was too small to be considered for the twenty pounds exchange. And so armed with that information the little money that they had on them had been divided into three portions. The man himself had deposited a part of the money separately. So had his wife, a second part while the remaining was deposited through Mrs. Nlemchukwu's younger sister, who was afterwards 'appreciated' with the sum of three pounds. So while some families were struggling with a few pounds and shillings they had nearly, sixty pounds safely slashed in the bank. "So why wouldn't they extend such benevolence to more than one person?" she hissed, deliberately making a sound which she hoped, would wake her already snoring husband. Yet he slept on.

In her mind's eyes, she replayed the pathetic sobs on the face of Martin when she visited them much earlier in the day. "Truly speaking," the woman pondered, "between Martin's face and his father's own, I can scarcely determine which one I consider as looking more pathetic. Was it not said that whatever could break a man's heart and spill tears through his eyes could bring about a woman's death?" She clearly saw in her mind's eyes, the tears that appeared in the man's eyes which were held back by sheer manly disposition.

What she did not see was the drama that was playing out at Martin's house that same night.

Martin had refused to eat that night. "Tell me," pleaded his mother, "what did you eat in the day time that could debar you from eating this night?" "Mama, please don't worry yourself, I just don't feel like eating, at all," replied Martin, trying hard to hold back hot tears. "Stop doing this to me, you didn't eat in the morning and now you also want to go to bed without food, do you want me to die at the altar of school?" demanded his mother, frustrated. "Then eat your food and stop sobbing, you can still make it in life, school or otherwise." This she said in order to pacify Martins, not that she liked the idea of not sending him to school. "Remember, it is not your father's fault. He was doing well before the war started. Have you forgotten how comfortable we were before the war started? I'm still optimistic that he'll soon rise again."

The woman seized this opportunity to drum back into the ears of her child, what she postulates that the lad had forgotten.

Martin was a pampered child in his younger days. His mother had refused engaging the services of a driver. She was not the type that turned down her husband's instructions, though. She however was so emotionally tied up with Martin that she preferred to take him with his siblings to school and bring them back again all by herself, rather than come and pick the child at one o'clock in the afternoon as was the right time, she would come by twelve noon, park her car under a tree and patiently await school's dismissal. Truth is that Martin alone of her three children at that time, was of school age. But their mother, who would pass for a homely woman, would neither leave her children in the care of a driver nor that of her nieces in the house who were living with them at that time. She preferred taking the younger ones along in the car while taking Martin to school or back.

They had all they needed to eat. They had biscuits, chocolates, ice cream and such other delicacies that children like to eat.

One day, as his mother went on to remind him, his father had driven into his school premises. As a matter of fact, the man had come to inform his wife that he had been assigned a duty outside the town and that entailed that he would not be spending the night with the family. But Martin had been so elated on seeing the father thinking that he had come to pick him from school and had rushed to meet him so carefreely that he only narrowly missed being knocked down by the unsuspecting father. "J-e-s-u-s…eh!" his mother had shouted, drawing the attention of all and sundry within the school premises. His father had been too stunned to talk. Martin himself had been disappointed with the way his father received him. His intuition had made him realize that his father had been unimpressed with him, but what baffled him was the reason behind that. The 'video' of that drama had lingered in his mind. Each time he remembered that incident, his mind wondered why his father who had come happily to his school, had abruptly changed at seeing him. Consequently, he had rejected the biscuits and sweets which his father later tried to give him. But when his mother walked up to the duo of himself and his father, she had succeeded in persuading him to accept the biscuits by trying to make him understand that his father meant well. Another reason why he accepted the biscuits arose when his siblings saw their father and started running to meet him. He had feared that they would collect them all if he went ahead to reject the biscuits.

Aside from this incident, Martin knew he had not had any reason to lose faith in his father, so "I'm not blaming my father for any reason," he had snapped. "In that case, you're nursing blames against me, your mother," returned the woman. "How can I bring myself to blaming you in this matter, mama?" he queried. "So why would you not have food before going to bed, do you realize it's getting to midnight?" "Mama," Martin began, trying to open up, "the truth is that I'm not blaming either you or my father in this matter, but I don't like the trade that I'm going in for, I prefer to go to school," he stressed, shaking his head in melancholy.

While mother and son were stressing their points, Jonah Nweke, who had been eavesdropping all along, began to feel relaxed, little by little. He had considered it a dangerous ground should his own son blame him for the down turn in the family's fortunes. "After all," thought he, "I've been up and doing, and I still believe that one of these days, I'll get employed, if not with the former establishment, it would be with a new one." With this in mind, he had gone to bed.

Chapter Thirty

"I'm so sorry that I disturbed your sleep last night," started Mrs. Nlemchukwu. Maybe, I should have brought the issue much later at a more convenient time, but the reason behind this is that the boy in question is one of the best brains in my class." She gently narrated to her husband, the reason why the boy should be helped. She had earlier taken time to rehearse what to say to her husband, and how to go about it several times over. "He's from a very poor family, and desperately needs help. Without our help, the boy's future, academically may be marred," she added, looking expectantly at her husband.

"So what is my dear wife trying to say?" her husband had humorously asked. But without waiting for the answer, Mr. Nlemchukwu had further demanded the reason why his wife would not settle with showing philantropism to one person at a time. "I'll advice you to choose between the boy and the girl, the one that best suits you for now. You can pick up the other person when we are through with the first one," insisted Mr. Nlemchukwu, fixing a glance at his wife with an air of finality.

Whatever efforts his wife had made in trying to stress her points was not really making an impact in Mr.

Nlemchukwu anymore. He belonged to the class of people not familiar with poverty. All his life, it was as if a proverbial benevolent spirit had cracked his kernels for him. His father, Amos Okere, had not been very rich himself, but had been married to the second daughter of a military officer from the Northern part of one of the countries in the contemporary European Union. This had enhanced his fortune. Amos Okere met Ian Robinson, a black military officer in Burma, during the Second World War. Amos Okere was also a soldier, but had served under the garrison of army, manned by Ian Robinson. Both were fighting on the side of the Union Jack. When the war ended, Ian had taken Amos to Europe, based on their relationship which had blossomed into intimate friendship from boss-subordinate relations.

One evening, as they were sipping champagne in a bar not quite far away from Lan's home, Amos had spoken to him "I like your daughter, Catherine," he said, but was cut short by his host. "Don't go further," Ian had snapped. "I'm civilized, I'll be dammed to speak to my own daughter for you, tell me something else."

However, time they say heals all wounds and so not quite long afterwards, Catherine knocked at the door to her father's bedroom one early morning. "Hi dad, had a nice sleep?" she said to him. And as if she was not expecting any reply from her father, Catherine had gone on to talk to him "there's something important I'd like to talk over with you," she said, pronouncing 'important' as 'impoorant'. "Yeah," replied her father, "I'm all ears," the 'ears', sounding like 'ers'. Catherine then told her father about her feelings for Amos, and the latter's proposal to her.

"Damn!" Ian had snapped, "you're not going to marry into Africa." "But dad, I'm sorry, I am. I love Amos and he loves me too." The nineteen year old Catherine had snapped at her father. Within minutes, she had run into her own room and shut herself up in the room, sobbing.

A couple of weeks later however, Amos and Catherine had become husband and wife. That was the parentage of Francis, Francis Nlemchukwu, the principal of Uzongbo Girls Secondary school.

Conversely, his wife Constance came from a not-so-rich background. Her parents, Mr. and Mrs. Olumba hail from the same village, but different kindreds in a nearby locality. She was the sixth child, out of the eight children born to Mr. and Mrs. Olumba. Her father was a Catechist in one of the Protestant Churches in their village, while their mother, as a house wife, took over the responsibility of taking care of her children and the local church women folk.

They had passed through the thick and the thin. Fortunately however, with the help of the church, Constance had passed through to University.

Once, Philip, the first of her two sons by Amos had gone to his father privately. He had wanted to dislodge a puzzle that had refused to be forgotten by his young mind. The puzzle was engraved in her mother's statement once, while stressing a point, to the hearing of her children.

"Dad," he asked, "Is it true that a boy or a girl can leave home for school without breakfast?" he had asked. "Yes," came his father's reply. "Some parents are so poor that they may not be able to give their children three square meals in a day. Under such circumstances, the family may eat two times, or even once a day."

"Dad," the little boy came up again. "Yes my boy," replied his father. "Is it also true that a child can die?" He asked next, brandishing a puzzled look. "Yes, in Africa, children die" replied his father. "What about other parts of the world?" further asked the boy, this time exhibiting anxiety. "In developed economies like Europe and America, they don't die, but in Africa and other third world countries, children die," replied his father. "Why?" he pressed on. "Children are not well taken care of in the developing economies as they're in Europe and America." "Will I die?" "Phill, you'll not die of course, why d'you ask such a nasty question?" retorted Amos. "Will Johnny die?" Johnny is Philip's younger brother. They both are the children of Mr. and Mrs. Amos Nlemchukwu. So John, who was not pleased with the last question from his elder brother, pointed a finger at Philip and took his own turn, "Will Phil die?" "Now children stop that rubbish and say better things to each other," snapped their father.

That was however, long after the couple were finally settled in Nigeria. Amos had applied for, and was posted to Uzongbo Girls' Secondary school while his wife, Constance had opted for a school nearer home, for the sake of the family care. That had placed her at Obazu Group school, the nearest to their home.

Not surprisingly therefore, Mr. Amos turned down his wife's plea for scholarship to Martin, on the grounds that since Nkechi had been favoured, Martin or any other person could wait until after Nkechi got through with her schooling. He did not want to 'over stretch' the family's income. Next, he did not want a crowded home.

Therefore when the final year students of a nearby Teacher Training College, who came to Obodoma Group School, for their Teaching Practice, arrived and were assigned to Mrs. Nlemchukwu's class, a drama had ensued. The former sitting arrangements of the class were rearranged. Under the new arrangement the quadruple of Osita, Martin, Nkechi and Nnamdi Odi were positioned at the four ends of the classroom.

Osita and the rest of the class members were surprised when a young man was introduced to them as the person to hold the class temporarily. They had feared that their regular teacher, Mrs. Nlemchukwu was going out on transfer or embarking on a leave, whichever case, they would frown at.

The monitor had passed his normal signal of producing a sound 'Kwam kwam, kwakwakwam kwam,' with his ruler against his sitting object, and as expected, the class had responded by saying, "good morning madam," "good morning sir." "Thank you class, and please sit down," responded Mrs. Nlemchukwu. "This is Mr. Geoffrey Umunna," she continued, "from a nearby Teacher Training College in Obodoma. He is a student teacher and will teach you on personal hygiene for forty-five minutes and at the end of the lesson, he will ask you many questions, so please pay attention very well so that you do not project yourselves before him, as a dull class. Is that clear?" she had said. "Thank you madam, and to you my own younger brothers and sisters, for the second time, I say welcome to school," said the new teacher. "And," continued he, "I'll give you a short lesson on personal hygiene, as Madam informed you earlier, and at the end of the lesson, we shall find out the best pupils among you through oral test. And for a start, who can tell us what 'oral test' signifies?" he had gone on. At this juncture, about three voices came up with an answer each, but no one heard distinctly what any of them had answered. "No chorus answers please," said Mr. Umunna. "If you have any answer, do raise your hand up like this," he said indicating with his hand raised up, "and if I want you to say something, I'll point at you, then that is when to tell us the answer, communicating?" "Stop the use of such words," a voice interrupted him, "use simpler words for easier understanding," the voice continued from behind. Surprised, everybody turned abruptly to take a look at the person who made the statement. "Sorry madam, I'll take corrections," the teacher answered nervously. Meanwhile, two hands already raised up in order to give answers to the last question were still up. "Yes?" resumed the new teacher, "you there, tell us." "Suspend that question," interjected the woman who shouted at the teacher earlier, "go straight to your topic." Naturally again, all eyes turned towards the direction of the voice.

There, sitted on one of the windows was the woman, eyes fixed at the student teacher. She was dark in complexion and average heighted. Once in a while, she would stroll along the corridors. She would take a few steps forward, and shortly afterwards, she would turn and take some steps in opposite direction, yet her eyes would always remain focused upon the teacher and the class. Seemingly, the only thing that was capable of removing her eyes from the class was her wrist watch.

"Don't direct your questions to only one or two pupils!" the woman shouted abruptly again, "spread your questions," "yes madam," came the student teacher, obviously jittery.

"Suppose your class is dull, do something to revive it," cried the woman again but for the first time since the lesson began, showed herself by standing at the door.

"Class stand!" commanded the teacher.

"I'm afraid, that's not what you should do in this circumstance," objected the woman. "You better ask questions." "O.k madam," said the student teacher, betraying further signs of being tensed up.

"Who can tell us what I said here that are the rules at meal?" Only two pupils raised their hands. "You there, no, you, yes?" "Eat at regular times" "yes, go on," encouraged the teacher, "Do not eat in-between meals," "yes continue", "drink plenty of water after meals." "Excellent, let's clap for him," "kwam kwam kwa kwa kwam kwam," came the class.

"Let other members of the class be asked some of those questions!" shouted the lady supervisor, "stop channeling all questions unto one or two persons only."

At the end of the lesson, the student teacher, Mr. Umunna, shook hands with Mrs. Nlemchuwku and they bade each other goodbye. As he walked out of the classroom and into the school premises, his face showed he was not impressed at the way the lesson had toed. Once in a while, he would look behind as if he heard what Mrs. Nlemchukwu and the rest of the primary three teachers were saying about him. His tall body structure, moving sluggishly as if the blue trousers he wore were only tied round his waist.

"I feel for the young man," said Mrs. Nlemchukwu, to the three other teachers of primaries 'B', 'C' and 'D'. "Yes, you're right, said one of them, "I heard several reprimands from his supervisor." "I hope he doesn't end up failing his practicals, added Mrs. Ogasi." "I know the cause of his problems," opined Mrs. Nlemchukwu, "the drama, you know, played out itself in my class." "The reason is that the school fees saga has reduced the number of students in each class, with my own class in the eye of storm. This is because, most of the pupils who dropped out from my class, were the intelligent ones. Last year," she continued, "the 'teaching practice man' asked a question and many hands would go up. He could point at any pupil from any part of the class, and the answer would be correctly given." "So, how does that relate with the man's practicals today?" enquired Mrs. Ebogu. "Listen," replied Mrs. Nlemchukwu, "this year only about one or two intelligent pupils are left in my own class. When the man asked questions, usually only this one or the other person would raise his hands. He had no option than to concentrate on the few." "O.k, is that the reason why his supervisor was always shouting at him?" asked the same Mrs. Ebogu. "Yes," replied Mrs. Nlemchukwu. "Once, the man had made a mistake of pointing at another person, and the child had opened his mouth wide only to vomit a wrong answer, and the man I'm sure, must have felt like slapping the stupid boy." "Well," said Mrs. Nlemchukwu, "they will probably, repeat that exercise, come next week." "If they do, can we arrange and help the young man before his practicals tear him apart?" suggested Mrs. Ogazi. "How do you mean?" asked Mrs. Ebogu. "Yes, we can bring together, from our various classes, some brilliant pupils to help answer his question, that's all I mean."

"'Ehe' least I forget," said Mrs. Ogazi, "my sister," she continued, pointing at Mrs. Nlemchukwu, "you blamed the school fees deal for all the maladies, I hope you're not against the introduction of school fees, otherwise how do you guarantee our salaries?" "Not at all my sister, well I probably should have blamed it all on the war," replied Mrs. Nlemchukwu. "Ehe" chorused her colleagues, "You have made a resounding point now," asserted Mrs. Ebogu.

To make herself clearer, Mrs. Nlemchukwu had pointed out that the war was solely responsible for the impoverished condition of the masses, and had so severely affected them, that most families could no longer provide food for the children, "how then could they source school fees?" she wondered. "I love and cherish it when there are many pupils in my class," said she, but right now, my class of about sixty five has greatly reduced and this is to my displeasure."

'Gam, gam, gam, gam', came the sound of the bell, announcing school's dismissal for the day. Then came the end-of-day prayers. "School dismiss," shouted Mrs. Nlemchukwu, "away" chorused the pupils.

Chapter Thirty One

"Good morning Madam," greeted Mr. Umunna. "Did you have a nice sleep?" "Yes, thank you," replied Mrs. Nlemchukwu "and how are you?"

"My supervisor said we are proceeding to primary four 'A' this morning, please can you show me the primary four 'A' classroom?"

Mrs. Nlemchukwu had called on a pupil in her class, for onward direction of the student teacher to primary four 'A' at the senior primary section.

"But before that madam, can you please lend me that my friend, Osita, he seems very intelligent," pleaded Mr. Umunna. "Of course, as a matter of fact, he's one of the best in the school, but what will he do for you?" asked Mrs. Nlemchukwu. "Not much madam," said Mr. Umunna, "it's just that I'd like to direct some of my questions to him." "I thought you said you were going over to primary four?" demanded Mrs. Nlemchukwu, "so how can he cope with the primary four scope since he's in primary three?" "You've forgotten madam that the questions I'll ask shall emanate from the lessons I'll teach," replied Mr. Umunna.

"Unfortunately," said Mrs. Nlemchukwu, "that boy is not in school today, he is among the pupils sent out of school for failure to pay their school fees." "Please madam," asked the student teacher, obviously taken off balance, "are you serious?"

At the student-teacher's request, thereafter a child was made to give the direction to Osita Tasie's house, and the student-teacher had speedily gone personally to pick him.

Mrs. Nlemchukwu had been taken aback. She was torn between two individuals in separate but desperate situations. "How do I help out now? She thought. "Suppose this man fails to convince Osita to come here and help, or suppose the boy's parents refuse to lend him and rather decide to withdraw him from school now? Suppose this young man comes back with or without Osita, but finds out that his lesson period had expired? If not for the war, she pondered, would life be as it were now, especially the school fees malady? Certainly not." She remembered the pre-war days, how parents and guardians worked hard especially in this part of the world to keep their children in school, because everyone knew the importance of education. She also remembered the saying that "children were the very purpose why parents toiled day and night." But the war had come, and although it had equally gone, many parents especially in this part of the globe, had lost their vocations. Most of them are trying hard now to find their feet.

"God please," thought Mrs. Nlemchukwu, "don't let Osita's parents decide to withdraw the boy completely from school now. He is an asset to this school and society although probably hidden at the moment." And as the woman spoke, she looked up to the heavens as if she were talking to a visible God.

Osita's house is not far away from the school. It is situated along the main road that leads from the main township of Owerri, and runs along the suburban town of Obodoma and beyond. It is a busy, but untarred road. The topography of the road is in consonance with the rest of the town, flat, almost all through, except of course a very few spots where the topography would rise up to a few yards. Even at such spots, there is a return to the original ground level as if directed to that effect. This makes it prone to the effects of erosion, and this in turn, results in the formation of water log intermittently along the road, making the use of the road both uncomfortable for the users and time wasting, too.

The ride to achieve his mission was made worse for the student-teacher by the bad nature of his bicycle. First, the bicycle had no seat. The man had to pedal from the rear, sitting on top of the carrier, rather than the seat proper. This did not make for comfort, however. Save for his long legs, his blue trousers which were slightly torn at the joint of his two legs would perhaps, have been badly torn. The silver-coloured iron bar meant to form the platform upon which the bicycle's seat was fixed, produced friction as the man pedaled. This is responsible for the slight tear under his flap. Once, he noticed that his trousers had hooked at the base of the position of the seat, Mr. Umunna, had tried to stop the bicycle so that he could release his hooked trouser. This had precipitated a discovery of another problem. The bicycle would not stop. More efforts as well as tact were made, yet the bicycle stubbornly moved on. Luckily for him, the spot at which he found himself was relatively dry, he had therefore brought both legs down on the ground. While the 'cycle', as he referred to it moved, his legs, both of which were placed on the ground, were used as additional brake device. Shortly later, the bicycle came to a stop. Hastefully, he deployed both hands into the business of trying to unhook his trousers. This had proved an uphill task and "Oh God, if this trouser tears here now," he had lamented, "what shall I do?" He made another patience-sapping move to unhook the trouser, yet the effort seemed to be one in futility. He felt the impulse to tear the trouser, and move faster so as to achieve his mission. "But suppose the tear ends up too bad?" he reasoned, "how do I cover myself up, would it not be tantamount to foolhardiness, trying to go home now from here, to change into another trouser?"

He later remembered his friend, Chike. True, Chike's house is not far away from here. "But Chike would not be at home at this time of the day," he reasoned.

Later, he made a last minute effort which yielded dividend for him, but with a short tear that would not be conspicuous. "Thank you God," he said, heaving a sigh of relief. "Gram, gram, gram," came the bell of an approaching bicycle from behind. A look behind showed him that he was almost at the centre of the road. Moreover, he had occupied the only dry portion of that part of the road, as both sides were water-logged. "Sorry please" he managed to yell, and waving his left hand at the bicycle rider, he tried to pull off the road, using his right hand in collaboration with his legs.

"Please madam, where is the Tasie's house, I was told to make enquiry once I got to this market square," Mr. Umunna asked a woman who was trying to crosscheck the ability of her worn out umbrella to perform. "Who exactly are you looking for?" asked the woman. "Osita." "Osita?" queried the woman, with both eyes fixed on the young man, at the same time wondering what the little boy would be having in common with this semi grown up man." "Anything the matter?" she demanded.

Mr. Umunna had to introduce himself, as well as explain the reason for his mission, before he was directed aright. While he was waiting for the boy to get ready to go to school, he started inspecting himself. "Is this what had become of my sandals and trouser tips?" he mumbled to himself. As he was trying to clean up his trouser-tips and legs, he suddenly became conscious of an impending rain.

Meanwhile, his supervisor had come into the primary three classroom to enquire for the whereabouts of Mr. Umunna. "Hello madam, sorry if I disturbed you, but have you seen Mr. Umunna here, this morning?" She asked. "Mr. Umunna? I'm not sure I'm familiar with that name," replied Mrs. Nlemchukwu, trying to buy time in favour of Mr. Umunna. "But, he and I were here last time for his teaching practice, remember?" she asked. "Oh yes, now I remember. Yes, I also remember seeing him around this place, this morning. But have you checked him up at the senior primary section? he must be around."

As the woman turned to move out, Mrs. Nlemchukwu smiled and offered her a hand shake. "You didn't want us to see how beautiful you were, at your first visit, but having seen you clearly now, I'd like to remark that you're beautiful, and by the way I'm Mrs. Nlemchukwu." "I'm Mrs. Opa," replied the woman," chuckling, her gaze fixed on Mrs. Nlemchukwu, her hands akimbo. "Aren't you beautiful too? Your gait and accent strike me as a non-Nigerian, are you European?" "Y-e-s," Mrs. Nlemchukwu said slowly but cheerfully, "somehow you're right … I'm Jamaican by birth, but born and bred in Europe, and married to a Nigerian, so can you say I'm not Nigerian?" The two women had burst into a hearty laughter. "You're not only a Nigerian my sister, you're a global citizen," joked Mrs. Opa. And they both laughed further and louder.

Mrs. Nlemchukwu had offered to get a boy from her class to go and look for the student teacher while Mrs. Opa sat down awhile. "Thank you madam, that is very thoughtful of you," said Mrs. Opa.

In a twinkle of an eye, Mrs. Opa, who had spent a good number of years in Europe as a student had recalled her stay in that part of the world. First and foremost, she had remembered her first day in Europe, specifically at the famous Heathrow Airport in England. She had previously been uninformed adequately about the climatic condition of Europe. She had heard that the continent had some four climatic conditions, viz-Summer, winter, spring, and autumn. What exactly they felt like however was not very clear to her at that time.

Her arrival had been in the winter season. She wore a beautiful black jacket on top of an equally beautiful red skirt and blouse. Her handbag was a combination of red and a preponderance of black background. Her high-heeled shoes were totally black. To crown it all, she had covered her head with a pretty hat, folded both sides upwards, with a combination of black and red colours. She had felt both confident in herself and on top of the world, fashion-wise.

Furthermore, she could remember that throughout her growing up years, she had nursed the vision of traveling to Europe one day. She had also considered it very ecstatic an experience and looked forward to having the experience of travelling in an aeroplane. The day she received her visa was one she could never forget in her life. She, in the company of her elder brother, had made efforts upon efforts without success. Once, she had gone on her own, thinking they would look her over with an eye of sentiment, thereby issuing her with one. Rather than do so and to her own surprise, the authorities had wondered why she wouldn't study in her home country, Nigeria, and had advised her to consider studying in Nigeria.

"Finally," she thought with a broad and reminiscenting smile, "I have not only succeeded in getting the hard-to-get visa, I also not only have flown in an aeroplane, but here I am in England. Europe here I come," she smiled to herself, high-spiritedly, bathing in the euphoria of success.

Suddenly she started feeling very cold and before long she had started shivering. She had thought that buttoning up her red jacket could spring insulation. How wrong she was she was later to realize. Within minutes however, she had felt contrition in her lungs that made her breathing more or less, labourious. "Hullow lady, d'you want to die? if you don't cover yourself up properly, you'll die," a man, she had never met before, had shouted at her.

That shout helped her a great deal. "It rebound me into consciousness. I remember grabbing my luggage and struggling along with it, hastened up into the travellers' lounge with an air of emergency," she remembered. She recalled also that while she was right inside the travellers' lounge, she still froze, and what she saw later had explained to her what that man was referring to as proper covering. She was the only person that was scantly covered and freezing.

Everybody seemed to be looking at her in amazement and pity.

"Are you a first timer to this part of the world?" a lady of about her age had approached and asked her, looking her over, not only into her eyes, but with an air of obvious concern. She remembered with amusement how difficult it was for her to understand this lady because, her accent was too heavy for a language learner like herself. "Can I lend you one of my winter suits?" the lady, speaking further, had offered.

While she was contemplating on accepting this lady's offer, her brother entered the lounge, and "oh thanks goodness," she exclaimed, he brought her a winter suit.

Conversely, Mrs. Nlemchukwu's thoughts flowed on and reflected on the sight of Osita as she saw him cry home from school that Monday morning. Although the headmaster had announced that pupils who had not paid their school fees for the term were not to enter their respective classes, many of them defied the order and went ahead to study along with others in their classes, Osita inclusive.

She had noticed the presence of about five of them in her class, but could not bring herself to asking them out. Her heart had gone out for Osita. "Last term this boy paid his school fees on time, one would therefore expect that his situation is not as bad as those ones who dropped out completely. So," thought the woman, "who knows what will spring up this term?" Her heart had been in turmoil. "Suppose the headmaster decides to go round the classes to personally send away the school fees defaulters as was customary with the school? God, please, let the man allow the sleeping dog lie."

Nevertheless, Osita and his defaulter-colleagues were not composed. Their eyes flashed out through one window or the other, in the look out for the approach of the 'second master' as they addressed him. They feared he might use a cane if he met them this time around.

"Who can remind us what we learnt last week in Mathematics?" asked the teacher. And without raising his hand, Osita had answered "Tangents and cotangents." Each time a pupil answered a question in her class wrongly, without first raising his hand up for her permission, Mrs. Nlemchukwu was sure to get irritated with the person. But if the answer was correct, she usually ignored the act of indiscipline as she termed it. So when the boy answered her question correctly, her heart melted the more. "Now who can define a tangent?" she asked again. There was subdued murmur among the children. Only Osita's hand went up. "Didn't you hear my question?" She further asked, ignoring the lone hand raised up. "I want somebody to tell us what a 'tangent' is", she cried looking at the pupils from one end of the class to another. "Only one person? Is this a sign that he was the only person in class when I taught the lesson?" she queried, and a conspicuous frown showed up on her face. "I know what to do," continued the teacher. "I'll give him a cane to flog all of you if he answers correctly," threatened the teacher.

She was at the verge of asking Osita for the answer when she noticed a faint shadow abruptly emerge in the classroom. Intuitively, she looked out and there he stood, a cane in one hand, and a sheet of paper in the other. The presence of the headmaster had precipitated an uneasy calmness in the class, while all eyes, including the teacher's own focused at the door where the man stood.

"Pay attention this way," came the hoarse voice of the vice headmaster. If you haven't paid your school fees up till now, leave the class now while I am still standing here. At the count of three, I'll disallow any movements, and give every defaulter, twelve-lash strokes of this cane. One ……." At the first count, all five defaulting pupils in primary three 'A' hurried out of the classroom. A few yards away, while silence still reigned, Osita's voice was ringing like a bell in the air as he cried out of the school compound. His voice sent a chill into many hearts including the headmaster's own, who now turned his head, took a look at the crying boy and shook his head in sympathy. This sprang up another unusual quietness in the class. Even the piece of chalk in the right hand of Mrs. Nlemchukwu dropped as if in sympathy to the boy's unchecked voice of crying, as it went on, piercing the air.

Chapter Thirty Two

"God please, help me quicken this boy up so that the rain does not catch up with us," mused Mr. Umunna. However, he could not hurry the boy up. He could also not exact any authority on him. This was because he knew that the school authorities sent him out of school for failure to pay up his school fees. Conscious of this fact, he resorted to pampering the boy. There was only one thing that he could do under that circumstance. He paced himself around, begging God that the boy would accept to come back to school and help him pass his practical examination. Of course he did not tell Osita the truth. He posed himself as one of his teachers. It was on this premise that he asked Osita to come back to school and resume his studies. As a matter of fact, he was not his teacher. But as a final year student in a Teacher Training School, he had taught in Osita's class in the course of one of his examination practicals. That was how he and Osita became familiar with each other. Incidentally, his next examination practicals are billed today, and at Osita's school, too. He had a reason for trying to bring Osita back to school. His reason is that Osita is one of the most brilliant pupils in the school. He needed him to answer some of the questions that he, the student teacher would ask in the course of teaching. If most of the questions that he would ask in the course of his teaching were answered correctly, his supervisor would certainly accord him with high marks. Of all the many pupils he had come across at the Obodoma Group School, he trusted Osita most when it comes to understanding his teaching and answering questions out of the theme of the lesson. He therefore could not imagine himself taking an examition in that school in Osita's absence. Moreso, an examination that is as important to him as his final teaching practical examination.

Unfortunately, Osita spent a long time inside the house. He had gone in to collect his books so that they would go back to school, together. But it seemed that Osita was not really willing to leave the house. This had really posed a source of worry to the student teacher. "What could be holding this boy for so long?" he mumbled, and paced around the compound. While he paced around, his eyes turned towards the direction of any sound. This was to see when the boy would emerge from the house. Unfortunately, he was not coming and his examination period was not waiting either. "My God, what shall I do now?" he sighed, his hands unconsciously placed on his head. Moments later, he thought that he heard a sound of a movement emerging from the hut. He stood still and listened very attentively. But the sound seemingly ceased. It was as if the person that made the sound discovered that someone was watching, and ceased moving. This added to his feeling of disappointment. At this point, he began to hear voices in his mind's ears. "You had better go back to school," one of the voices, suggested. "The boy is not willing to go with you afterall," the voice added. He shrugged, glanced over his shoulders and back again. "Okay," he mumbled, and made to leave. "Excersice more patience," he heard another voice from within his mind, say. At this impulse, he waited a little longer. There was still no sign of the boy. Suddenly his mind began to play a trick on him. It began to show him a picture, where the boy was hiding away from him right inside the house. So, at this impulse too, he began to pray in his mind. "God," he said, "please let my coming here be not in vain. Let this boy not hide himself in the house. That would mean to keep me waiting here all day long while my examination period whiles away." Little did he know that the boy, on the other hand, was collecting all his books, pencils and biros in a haste, and was also praying in his own heart that the teacher might not change his own mind and leave, thereby dashing his hope of resuming school that day. "I hope am not forgetting anything else," Osita mumbled. Satisfied that he had collected everything that he needed, he headed to the door. Moments later, he came out from the house, bearing some books in his hands. This gladdened the student-teacher's heart. "Hmmm," he heaved a sigh of relief. He could not afford to wait for Osita to meet him where he stood. Instead, while the boy moved towards him, he too tried to also move towards the boy, rolling his bicycle along. Moments later, he stood face to face with Osita, and so steadied his bicycle against a dwarf mango tree just at the entrance to the compound. "Can we move now?" he asked, putting on an awkward smile on his face, while reaching out his hand to collect the books from Osita's hands. "Sir, please let me lock the doors and go and tell my uncle that I'm leaving for school," Osita pleaded, and without waiting for an answer, he hurried back into the house, locked up the house and hurried to meet his uncle. "Uncle, my teacher has come," he said, his face expressionless. "Which of your teachers?" asked Michael, his lips apart. "I do not know how to describe him to you," Osita replied, "but…." "But your head?" Michael snapped, fixing a hard look at Osita. "You do not know how to describe your teacher, and you make bold to say it out," Michael went on, his face slightly furrowed. "Come and show me the person," he added, leading the way. Osita reluctantly followed behind him. Uncle Michael was used to receiving Osita's teachers in his house. They usually came to ask him to give Osita an opportunity to exploit his brain in the educational. He had come to know the names of some of them, especially the more frequent ones. He was therefore no longer perturbed at their visits. But not this one. Osita seemed not to know the name of this one. He could not describe him either. "So let me go and see who he is," he mused as they moved.

While Mr Umunna waited for Osita, he examined the books that Osita brought out. "What on earth would this boy be doing with all these books," he mumbled, but kept the matter in his heart. Suddenly a thought flashed through his mind. He remembered the ordeal he passed through while coming to Osita's house. This made his heart skip a beat. He glanced at his wrist to check the time. That was when he remembered that his watch does not actually keep to appropriate time. There were times when it moved behind the right time. There were times too, when it moved ahead of the right time. It depended on whose chronometer he based on while setting the watch. He became restless. He was not sure whether his watch was really moving late or ahead of time. “Whichever way,” he prayed, “God, please let this bicycle behave better this time around, so that we can get to the school before my supervisor comes looking for me.” He had hardly ended his prayer when Osita came back to him, accompanied by an elderly man whom the teacher presumed to be his uncle. “Good morning sir, he quickly greeted, slightly bowing down his head and at the same time praying in his heart that the man does not spoil his day. “Morny, my son,” the man greeted back, pronouncing ‘morning’ as if in ‘money’. “Did you say that you are going to school at this time of the day?” Osita’s uncle asked, glancing first at Osita, then at the teacher, and back at Osita. “Yes uncle,” Osita answered, lowering his face to the ground, but quickly added, “this is my teacher. He came to take me back to school.” “Y…yes he is right, sir” the teacher stuttered, trying hard not to betray his inner feeling of fear. Osita’s uncle said nothing at this point. He took a scrutinizing look at the teacher. Satisfied, he felt that there was no point in asking further questions. He therefore stood there while Osita and his teacher prepared to leave. And as if in unison, Mr Umunna’s mind began to relax. He felt assured, for the first time since he entered Osita’s compound, that he was really going to succeed in his mission. His face began to brighten up. In the same vein, Osita’s own heart began to feel elated that he was finally resuming school. He wished that he could just close his eyes only to find himself in the school. “Thank God that I did not go into the rigours of trying to explain to uncle, that Mr Umunna was a student teacher from the nearby Teacher Training College,” he mused. Uncle was certain to have problem understanding me. And of course, that would spell flop for this outing.”

"Please bring the books up quickly," Mr Umunna said, thereby breaking the flow of his thought and at the same time, stealing a glance at the old man as he stood there, his hands akimbo, watching them. "Alright sir," Osita replied, trying to bring up all the books at the same time. And so a little while later, both the teacher and the pupil embarked upon the bicycle, before the watching the eyes of the elderly man. "I hope you can ride a bicycle?" asked the teacher, looking enquiringly at Osita, while holding the bicycle in one hand. "Yes sir, I can ride very well," Osita assured him. "Then give me the books," the student teacher had said, reaching out to collect the books with both hands.

Mr. Umunna placed the books in between his flap and the protruding shaft. The shaft was what held the seat in place. But the seat had torn to shreds and had long been detatched. This had exposed the silver coloured shaft that held it in place. That was the spot where Mr Umunna squeezed in the books. The absence of the seat had left any adult using the bicycle with no option, than to sit on the bicycle's carrier. That was how Mr Umunna rode down to Osita's house. On the other hand, children of Osita's height would ride in 'monkey' style. The reason is that they would not be able to pedal the bicycle, sitting on the carrier. Their legs would not stretch that long. This was what style that Osita adopted.

And to accord stability to the bicycle, Mr Umunna placed both legs on the ground. "Now mount on, but bear in mind that you are the one controlling the bicycle. I will only place my hands on the handle bar for more stability, do you understand?" "Yes Sir," Osita answered, nodding his head at the same time. Thus the 'journey' back to school commenced.

Osita did not find the ride very difficult. This was because, the bicycle was the ladies' own brand. He mounted on and remained in 'standing' posture while pedaling. While in motion, the front wheel shook and thrust itself unsteadily, tilting either towards the left or the right, but was each time stabilized by both the continuous pedaling made by Osita and the long legs of the teacher which he thrust down when the need arose.

"Please do not pedal hard," the teacher warned, adding, "the brakes are not efficient." Once, Osita had tried to apply the brakes. Although it did not function very well, it pressed against one of the teacher's fingers. This had precipitated a very sharp pain. "J-e-s-u-s," he yelled, as he drew back his hand. "Sorry Sir," Osita appologized.

Osita quickly remembered the day he sustained such a wound. He had bumped into a friend while riding his bicycle along the road to the market. As suddenly as he noticed the boy, he applied the brakes. Unfortunately, the bicycle did not stop. It rather slowed down. The boy noticed that he was having problem in trying to stop the bicycle. And so had tried to help him out by applying the same brakes. This pressed hard on Osita's fingers. That was not all. As the brakes handle pressed hard on Osita's fingers, he lost control of the bicycle. Consequently, both he and his bicycle crashed on the road. He was lucky that the vehicles that were coming towards his direction, were not very close. One of them had however, hooted very loudly. And the sound of the hooting so jolted him that he felt his heart jump into his stomach. Inadvertently, he jumped off the road. No sooner had he jumped off the road, than the Peugeot 504 saloon car, sped pass him, dodging his bicycle as it sped. This had aroused a sponteneaous shout from among the people that were nearby. Some of them termed him naughty, while others pronounced him lucky. As he stood by the roadside shivering, he began to feel his heart beat hard against his ribs. Soon his head began to throb too. What a painful and shameful experience that was. A couple of minutes later, Donald sluggishly went and brought the bicycle out of the road. Guilt conspicuously covered his face. "I'm sorry," he had pleaded, his eyes fixed on Osita. "I hope it didn't spring up blood?" he added. And as he spoke, he tried to inspect Osita's hands and legs. "No," Osita muttered, trying to act as if nothing happened. But that experience was not one that he could forget in a hurry. What with the pain emanating from the fingers where the brake handle tried to crush. What also with the pains emanating from his knees and elbows where the rough tarmac brushed hard and wounded him.

Chapter Thirty Three

Suddenly, he heard a voice. It was at the time when he was immensely engrossed in thoughts that he heard the voice. And it made a dual impact on him. First, it jerked him back to consciousness and he remembered that he was on the road. Second, it reminded him that he was headed to his idol, the school. He grinned and began to long for the school. "Go straight to primary four 'A' class room," the voice had said to him, once they caught view of the school. "I am not in primary four Sir," Osita replied, trying to glance across his shoulder in an effort to glance at the teacher. "But that's where you'll learn today," the teacther pointed out. Soon Osita and the teacher arrived at the primary four classrooms' block. "Primary four, here I come," Osita mused. But as he stood near the teacher, he began to feel his heart skip a beat once many times over. "Why did this man bring me into primary four instead of primary three?" he mumbled and stole a glance at the teacher. He could not make out the reason for that. "Did he not understand me when I told him my present class?" he wondered. He looked at the teacher once again. "How would he feel if I repeated myself?" he mused. "I think I should repeat to his hearing what my present class is, for better understanding." However, he noticed that the man was busy looking around the premesis as if he was trying to remark the place. He would certainly call his attention to that issue later. He was not going to keep mute and disgrace himself when the chips were down. He was in this state of mind, when he heard his name. "Hello, Osita, the new big boy," the voice called. He looked up, and saw Eze already closing up on him. "Hello, Eze," he greeted back, "it is good to see you again." Osita and Eze were still holding each other's hand after a hand shake, when the teacher looked their way. Intuitively, Eze disengaged his hand. It was as if the teacher would frown at that. He walked briskly towards the teacher and slightly bowed his head. "Sir," he said, looking down on the rough cement floor as if the teacher were seated on the ground. "Madam sent me to go and find out where you are staying." "Which one?" he asked, as he fixed a glance at the boy's head as if inspecting his hair cut. "The one that came with you the day you taught in our class," Eze tried to explain, looking up at the teacher now, as if noticing him for the first time. "Okay, you mean my supervisor?" the teacher asked, apparently elated, adding, "tell her that I am waiting at the primary four classroom block in accordance with her directive," And as he pronounced the last word, a smile appeared on his face. "I will do that Sir, good morning," Eze replied, and turned his back to leave. But as if he had consulted with himself, he turned again and waved at Osita. But, he did not stop at that. He continued to wave at him while slowly moving backwards. Suddenly, he stopped waving his hand and switched over to something else. He began to gesticulate a sign of solidarity to Osita.

Eze finally ran back to the junior primary section. On his way back, he began to spread the good news. "Osita has been promoted to primary four," he told all that he met on his way. Within a few minutes, the news had circulated all round the junior section. "Osita has been promoted to primary four without finishing primary three." This became like a song. One that was in everybody's lips. Pupils in the junior primary began to troop into the senior section. Every one wanted to take a glimpse at their hero, Osita. "Are you surprised?" Uchenna asked, trying to engage many pupils in his word. "That boy's head is a magnator," he enthused. "Supu ya," Nwanna mocked. "Ehe, what should I have said?" Uchenna querried, looking askance at Nwanna. "You should say, that the boy's brain, not head, is a magnet," adding, "take notice that I said 'magnet,' not 'magnator'," Nwanna tried to correct, pronouncing both 'brain' and 'magnet' with an air of emphasis. "It does not really matter whether I used the word 'brain' or 'head'," Uchenna retorted, glancing here and there for a possible supporter. "The issue is that you and all here understood me clearly. As for the word, 'magnet' and 'magnator'", he went on, "both are the same." At this juncture, all the pupils that were gathered there began to laugh. They took sides. A handful of them commended Uchenna for his smart defense of himself. The other divide, however mocked his poor command of English Language. From that day onward, Uchenna bagged the name 'magnetor'.

"Gam gam gam gam," sounded the bell for a signal that the short break period had commenced. Mr Umunna's practical examination was slatted for the long break period. This arrangement suited the pupils. It was as if it was arranged for their pleasure. Those who ran to the senior section at the instance of the news of Osita's promotion did so, defying the school's regulation. They constituted a little percentage of the school though. But with the long break on now, it had become a free for all adventure. None feared any reprimand. So as the bell began to sound, the picture of the school equally began to change. Those who did not want to flout the school regulations were more in number. Although they were tempted to join the first group, they did not want to defy the school's regulation. These ones were law abiding. Now that the bell had allowed them to do so, they began to run to the senior section. Before long all the windows in the primary four classrooms' block, began to play 'host' to pupils in the juniorate, especially those in primary three.

After the formal introduction of Mr. Umunna by the class teacher, all became set for the commencement of the lesson. He took good charge of the class today. A look at him showed a greater self confidence than what obtained previously. It was as if he reoriented himself this time around. He positioned Osita at the right end of the class. There were three other brilliant pupils recommended to him by the class teacher. These comprised of a boy and two girls. He placed them at other strategic positions.

"Our lesson today is captioned 'Digestive System in Man'. Can we all say it?" "Digestive System in Man," the class chorused. "Look up here, and pay genuine attention. This lesson promises to be fantastic," he said pointing towards a boy who was fondling with God knows what, and inserting his left hand in his trousers' left pocket. Suddenly he began to move. It was as if he decided to inspect the class. Taking off with his left foot, he strolled from one end of the class to the other, beaming with smile. He suddenly turned and faced the opposite direction. He held a piece of chalk, in his right hand, while his left hand remained dipped in his trouser's left pocket.

Suddenly too, he coughed slightly. He quickly pulled out his left hand from his pocket, and covered his mouth while the cough lasted, as if in consonance with etiquette. This revealed a worn out chain wrist watch, which he wore on his left wrist. Ordinarily, the watch was partially covered. It was covered by the worn out, but neat white long-sleeved shirt which he put on. The shirt was neatly folded up in a single fold. Looking downward, one noticed how neatly too he tucked the shirt into the equally worn out, blue trousers. Noticeable also, is the leather belt he put on his waist. Although black, the belt had blended well, with the white shirt and the sky-blue trousers he was putting on. The black sandals on his feet equally, matching in colour with the belt on his waist, had also added to his elegant looks.

"Digestion is the process by which food substances are broken down into smaller molecules that can easily be absorbed into the blood stream," he had begun, face up and looking straight at the black board, where he had drawn the digestive system of man. After defining his subject matter, he made ample efforts to inculcate the lesson into the memories of the members of his class. This he did, by severally repeating himself.

"Look on the board," he stressed once again. "The diagram on the blackboard is segmented appropriately. Each segment is given an identification number, for easy understanding." "Ask questions on the magnitude you have so far covered." A voice sounded suddenly, from outside the classroom. It was the voice of Mrs Opa, Mr Umunna's supervisor. Her sudden intervention had interrupted the lesson. That was not all, it had also distracted the attention of the pupils. Virtually, all the pupils turned towards the direction of her voice. This was however with the exception of two persons only, Osita and the teacher. They had gotten used to her sudden interventions. "Alright, thank you, Madam," the teacher replied, fidgeting. "Now, class," he began again, obviously conscious of the Supervisor's presence, "what did I say that digestion meant?" Now only a few hands went up. This had made Mr Umunna feel very unhappy. He had expected that many hands would go up. Afterall the question he asked was not a difficult one. And more over he had taken time to teach even from the very beginning. "So why would only a few persons know the answer?" He hissed silently. Of course he could tell the reason. "My supervisors' interruption is behind it," he grumbled in his heart. "The children's brains need more time to focus again."

He however, pointed at one of the few hands that went up. It was Osita's hand. "Yes, you there," he had said, even as his heart jumped into his stomach. Fortunately, his fears were allayed. The question was answered correctly. "Correct, thank you," the teacher gladly admitted. "Class, what we do to him?" he asked, trying to keep his face expressionless. The class did not give him a verbal answer. They were not expected to answer verbally. They were expected to do something else. That was what they did. They gave a clap ovation. "Kwam, kwam, kwa, kwa, kwa, kwam," sounded the pupils clap ovation. Minutes later, he asked another question. When he looked around, he saw many hands up.

This immensely gladdened his heart. “This class is lively,” he thought. “I shall surely enjoy my lesson here if this woman would let me alone.” He was however, disappointed. The first person he called up, had failed the question, and the second person had followed suit. “I must stop this gamble,” he had said to himself and had therefore, hurriedly returned to Osita, who then gave the right answer to the question. However, this did not go down well with his supervisor, and she spoke out again. “Don’t throw many questions at a singular person. There are many other children in the class, let all of them be involved,” his supervisor retorted once again, rising on her feet as she spoke.

When she rose up, she gently walked up a few feet ahead. That was when Osita and his freinds took a glimpse of her.

Her dress was also blue in colour. But not exactly the type that Mr Umunna was wearing. Hers was the type that Osita’s class teacher, Mrs Nlemchukwu, called ‘violet’. Violets are sparkling. Perhaps, more sparkling than Mr Umunna’s type of blue. Osita loved that name. Was it not his mother’s name, afterall? Suddenly, a thought flashed through his mind. His mother must have been a good looking baby girl, during her growing up years. That must be the reason why her parents named her Violet. If that is the case, he must name one of his own daughters after his mother.

In that split second, Mr Umunna, replied to the woman’s objections. “Alright, thank you madam,” he had replied, drawing in a long, slow breath. However, after further gambling with other pupils whose hands showed up in the quest to give answers to his questions, the teacher had resorted to concentrating on Osita alone. "After all," he said to himself, "I would rather be scolded for using only one student to pass my examination, than throwing questions liberally, but fail the examination when the chips are down."

Mrs. Opa was of the type that would test her students all round the course to ascertain that such students come out, 'pure as gold' as she would say. She would however, not hesitate to score any student his due marks on other grounds where the student makes up for his shortcomings. And so, although Mr. Umunna had not done very well in the style of disseminating questions, he had made up for that in the area of being able to teach some what effectively, that most of the questions he asked had been correctly answered.

Chapter Thirty Four

"I wonder how far I would have gone without that your boy, madam," Mr. Umunna said. He had gone straight to Mrs Nlemchukwu's class immediately after the practical examination. As he spoke, he stole glances this way and that one, as if trying to avert being heard by someone else. "The other children," he went on, "recommended to me by their teacher, Mrs Adielle, largely disappointed me. At a point I threw away the caution against directing questions to a selected individuals, and deployed the tactics of scoring high marks in the number of questions answered correctly." "And how did you fare, then?" the woman asked, fixing a glance at Mr Umunna. But as if Mr Umunna had no direct answer to give, he began to brush his trousers, using a handerkerchief he had brought out from his trousers' pocket. Mrs Nlemchukwu followed the movement of his hands for a while. But moments later, she raised the same question up again. "How did you fare?" she repeated, her eyes still focused on him. As she spoke, she tried to push a chair to Mr Umunna. And the later, quickly pulled the chair closer to himself and sat down. But he did not say a thing. At this point, Mrs Nlemchukwu looked enquiringly at Mr Umunna. That was when he began his story. "My supervivisor is a stern woman. Everybody in our school knows that……." He seemed to have said much longer than Mrs Nlemchukwu wanted to hear. So she made to mind her pupils instead of the teacher. "Kelechi, will you stop playing in class?" she yelled, a frown on her face. However Mr Umunna did not stop his story. He talked on. Suddenly, she interrupted him. "And where is the boy?" she asked, this time, she tried to avert his eyes while talking to him. "I think he has mixed up with his friends up there," replied Mr. Umunna, pointing at the direction of the primary four classroom block. "You ought to have come back here with him," Mrs Nlemchukwu pointed out, a frown on her face. Soon, Osita appeared. "Good afternoon, madam," he greeted looking exhausted. "Good afternoon, Osita," Mrs Nlemchukwu answered, strictly watching the boy's demeanour. Osita opened his mouth to speak, but felt a lump in his throat. He felt confused. "Was that all that they had to learn today? Is it what it feels like, to be in the senior section?" he wondered. If primary four learns only a subject each day, he woundered, it would be very unfulfilling. However, no one explained what was going on to him.

Mr. Umunna was still talking, when Mrs Nlemchukwu suddenly felt a strong sense of foreboding sweep through her. Her eyebrows suddenly parted widely. Moments later, she sluggishly rose on her feet, stretching her body as she did. She however, sat down again, shortly after. But her demeanour was no longer the same. She began to look withdrawn. "Is anything the matter?" Mr Umunna asked, looking concerned. She could not give an answer. It was as if she was taking her own turn to ignore Mr Umunna's question. Without doubt, her mind had become restless. She tried as much as she could, to 'fold her legs', but the efforts apparently were all futile. At this point, she felt that she could not continue the conversation. Stretching her body once again, she rose on her feet. "Mr. Umunna," she said, suddenly, her voice sounding shaky. "I do wish you could hold the class briefly for me, while I rush home and check my kids. I wll soon be back, please." And as she made the last statement, she opened her hand bag and brought out something that was black in colour. It was a long comb. She began to comb her hairs with it. While she was busy doing that, Mr Umunna tried to respond to her question. "That will be my pleasure," he replied, grinning. And as soon as the woman stepped out of the classroom, he stepped in. Soon he began to move round the classroom. And in the course of doing so, he took time to look at the faces of some of the pupils. There were some among them whose head he caressed. He also caressed the shoulders of others. But at most times, he cracked jokes with all on the flat level. This one evoked an atmosphere of general laughter. But as if he remembered what he had forgotten, he suddenly cleared his throat and became serious. "Class, can anybody tell us what subject we have at this period of the day?" he asked, looking at no one in particular. "Sir, English Language," shouted a boy from the rear. "Yes, it is English Language, sir," another boy tried to confirm from in front. But as if he was stung by a bee, Mr Umunna quickly turned towards the first boy. He strolled closer to him and asked him a question. "What is your name, boy?" he asked, looking straight into the boy's eyes. "Kenneth, sir," answered the boy, his face lowered, as if he were addressing the cement floor. "Kenneth stand on your feet," Mr Umunna directed, his face slightly contorted.

While Kenneth was standing, Mr Umunna placed his hand on his head, made him raise his face up and took a closer look at his face, as if trying to remark him. "Kenneth what is your surname?" "Opara, sir," he answered, his face still lowered. "Listen class," Mr Umunna said, this time, he addressed the class. "There is a mistake that Kenneth Opara has made a number of times now, who can tell us what the mistake is?" Having said that, Mr Umunna began to roam the class with his eyes. There was silence everywhere. "No one?" he asked again, but kept looking around. "This is serious," he said, now lowering his voice as if he were talking to himself. Just as he kept looking around, Osita stole in and made to squeeze himself in between two other boys. He was surprised when the teacher called his name. "Master Tasie, can you answer my question?" And as if he had been rehearsing what to say, Osita answered right away. "Sir," he answered, "he did not give his answers in complete sentences." "This is great," replied Mr Umunna, as he shook his head in amazement. "Now, class did you all hear him?" he asked, looking around, as if trying to take notice of those who would respond. Then he turned to Kennet. "Can you see where you got it wrong, Master Opara?" "Yes sir," replied the boy. "You may sit down," he added. "Have you been eavesdropping upon us this while, Master Tasie?" asked the teacher, as he strolled back to the blackboard. "Sir, I was not eavesdropping on you, but I could hear you from outside," Osita replied, frowning. "This boy would go places," Mr Umunna remarked. "Sir, he is the one that takes the first position in all our class' examinations, every year," a voice pointed out. Mr Umunna was however not mindful of who made the remark. He was rather overwhelmed with admration for Osita. Ordinarily, Mr Umunna like Mrs Nlemchukwu, frowned at someone who tried to answer a question in class without the teacher's permission. He termed it unauthorized talking. However, a few minutes later, he took up the class in English Language which was the right subject for that time of the day.

While the lesson was going on, Osita's mind was ill at ease. He reflected on the events of the day. The more he did, the unhappier he became. He could not reconcile the issue of learning in two different classes the same day. "Now, am I in primary three or in primary four?" he pondered, gazing up. He tried to imagine himself going over to primary four the next day. He could not imagine himself learning again in primary three. "Afterall, had he not been promoted to primary four?" As he pondered over this, he remembered 'Dee Raymond'.

Dee Raymond lived close to his house as a tenant. He was a student though. A student in secondary school. Once, Dee Raymond had organized a questionaire at home. It was not meant for any particular school grade. Anybody who knew the answer to any of the questions he asked could come up and say it out. He did not give any prices though. He rather made the whole participants to give a clap ovation to anyone who answered any question correctly. And at the close of the exercise, the overall winner was applauded. "Did I not win the contest?" he mused. Did the exercise not comprise of pupils even in primary six?" So while would anybody demote him after he had been promoted to primary four. "Is that not a promotion to the very next level? One of a mere one year difference?" He fancied that he could even cope, if he were promoted three classes ahead.

He was sure too that he could do better than most students in secondary school, especially in English Language. But was he really promoted? Where would he learn the next day, and the days ahead?

After the lesson, Mr Umunna wiped out what he wrote on the blackboard while he was teaching. He cleaned the blackboard by himself. "Now look up," he said, holding the board with his left hand, and the chalk in his right hand. All eyes focused forward. However, while some were fixed on the board, others were fixed on the teacher. Osita's own eyes where fixed on the board. "Look on the board all of you," he said again, his own eyes moving round the class. "I shall write down on this blackboard as many as twenty five questions. Be careful, therefore to read out the questions correctly. That will, of course enable you to answer the questions correctly. Each question bears four marks." He allowed a brief pause before continuing. Moments later, he began again. "Finally," he said, "ability to read the questions correctly shall be part of the test, so do not ask me to read out any question for you." At the appropriate time, the test was over. As was expected, Osita scored the highest marks. He scored 85%. "Class, what do we do to him?" the teacher asked, smiling. No sooner had he ended the question, than the class brandished a resounding clap ovation. "Master Tasie," said the teacher, "please come and take your sheet." There was silence. Mr Umunna thought that Osita did not hear him. "Master Osita," he called again. This time his voice raised a little higher, while looking at his wrist, for what time it was at the moment. Yet there was no response from the boy. He frowned and called his name for the third time. When the lad would not come, Mr Umunna moved in anger and ordered him to go to his table and take his sheet of paper. Osita rose on his feet. Rather than move, he let out many drops of tears down his cheeks. Meanwhile, all eyes were fixed on the teacher and Osita. There was murmuring every where. Every pupil in the class knew the reason why Osita was weeping. All, except Mr Umunna, knew. He stood beside Osita. He did not realize that his hand was shaking. His hands were shaking out of emotional anger. He was angry because he thought that he had been slighted. But he discovered that there was a second emotional impulse that was sweeping down his entire being. That was an emotion of love. He could not punish this angel, although the angel was slighting him in the presense of the whole class. Was the angel really slighting him?

Soon afterwards, Mr Umunna dragged himself to Mrs Nlemchukwu's table and sat down, looking downcast. Soon his mind began to race around. Why on earth would this boy slight him in this way? Did he think I would not have passed my examination without him? What.., why..? However, he could not ask his question. The class had heen enmeshed in high scale murmuring and it suddenly occured to him that some senior teacher could come around to see what was going on. That would not paint a good portrait of me, he reasoned. And for that reason, he tried to put his emotion under control. He got up from the chair and walked up to one of the pupils he had observed to be in the forefront of the noise making. "What is the noise for?" he demanded, his voice rising. He had wanted to lambast at the boy. But that was not to be. The boy's name is Chidi.

Chidi sat next to Osita. He was one of the biggest boys in class. Mrs Nlemchukwu had allotted a seat for him at the back roll. But he seemed bent on seating next to Osita. There were times when Mrs Nlemchukwu had flogged him for leaving his own seat for the one next to Osita. But he would take advantage of the least opportunity and go for the seat. Mrs Nlemchukwu's absence from the class, as in this case, offered him such opportunities.

Chapter Thirty Five

"Be careful, otherwise I will flog that madness out of you now," Mr Umunna bellowed, fixing a hard look at Chidi. While his gaze was on Chidi, Mr Umunna tried as much as possible to avert Osita's face. "He is a kid to me. So, I will guard my eyes against meeting with his, so that he does not think of himself more than he should," thought Mr Umunna and turned his back. "Sir, I was not making a noise. I was trying to tell Osita to…." He could not say immediately, what he wanted to tell Osita. He was interrupted by Mr Umunna. The latter abruptly turned and shouted at Chidi, "you told him to do your head," Mr Umunna shouted at him. As if he was desperate to pass information to the teacher, Chidi went on in spite of the odds. "I told him that I will tell you the reason why he is crying." This statement softened the teacher's mind, and so he kept quiet. He did not expect such from a boy he had just threatened to flog. "What could be the reason why Osita behaved the way he did?" That was what concerned him, not the reason why he cried in the class. He could go ahead and cry even in the church if that was what he wanted. He said, hissed and tried to put the matter behind him. But as if he had a second thought, he glanced back at

Chidi. Could his reason for crying in the class be the same why he behaved the way he did? If yes, could he ask Chidi to say it out here in the class? Or should he call Chidi out from the class?" One thing was sure. Mr Umunna was keen to know the answer to that puzzle. He was sure that it must have to do with him, but could not determine what exactly it was. However, a few munites later, Mr Umunna mustered courage. "Why is he crying?" he asked curtly. "Sir, it is because he did not get hundred percent in the test." "That is true, sir," echoed his mates. Some of the pupils tried to get into more details to tell the teacher that that was Osita's attitude. Mr Umunna was taken aback by this revelation. "Are you serious?" he asked. "Yes sir," the children chorused almost in unison. This was something that he never dreamt about. He therefore turned his back and went back to Mrs Nlemchukwu's chair. "That boy will really go places," he mused again. His mind suddenly began to reflect on the remarks that he had heard Mrs Nlemchukwu make about the boy. "Once, she told me that he was one of the best in the school." But is it not incredible?" he thought. He tried in his heart to analyze the implication of that assertion. Two schools of thought emerged from the analysis. If the boy was brought together in a class and taught the same lesson with his senior, he could defeat them in a test. It would not matter what the age difference between he and the others was. It would not matter too what scope of lesson that was involved, either. At least the latter was established before his own eyes earlier this morning. At least, about forty four pupils in primary four were beaten by this boy in his own class. "God, you must be a wonderful creator," he mumbled. Otherwise, if not for a special favour from you, how can some brains be a lot larger and more active than other peoples' own. He was however pondering over this thing, when the school bell sounded.

"Monitor, what do you have next in your time table?" he asked looking around the class. To his surprise, rather than give him an answer, all eyes tuned towards the backside of the class. "Who is your monitor?" he demanded, lips apart. "Sir, it is Osita." But before he could open his mouth again and ask, Osita rose up and told him. "Sir, this is warning bell. It is meant……" But he could not tell what the bell signified. This was because the teacher interrupted him. "Never mind, I know what that means. I only needed to have an idea of what the bell was about." He had hardly pronounced the last word when Chidi raised his hand. "Yes, what is that your name?"

Chapter Thirty Six

Mrs. Nlemchukwu had hurried home at the impulse of foreboding. Sadly, no sooner had she opened the gate leading to the back of her house, than she heard her mother-in-law fume with rage, as she spoke in very high tunes. "If you don't want to stay, you can go back to the land of your fathers," mama Nneoma fumed. "Anyi awuhu nwa bekee" – "We're not whites." "My son is an only son and so he should give me as many children – boys and girls as God allows him."

Mama Nneoma is Mr. Nlemchukwu's aged mother. She, in collaboration with her sister, who was married into the same kindred with Nkechi's mother, had pressurized both Mr. Nlechukuwu and Nkechi's mother, and they had succeeded in bringing both Mr. Nlemchukwu and Nkechi together. The inevitable had taken place and while Mrs. Nlemchukwu was going home that afternoon, induced by an unexplained urge to do so, Nkechi was in distress, vomiting. The cause of the illness could not be hidden perpetually. "So Nkechi, you, even you of every other person, could do this to me?" Was all the benevolent Mrs. Nlemchukwu, could say to the recipient of her benevolence. The statement had struck the girl in her heart, so severely that she could not stand it. "Mama o-o," was all she could utter before collapsing.

The St. Monica's Maternity home was not very far away from the Nlechukwu's home. The road however, was in a mess. Nonetheless, an arrangement that succeeded in bringing an old Peugeot 404 saloon car was made. Nkechi's mother, who had been brought in haste, was to hold Nkechi's lower trunk, while Mr. Nlemchuwu held her head. Confusion and apprehension held sway in the home of the Nlemchukwu's all through the night. Early in the morning of the next day, an embattled Mrs Nlemchukwu hurriedly parked her personal effects as well as those of her kids. She was however pondering over what her next line of action would look like, when her first son interrupted her flow of thoughts. "Mum," he had called, "where are we going?" The woman had opened her mouth to speak, but could not form the right words and so had swallowed the lump that suddenly appeared in her throat. "Mum, please, what is going on here?" her second son asked, when his elder brother's first question failed to attract an answer. "Phil, Johnny," she finally found herself saying, "we're going to meet your grandfather, okay?" "Is he coming to see us here?" the innocent boy had asked. "I said, we're going to meet him where he is, don't you understand"? she snapped.

The next morning, the authorities of the famous Obodoma Group School continued their daily activities oblivious of what was going on in the home of the Nlemchukwu's. "The form for the forthcoming entrance examination into secondary school, beginning from the next academic session, is out," began the headmaster, after prayers that morning. "Inform your parents, so that you may buy your own at the bursar's office, from today." "How much is the form?" asked a boy in primary six, rather in hushed tunes. "What is the noise for?" asked the headmaster, on account of the underground murmuring. "Say it louder," advised another boy, "so that the headmaster will hear."

"Never mind Mr. Nlemchukwu, we're doing our best so your wife'll be alright. She's is still unconscious at the moment, but we're still making frantic efforts to revive her. However, your baby girl could not make it. We think she was aborted by a heavy shock that affected her mother very strongly. Meanwhile, we've ordered for a team of experts to help unravel some intricacies in this matter, and they would soon be here," stressed the doctor. "B…... but, suppose we send her up to them, rather than wait for them to come. I… I mean for faster treatment" Mr. Nlemchukwu stuttered. "No, please" replied the doctor, "she," referring to Nkechi, Mr. Nlemchukwu's 'second wife', "is too fragile for that experiment," the doctor explained

Meanwhile, all the doors at the house of Mr. Nlemchukwu were securely shut by the time he got home. "Koi, koi, koi, koi, sounded the knock on the door. Of course he did so very many times over. This is in addition to several other attempts that had been made to bring his wife to open the door, without any success. "Come and pass the night in my house," offered Nkechi's worried father, adding, "she would have no option than to open the doors when she would be going to school tomorrow". Two days after, however, the doors had remained locked. Mr. Nlemchukwu would not want to hurt his wife any further so he had accepted to sleep outside for the two nights rather than force his way in, howbeit in discomfort. “Let’s break the doors,” suggested concerned neighbours. Mr. Nlemchukwu would not oblige to this, not even when his mother had added her own voice.

Meanwhile, Nkechi’s health was still hanging on the balance. She was still unconscious and a set of double drips hung in her hands, one at the left, and the other at the right.

Five days later, a motorcyclist arrived at the Nlemchukwu’s compound. “I’m looking for one Mr. Amos Nlemchukwu,” the man had asked. “Sure I’m the one,” replied Mr. Nlemchukwu hastily, just as he fixed a glance at the motorcyclist. “Please sign the receipt of this letter,” the motorcyclist said, passing a booklet to a visibly shaken Mr. Amos Nlemchukwu. “Are you… please, where are you coming from?” Mr Nlemchukwu stuttered, and without waiting for an answer, he hurriedly tore the white envelope and right away began to read the letter therein. Sadly speaking, he had hardly read the letter for a few minutes, before he exclaimed, “I’m finished” and slumped, while the envelope fell off his hand alongside the letter. The envelope handed to Mr. Nlemchukwu was written by his wife. He had identified the hand writing on top of the envelope and so had read through the missive in a mad haste, but the message turned out to be nothing close to his expectation. “Mr. Amos Nlemchukwu” the letter had begun, “I thought you loved me, so I acted against my parents’ wish and married you. I adapted as much as I could to the African culture because of you. Unfortunately, I’ve discovered, though late, that you do not in any way deserve me. You have unfairly treated me. Please, count me for a stranger, henceforth. Meanwhile, the children and I are in safe hands in Europe. Bye for life!" The last two statements in the letter had hit Mr Nlemchukwu as a thunder bolt, tearing his heart in shreds. He had collapsed as a result.

Meanwhile Nkechi had barely opened her eyes, and had managed to ask the nurse on duty, "what am I doing here?" "Don't worry, you …." The nurse had begun but could not however, fully explain to her patient what the matter with her was, but was cut short by a distress call that was accompanied by series of harsh knocks on the door, giving an impression of an emergency situation."N-u-r-s-e, n-u-r-s-e, doctor!" the voice yelled from outside, and in apparent distress. Seconds later, Mr. Nlemchukwu was brought into the ward unconscious.

Meanwhile, the common entrance results had been released. Many pupils passed the examination. Speculations had it that, unlike previous years, the examination board acted liberally to allow as many candidates as could make efforts to secure admission into secondary school. As expected, Osita's score was about the highest marks in the divisional area. "Our school, I mean, a candidate of our school, scored the highest mark in all the entire division," the headmaster announced happily, "so let's give the school seven happy cheers. "Hip-hip-hip." "Hurray," came a resounding reply, followed by a prolonged applause. This was also mixed up with whisperings here and there. Many pupils and teachers had started speculating who the person could be. "It's Osita Tasie, who else do you think it would be?" speculated one primary six girl. "Did he sit for the last common entrance exams? I thought he is in primary five?" pointed out the girl. "Yes, he took the examination along with us that is the reason why I said it must be he." "Hold on, lessen the noise," cried the headmaster once again. "The person in question has therefore been offered provisional admission, into the prestigious Government College Owerri. While we celebrate this genius with a clap of hands, can you come out here, Master Osita Tasie for your result slip?" As the boy was coming, his expressionless face should have been a sign to the entire school that he was enmeshed in thoughts. A mixture of happiness and doubts had swept through his mind. Happiness because God had granted him this huge success. Doubt on the hand, about who would sponsor his secondary school education. However, neither the staff nor the pupils could read his mind. The headmaster had recalled to the listening ears of his audience for the second time, the events that unfolded the very day this boy was registered into the school. He had concluded by absolving himself of any blames in taking the decision to register him in primary two when there was no vacancy in primary one. "Posterity will rather extol my futuristic vision," he had asserted.

That night, Violet, Osita's mother had cried her eyes out. "I know what to do," she reasoned. "I shall go back to both Chief Ekwebalem and Mr. Okparaji, and renew my plea, I hope at least, one of them would oblige me. This decision had offered her a reprieve that had resulted into a deep sleep that precipitated a dream. Unfortunately, by the time she woke up early the next morning, she had forgotten what the dream was all about, "Wake up, Osy, wake up," Violet called in hushed tunes, shaking the boy gently. "I almost over slept my time," she said. "Wake up, Osita," the woman went on silently, trying hard not to wake the sleeping world. Later that morning, mother and son had visited both Chief Ekwebelam and Mr. Okparaji, respectively. "Let me start by congratulating you my son for the success that God has granted you," remarked Chief Ekwebelam, after Violet had explained every thing to him, "however my wife," he continued, "No one ever tells his people to preserve boiled water, because he was going to fall down from the tall tree he was intending to climb." In that case, I can accept to take the boy, but he will start school, not this academic year however, but the next one," the man had summed up.

"Welcome to Government College Owerri. Each morning, the form master of class one 'A', the Reverend Jim Smith, a Canadian Nigerian, would come to class before normal lessons would start at eight o'clock. Rev. Smith was a man of his words. He never joked with his time, and he abhorred lateness. Each time a student called 'Time', he was referring to Rev. Smith. So, at exactly eight o'clock each morning, he entered class one A for normal roll-call.

"Who is this number one name in my class register, Osita Tasie, who has not reported to school up till now?" he queried, pronouncing 'Tasie' as 'Tesie'. His entrance examination score is very impressive – does any one know about him?" "Yes, Sir," said Iheanyi Okparaji. "Has he changed school, or what?" Rev. Smith asked further. "Sir, I don't think he'll be attending, he lost his father during the war." "That's Africa's greatest problem," remarked Rev. Smith, "the best of brains are not exploited, and until this malady is corrected, the continent cannot …."

….. THE END ….

AN AEROPLANE, AGAIN?

Printed in the United States
By Bookmasters